BENEATH THE ASHEN SKY

BOOK 1 IN THE TESTAMENT OF TORMENT

T.L. BELLIA

ISBN: 978-1-7640998-0-6

Cover design by: T.L. Bellia and Microsoft Copilot
Printed in Australia

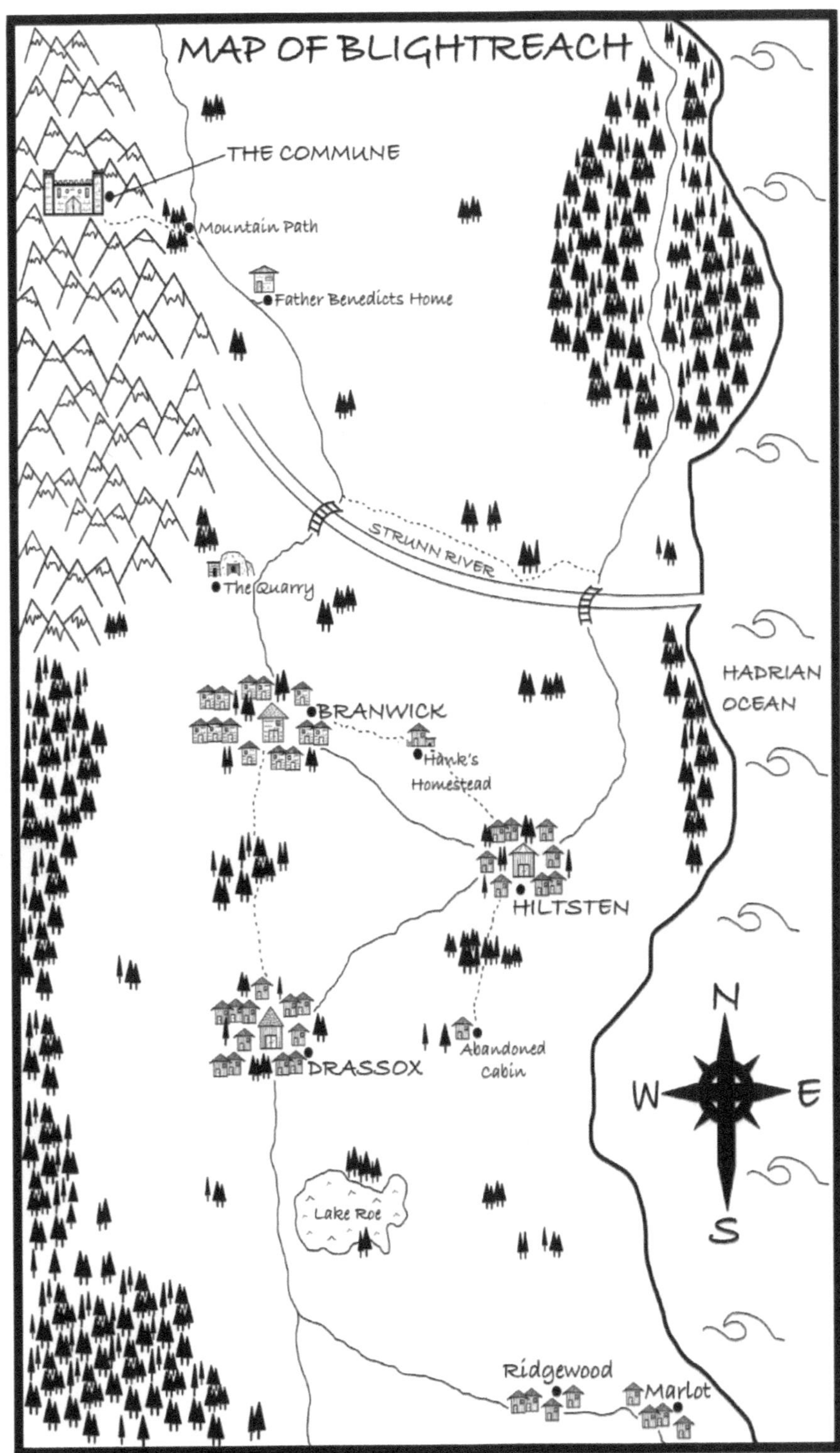

MAP OF BLIGHTREACH
THE COMMUNE
Mountain Path
Father Benedicts Home
STRUNN RIVER
The Quarry
HADRIAN OCEAN
BRANWICK
Hawk's Homestead
HILTSTEN
DRASSOX
Abandoned Cabin
Lake Roe
N
W
E
S
Ridgewood
Marlot

'For we do not wrestle against flesh and blood,

but against principalities, against powers,

against the rulers of darkness and wickedness'

CONTENTS

PROLOGUE
THE DREAM

'You will not fear the terror of the night, nor the arrow that flies by day, nor the pestilence that stalks in darkness, nor the destruction that wastes at noonday'

"CLUNK." The shrill, metallic, clang of steel against steel crashing together, pierced my eardrums as my opponent's sword struck my metal vambrace—sharp pain immediately followed.

Better not be fucking broken, I thought.

I'd intentionally blocked the blow with my forearm after snapping my own blade parrying off the previous attack, not the wisest move, but a necessary one.

As his blow glanced off my armour, I looped my forearm around and under my attackers, flexing upwards with a sudden jolt, popping his elbow at the joint, and causing the distinct, audible 'click' of bone snapping.

His expression twisted into agony, shortly before I violently rammed my mailed fist upwards into his face.

Bits of teeth, blood, saliva, and what I'm sure was a piece of his lower lip spewed from his face as I then booted his ankle out and slammed him down heavily onto his half-decapitated companion I'd just recently dispatched.

WHY HAD THEY COME.

WHY HAD THEY DONE THIS.

THEY'RE GOING TO LEARN WHO THEY ARE FUCKING WITH.

A rage was bubbling inside of me, overwhelming my senses, and momentarily blocking out the stench of the blood and burning flesh, lingering in the air around me…

"THWACK!!"

"THWACK!!"

I was hardly aware of the dull thudding impact, becoming sloppier as I continued to repeatedly bring my heavy, leather boot down on top of his face. I kept stomping, watching it rapidly turn into an unrecognisable mix of teeth, bone, brain, gristle, and mud.

"Lothar!"

"THWUCK!!"

I WILL MAKE THEM ALL PAY.

"THWUCK!!"

Out of the corner of my eye, I could've been sure the sky had just darkened, as though an object had moved into the path of the sun rays, blocking out their purifying light, and ominously casting a black shadow upon me.

I may have taken more notice, if I wasn't too absorbed in my rage to care. The weather was a rather small matter right now.

"THWUCK!!"

"Lothar! Behind you!"

That voice…

The boy?

The fear and urgency in his tone snapped me free from the paralysing frenzy of my bloodlust, allowing me to spin around just in time to meet the deathly gaze of a third attacker, raising a loaded crossbow in my direction.

Too far away for me to reach in time.

DAMNED COWARD.

I braced myself, preparing my body for the penetrating thud of the bolt, when suddenly, without cause, the man jerked and clutched his chest, his face contorted into a spasm of extreme pain, and his veins began to bulge from his skin as though they might rupture.

He shuddered—his final movement… right before he collapsed in a heap where he was standing on the edge of the town square.

Falling stiff as a board to the ground, with thick, dark blood, oozing from his mouth, nose, ears, and eyes.

CHAPTER 1

A MAN'S GRIEF

'For every battle of the warrior is with confused noise, and garments rolled in blood will be burned as fuel for the fire'

I rolled over in my makeshift bedding as I awoke, drenched in sweat, my heart still racing from the terrible images of the dream flashing through my mind.

It seems yesterday's events, are now today's nightmares.

The first thing I noticed was how much my forearm throbbed, I could feel the swelling had already set in.

It was not broken, luckily. I'd been sure to check the bone for deformities before I fell asleep.

What had killed that crossbowman though?

Sickness?

Plague?

It was unnatural, the timing almost too uncanny to be mere luck. Not that I felt bad for him, few men deserved it more than one of that lot.

I shouldn't look a gift horse in the mouth I suppose, he is dead, and we're not—that's all that matters today.

I saw it was still dark outside, the sun hadn't yet risen. I relaxed a bit and pulled my sheets up to my chin feeling a shudder run through my body from the frigid morning air.

The home we'd taken shelter in smelt of mildew and mold, but that was a small relief when compared to the stench of blood…

And the BURNING…

No.

Stop it.

Don't dwell on that, you fool. Nothing good will come of it. God, I wish I could forget that smell though…

Laying there, I took a look around the dimly lit room, my eyes quickly finding the boy resting on the opposite side to me.

He didn't move and appeared to be sleeping soundly still, tangled up in his own bedding, clutching that wooden toy sword he had when I found him hiding in the town hall.

His scruffy, medium length black hair resembled a bird's nest. He seemed small for his age, but then again, I wouldn't really know how big a boy should be at eight or nine summers.

We'd stumbled across this small, desolate cabin in the middle of the night, after we'd fled the town, heading east.

By the time we arrived, we were both completely exhausted.

I broke the flimsy lock off the half rotted, wooden door, and we'd taken shelter inside from the unforgiving chill of the night.

As soon as we entered the abode, it was clear it had been abandoned by its earlier inhabitants, anything of value was already taken, or possibly looted. A few loose items of clothing lay strewn about the interior which we had used to make our bedding on the floorboards.

The cupboards had been practically stripped bare, however, luckily for us, the previous owners missed one pantry.

Or they were in too much of a rush to care.

Regardless the reason, we'd found a half loaf of stale bread in it, somehow still free from mold. It hadn't been much but provided us a meal at least.

The most likely reason for the empty cabin, at least I believed, was that the owners had fled in a rush when the rumours of the soldiers reached their ears.

Must have been smart people.

Anyone wise enough had fled early as the reports came in of an unknown group prowling about, seemingly, indiscriminately executing the children of neighbouring towns.

The message had been brutally simple, hand the children over to them, or be massacred.

For reasons unknown to me, the bodies of the little ones were being decapitated, and then the remains stacked in piles and…

And BURNT.

Oh God, how I wish I could forget the BURNING…

All the reports we'd received told us that anyone who put up any resistance whatsoever, or objected to the group's demands, was being struck down ruthlessly, without further question.

That is at least, if they were one of the lucky ones.

The unlucky ones, like those poor souls in Ridgewood to the south… had been tied to stakes that were hammered into the ground, and mutilated. Reports spoke of both men and women, partially flayed, yet still alive, left barely clinging to life for the crows, vultures and fuck knows what else to feed on their exposed muscles and tendons. Clearly, it was a scare tactic being used to persuade others to submit, rather than resist. And a hell of a bad way to go.

People began packing up and heading north when they heard, as anyone would expect.

Over the past few weeks, I'd sent scouts out on multiple occasions for some hint as to who the group was.

Yet every time, they'd arrived shortly after the massacres had taken place. Not that they could've stopped them, even if they had arrived in time.

In truth, we barely housed enough men at arms to look after ourselves, let alone defend our neighbours.

From the reports the scouts had brought back, the group never revealed what they sought from the children.

AND WHEN THEY CAME, I DIDN'T CARE TO ASK.

***

As far as I was concerned their lives were forfeit the moment they stepped foot into our township with such an agenda.

Word had quickly spread through the settlement that the advancing force was less than a day's ride out from the outlying homesteads on the skirting edges of Drassox, a small, isolated town, situated on the great continent of Blightreach.

Drassox was home to almost sixty villagers, protected by a garrison of twenty men at arms, all governed and led by our elected official, the aging

Duke of Drassox, Lord Edmund.

It was here, beneath his house's banner, that I had served with honour as the Captain of the Drassox guard for near on the past two decades.

I'd been born and raised in Drassox by my father, my mother died when I was young and truth be told, I possessed few memories of her. My father hadn't spoken of her much, as was his way. I believe it pained him to do so, hence I didn't ask, even as he passed away a few summers back.

I'd been with Lord Edmund when one of my scouts returned carrying word of the soldiers approach. Lord Edmund reacted with the calm demeanour of an experienced leader, and immediately ordered the muster bells to be rang, directing all of the villagers to seek safe haven within the town hall. While it wasn't a large building, nor impenetrable by any means, the hall was partially constructed using stone foundations and had large, reinforced, timber double doors, able to be barred from the inside. The building offered the most protection within the settlement, especially when compared to the cruder, wooden cabin design of the surrounding homes.

Under Lord Edmunds orders, I had the Drassox guard mobilised, in preparation for the defence of the town. I instructed my second in command, Lieutenant Elias, to empty our armoury and begin outfitting any able townsmen to aide in the battle if necessary.

Elias had just passed his thirtieth summer, almost a decade younger than myself and as such, less seasoned in warfare. He did, however, show great promise, and I had confidence in his abilities. He was also my closest friend in town.

I had been personally responsible for training all of the men at arms, due in part to being the most senior in not only age but also experience, and battle prowess—credit to my father and his strict training regime. In his younger days he'd been a warrior of some renown, and a veteran of the Great War, which had decimated and divided the lands of Blightreach in the years before my birth.

Due to having a rather talented town blacksmith, a stout, balding man with a thick beard by the name of Rupert, our town guard was well equipped when compared to the smaller towns to the south, and thus far had been more than capable of dealing with the groups of common brigands that normally stalked the wilderness.

Stupidly, I'd thought this time would be no different, having spent many summers preparing the men mentally and physically for combat, forcing them to train regularly and rigorously as my father taught me.

On top of that, Lord Edmund had made it clear to me, that this group would leave empty handed and peacefully, or they would meet fierce resistance.

I'd passed the message to the men without reserve. The alternative would not be considered as a choice. Not that I, nor any of the men needed to be persuaded about that.

Drassox looked after its own, we wouldn't be intimidated, bullied or enslaved, and we wouldn't allow harm to come to our children.

Truth be told, I wanted to make these men pay for what they'd done anyway.

As our settlement lacked a defensible wall, and the approaching force not now far away, I ordered the men into the town square, taking up a defensive position in front of the hall.

They formed into two lines, sixteen abreast. Each man in the front column had been equipped with chainmail armour, a short sword, and wooden shield. A row of spearmen, made up mostly of the recruited townsmen, had been clad in leather armour, and made up the second column, reinforcing each shield bearer in front of him.

Elias and I had taken place in front of the men.

He'd appeared concerned at the time, and glancing at my friend I'd tried to lighten the mood, jokingly saying, "You look worried, Eli. Losing faith in your Captain?"

He looked to the ground in an attempt to avoid meeting my gaze, and had replied, "Of course not. I… I just have a bad feeling this time, Lothar. The reports we've gotten back from the scouts… these men are like fucking savages. Why the hell are they doing this? Why the children?"

I recall thinking on this at the time, unable to come up with a reason, even though I'd wondered this myself.

So instead, I'd said confidently, "I don't know. And I don't give two shits. These animals will pay for what they've done, worrying won't stop them coming, and it's fallen on us to deal with them. We've kept Drassox safe in the past, and today, will be no different," I paused, and then continued, "You remember three summers ago, when that company of brigands kept attacking Hiltsten?"

He'd rolled his eyes while he continued looking at the ground, still not wanting to meet my gaze.

"How could I forget, with you always reminding me? They asked for our aide. I argued with you and said we should use the chance to look to our own defences before sending our own to die, for people who haven't helped us in the past."

"Ha! I'll remind you until you understand. But you're right, and I said to you, 'These men deserve to pay for what they've done, if we don't help stop them now, we'll only have to deal with them alone one day'. We're not cowards, Eli, we're warriors. And these men, like those brigands in Hiltsten, will pay for the crimes they've committed with their lives."

His gaze finally strayed from the ground, and back to me.

"I'm not scared, Lothar, I'd follow you anywhere—you know that. I just like to see that at least one of us is so confident," he'd said with a half smirk.

I'd grinned back, then become deathly serious.

"I know you're not scared. Confident or not though, we're not handing over our little ones to be butchered like a pack of cowards. These butchers will suffer for what they've done. Today."

I had no idea how wrong I was at the time, how foolish I was being… But my little speech worked.

Elias had nodded and looked on with a new gaze of determination in his eyes, ready to fight.

At the time I'd said the words with complete conviction and seeing him inspired had made me feel a little better… but deep inside, I shared his ill feeling. That this time, maybe things wouldn't go so smoothly. A gnawing doubt and sense of impending dread invaded my mind, a foreign feeling that my pride refused to give the time of day.

Maybe it was just the stubbornness that I'd been accused of in the past, a trait I no doubt picked up from my father.

Regardless, with any man old or strong enough to hold a weapon now armed to join the defence, our meagre force had been bolstered to thirty-four. If the reports were to be believed, Drassox would need every fit, able body we could muster, so that was exactly what we'd done.

The women, children, and those too old or frail to join the defence, including Lord Edmund himself, had taken shelter behind the protective walls of the town hall.

The men had said their goodbyes to their loved ones and then Lord Edmund had given a short speech, wishing us luck in battle as he joined the others, and retreated to safety last, closing the doors behind him. I heard a firm thud as those inside dropped the heavy wooden cross bar in place, sealing us outside.

Earlier this day I'd sent our fastest scout, a young hunter named Orin, north. He was a very reliable lad. His orders had been to trek to Branwick, the largest nearby settlement, and request mutual aide. It was a journey of almost two days. Branwick, and Hiltsten which was to the northeast, were the two closest settlements that were friendly with Drassox.

Standing there in the town square I knew that it wouldn't do us any good, even at his fast pace it would take Orin at least a day and a half to get to Branwick, plus the time it took to return with help. Far too long.

Aside from these two nearby populaces we were isolated out here, far from the larger settlements to the north, across the Strunn River.

Not that those settlements would send us aide, even if they could. Alliances were an uncommon thing in this harsh, divided landscape.

FUCK IT. LET THEM COME, I'd stupidly thought while standing there. I had no real fear at the time, even with the gnawing doubt in my stomach I still expected this to be another group of common brigands, just like we'd dealt with countless times before.

So, we had waited, and sure as the sunset goes, the men had come.

Marching five abreast, ten columns long, up the main dirt road from the south that trickled into town. Numbering no less than fifty. A large band for Blightreach, especially coming from the south… and much more than I would've liked.

We were outnumbered.

All footmen, although this hardly came as a surprise at the time. Horses were a rarity since the Great War, back then they'd primarily been used for battle and as a result, nearly all had been slaughtered along with their riders. I'd never seen one and doubted I ever would, although I'd heard stories from my father of their magnificence.

As the gap between us and the enemy shrunk, I begun to make out a clearly well trained and organised force of men. All adorned in matching sets of gleaming chainmail, black gambesons, and open-faced conical basinets.

Each soldier carried a sword or studded mace, with

a wooden shield, and was draped in a matching white surcoat largely emblazoned with a strange symbol I hadn't seen before.

My best description would be that it was a black four-pointed cross, with a circle in the centre of which another four smaller points sprang off diagonally. Although I didn't recognise the symbol, if I had to guess, I would say it'd appeared religious in origin.

I will never forget the man's face that had led the columns of soldiers. He was tall with a chivalrous look to him, he had chiselled features and long, golden blonde hair, which he wore tied neatly back in a ponytail. He'd appeared to be slightly senior to myself, yet still fit, and broad of shoulders.

His whole demeanour stank of arrogance.

He wore a scowl upon his face, as though the mere presence of our resistance had offended him. He radiated hostility.

I immediately disliked him. I wanted to kill this man.

His armour, however, was striking, a style of light plate mail of which I hadn't seen before—far better constructed than my own heavier plate mail. It appeared that it'd been forged by joining a series of small, interlocking plates to allow more fluid movement with minimal gaps, then polished to a mirror shine. It gleamed as the sunlight reflected off of it. The smith that had forged the armour must've been very skilled, far more so than even our Rupert.

I noticed the man hadn't draped the white surcoat of his men, but rather wore a white cape, emblazoned with the same unique cross symbol as his men. Like I, he donned no head protection.

This was no common band of brigands or raiders, that much had become clear. They were far better equipped than any group I had seen in some time, possibly ever, and it only added to my growing concern.

As they approached within fifty paces of us, I had raised my palm and called out loudly to the leader, "That's far enough! You have no business here in Drassox, nor are you welcome here. Take your men and leave!"

I'll never forget the way his scowl instantly deepened, and he immediately reacted by raising his fist, bringing his company to a sudden halt. Or how, without further word, they'd begun to spread out in three neat columns within the town square.

I observed two men with compact crossbows take place at each wing of the front column.

Undeterred by my command, the leader had then continued to approach alone, glaring menacingly at me.

Like a wolf, eyeing its prey.

His left hand oddly clenched into a fist by his side as he strode forward, while his right hand rested on the hilt of a jewelled sword pommel seated within a mahogany brown leather scabbard attached to his waist belt.

Unperturbed, I'd matched his hostile gaze, and strode forward to meet him between the two detachments. Elias had followed behind, slightly to my left.

We continued to glare at each other as I awaited his answer, the tension, hanging so thick in the air it could be sliced through with a blade.

"I disagree. I have particularly… important business here," he had finally answered slowly, in a low, deep authoritative voice with an accent that was foreign to me.

His voice, as dislikable as the man himself, only made me want to kill him more.

My body tensed, ready for battle as I replied, "I've heard reports about your 'business', Butcher. And I suggest you leave, now. There's nothing for you here."

He'd hesitated for a short moment continuing to stare back at me and then slowly, a cruel masochistic smile crept onto his face, his eyes darting to Elias and then back to me.

"Well… I suppose that is too bad… clearly you have not learnt from the lessons we taught those to the south of you during our journey. Allow me to… educate you."

Although I could sense his anger, he spoke calmly.

Then he very obviously, unclenched his left hand.

And our brief exchange was over as fast as it'd begun.

What followed was a chain of events I will never forget for the rest of my life, as much as I wish I could.

I flinched, as an object suddenly whistled by me like a bird and struck Elias hard in the face with the sickening wet crunch of bone shattering into fragments.

A bolt.

The fucking crossbow men!

My close friend collapsed to the ground with a heavy thud as a second bolt skimmed off my shoulder pauldron and collided with one of my charging men's shields advancing behind me.

Immediately I'd drawn my blade, and in one fluid motion swung for the leader's head, he had however expected this, swiftly stepping back. Although not quite quick enough, with my sword tip narrowly skimming his face, opening a thin gash across his forehead.

He showed an expression of brief shock and awe for just a split-second, before resuming his prior calm, cold demeanour, then drawing his own weapon, and returning with a lightning fast, well-practiced attack of his own aimed at my throat.

My reflexes kicked in and our blades clanged together as utter chaos had erupted in the town square.

Both cohorts charged forward and clashed together all around us while the man and I had exchanged blow for blow, equally matched in skill. Never have I fought a more harrowing fight, his every swing intended to shatter my defence and end my existence on this plane.

Formations were abandoned and blood littered the earth around us as combatants engaged one another, and men from both sides fell to mortal wounds.

I recall raising my sword and blocking another heavy blow from my opponent, our blades locking together momentarily with fury clouding the air between us, both of us still refusing to break eye contact as though to do so was a loss in itself.

It was at this moment, I was struck heavily in the head from the right side.

My last memory before the battle was stumbling back and tripping, as the world spiralled aimlessly out of control.

Then blackness overcame me.

***

When I'd awoken sometime later, I was covered by the body of a dead comrade. His head had been crushed, most likely from the swing of a mace. Bits of bone protruded through the skin around his bulging eye sockets, the mashed face was unrecognisable.

A throbbing headache pulsed through my own skull, which as I probed with my fingers discovered wore a deep, swollen gash.

I was covered in blood, though I couldn't tell how much of it was my own, or that of the ally who'd perished on top of me.

The nauseating smell of death was all around, the metallic tang of blood and something burning combined to resemble a living hell.

The smell of war.

I clambered unsteadily to my feet, my vision still spinning. I glanced to the ground to steady myself and found my sword, its familiar blade well-worn and notched from years of fighting.

I bent down and collected it, sliding it back into its sheath on my back.

Looking about, I'd scanned hopelessly around the town square for survivors from my company. The corpses and detached limbs of my men, and some of those of the enemy, lay scattered all about the ground in a visceral display of gore.

But there appeared to be no survivors, bar myself.

It felt as though I'd died and awoken in hell.

Frantic, I'd stupidly wondered at the time...

What about those who took shelter?

Better I'd died in the town square than witness what that thought led me to find yesterday.

That was the moment when I first became really aware of THE BURNING SMELL...

I'd felt my heart drop when I suspected it

originated from the town hall. Quickening my still unsteady pace I stumbled towards the charred, broken double doors, carefully treading around the hacked-up corpses of what I quickly recognised was the villagers.

Every single one of them wore horrific wounds. It appeared a few had tried to fight back when the doors were breached.

A valiant effort. But hopeless against such odds.

All people I'd known. People I'd swore to protect. People I lived amongst.

It was a massacre.

A pregnant woman lay in front of the entryway, her bloated stomach had been savagely cut open, her entrails and umbilical cord strung out on the dirt next to her.

The baby missing.

I dry retched, almost vomiting at the site. I'd known who this woman was… Tanya, wife of Broderick… one of the farmers, who now certainly lay dead with the other men in the town square.

Splayed out unnaturally next to Tanya, lay the body of Lord Edmund, sword still clutched in his hand. He'd been slain bravely attempting one final defence of his people.

These people had been my neighbours, people I knew my whole life. I'd known everyone in Drassox, we were a small community, and although in denial at the time, I'd also known in the dark recesses of my mind what the burning smell was…

Cautiously, I ventured further inside the blackened interior, stepping around the bodies of the townspeople that further lay scattered on the floor everywhere throughout.

My heart sinking further realising it was all the women…

But none of the children…

It hadn't been much further when I found the source of the smell. An image that has forever seared itself deep into my memory for eternity.

Stacked carelessly on top of one another in the centre of the hall, still smouldering… lay the blackened and charred remains, of seven, small bodies of different proportions.

All decapitated. The tiny burnt heads, mixed in among the ash and soot… the children.

I am not ashamed to admit I fell to my knees in grief, feeling like I was suffocating. Barely able to breath as I sobbed.

I should've stopped this.

All of it.

CHAPTER 2

A CHILD'S INNOCENCE

'Be strong and courageous, do not be discouraged. For I am with you wherever you go'

I couldn't sleep, but I didn't want Lothar to know. I knew he'd woken up because he'd finally stopped snoring like a big, giant bear.

I lay there, wishing I could sleep like that after what happened, but every time I closed my eyes I…I saw her face.

I'd tried to sleep all night since we found the cottage but no matter how tired I felt, I couldn't stop thinking about it.

I wanted Lothar to see that I was brave and strong too, like he is, I don't want him to see me cry. It's hard though so instead, I pretended that I was fast asleep and hugged my sword.

It's not a real sword, just a dumb toy I made in the village before all this happened… when everything was still good… before I saw Mother lying there… before I lost Pa.

Before the bad men came and hurt everyone.

***

It was just a normal day in the village when I heard the sound of bells ringing. I had no idea what it meant, I couldn't remember it ever happening before, but all the adults seemed to know and they started panicking, so I'd started to worry too.

I was out hunting goblins with my sword like most days, and Mother had come running over to grab me, and then rushed us to the town hall.

I'd never seen her run like that before.

Catherine wasn't my real mother but her and Elias, who I call Pa, had raised me since my real mother died giving birth to me eight summers ago. Well, almost nine now.

My real mother and Catherine had been friends, I was told.

"Will Pa join us?" I'd asked Mother, as we ran.

"He's busy with Lothar, organising things, Kael. I need you to do as you are told. Right now—and not ask questions! Now move!" She'd snapped back at me.

I could tell she was scared, because she didn't

normally tell me off like that, so I gripped my sword tightly and did as she said, even though my legs were sore from trying to keep up with her. I didn't know Mother could run so fast, I'd always thought I could run quicker than her.

When we finally made it to the hall everyone from the Village was there, even Lord Edmund.

"Edmund, thank God. What is happening!? Do we know how many there are?" Mother had asked him as soon as we walked inside.

They knew each other well so she was allowed to call him by his name without saying Lord first, I wasn't though. Mother always said it was disrespectful for a child to do that.

"I'm not sure Catherine, but it isn't good. Lothar and Elias are organising the men now, they should arrive here shortly. Please take a seat inside with the others. I will address everyone together once they arrive," Lord Edmund had replied.

He seemed worried too and was sweating a lot.

Mother had nodded and we went inside together. I'd been scared, I knew this seemed serious, and it was also very loud in the hall with everyone in there yelling.

I saw Matthias and the other kids from the village grouped together in the corner, but I didn't go over to them.

They'd always been mean to me, they would tease

me because I liked to play with my sword and hunt goblins on my own most of the time.

Well. I guess that wasn't the only reason.

One-time last spring I'd been out playing, and Matthias's dog had nipped at me and chased me, I ran as fast I could to get away, but it cornered me near the quarry. I yelled at it and screamed for it to leave me alone. I yelled as loud as I could hoping someone would hear me but no one did, so I yelled even louder… and then blood had come out of the dog's nose and ears, and it just fell over.

Pa had said it must have had the 'madness disease' that dogs and some animals can get, and that it wasn't my fault. He said lucky it didn't bite me because the 'madness disease' could be caught by humans from animals.

Matthias and his friends blamed me for what happened anyway, even though Pa had said it wasn't my fault.

I was just glad I didn't catch the 'madness disease'. Sometimes I wished Matthias would catch it though and leave me alone.

I waited with Mother and everyone else for a while before a loud noise outside made me spin around, Pa and his friend Lothar had arrived! They weren't alone either, it looked like almost all of the men were with them.

Everyone carried weapons and even had armour

on, this was definitely serious I'd thought. All the people inside were happy to see the men had arrived though and seeing that Pa was alright had made me feel better as well.

I watched them all gather outside in the town square and then Lord Edmund went out to speak to Lothar, Pa and the rest of the men, before coming back inside the hall with the rest of us.

A few of the old men that were inside with us helped Lord Edmund lift the door bar in place, it looked really heavy, but they managed to get it in the latches.

After it was in place everyone had followed Lord Edmund to the middle of the hall and started asking questions, he was trying his best to answer, but people were all talking at once which I thought was rude.

I still had no idea what was going on, they were all yelling over each other and it was impossible to understand so I ignored them, and snuck over to the doors hoping I could peek through the gap.

Outside I could make out Pa and Lothar standing in front of all the men, Pa had a worried look on his face and Lothar was saying something to him that I couldn't make out. They spoke a bit, back and forth and Pa seemed to look more relaxed after they finished.

Not long after, all of the men outside suddenly turned their heads at the same time, looking at something in the distance I think, but I couldn't see what it was through the gap.

I shuffled my body across trying to get a better look, when I'd heard Lothar yell something out, but I hadn't been able to make out what it was. I kept watching and saw him start walking forward, standing really tall. He looked scary, but also brave, like he wasn't worried at all. I noticed Pa followed just behind him, but he didn't look as sure as Lothar did.

I could almost see what they were walking over to when Simon, one of the town elders walked over and told me to 'get out of the way and go back to my mother'.

Mother heard him and turned from listening to Lord Edmund, then grabbed me, and dragged me down towards the back of the hall.

Everyone started crowding at the doors and trying to peek through the gap like I'd been doing. It wasn't fair because I wanted to see what the people were looking at too, but Mother wouldn't allow it.

We made it to the far back corner of the hall, away from everyone, I watched as Mother felt around the wooden wallboards and then somehow, she pushed it aside like a door, showing a small, hidden closet behind.

It was smelly, and dark and I didn't want to go in there, I'd begged her to let me stay with her, but she'd gotten angry.

"Listen, Kael! Do not argue with me! There are bad men outside, I need you to hide. You are not to come out until I, or your father, says so—do you understand!?"

I knew she was serious, so quietly nodded my head at her. I felt sick, I was scared but I wanted to look brave.

"Good boy. Stay back here and keep as quiet as you can, no matter what. Please, do not disobey me. I love you, Kael," she had said, and then kissed my forehead, before hugging me tightly.

I didn't know it then, but…

That'd be the last time I would ever hear Mother speak.

She closed the door behind me and blocked out the light.

It was pitch black and cramped inside, even for me. My knees were pressed up against my chest, and I'm kind of small for my age.

From where I hid, all I could hear was muffled yelling and the sound of metal making clanging sounds. Like when I watched Rupert make stuff in his smithy.

I couldn't tell what was going on, but I knew it was very bad.

I held onto my sword, feeling the wooden handle Pa had helped me carve into shape out of an oak branch, then shut my eyes as tightly as I could. I wished Pa was with me.

I don't know how long it'd been, but eventually the metal banging sounds outside stopped, and everyone in the hall began whispering quietly.

Suddenly, a voice that sounded like Lord Edmund hissed, "Lothar and the men have been overwhelmed. Emeric! Simon! Begin handing the weapons out to the women, now!"

Lord Edmund sounded different than normal, his voice shook, he was scared.

From my hiding place I heard some of the townspeople sobbing, and others telling each other it would be fine.

I believed them at the time, because I wanted to be true so badly... but it wasn't fine. They'd lied. They were all liars.

A loud crash suddenly made me jump, and I remember I nearly wet myself. I was brave though and I didn't, Mother or Pa wouldn't have liked that.

"Prepare yourselves! The door will not hold!"

Someone had yelled, I think it was Lord Edmund again, but I couldn't be sure.

All the voices had gotten louder, and I wanted to cry, I wanted this to be over and things be how they were before.

It was dark, and loud, and I was scared. I was realising that being brave wasn't as easy as I thought and I didn't like it.

Where was Pa? How could Lothar be overwhelmed?

Lothar was the strongest fighter in the town, everyone knew that. Even Pa had said so before, and he was really strong himself, he told me Lothar had saved his life once and he had never seen Lothar lose a fight.

I'd jumped when I heard another giant crash, and then it got really noisy, I could hear new voices shouting angrily.

Then the metal clanging sounds started up again and people began screaming… I've never heard people scream like that before, and I hope I never do again. If I was bigger and not scared, maybe I could've helped.

But I did as Mother had said, and I never came out.

The screams and sounds went on and on, I thought they'd never end. I was glad when eventually they did, but I knew deep down that this didn't mean anything good.

When the sounds had stopped, I heard men I didn't recognise start talking to each other and I held my breath, too terrified to make a sound.

They spoke funny, their voices sounded different to the men in our village.

"Cleric Gildred, give me a status report. How many men did we lose?" A bossy sounding voice had said.

"Ah… eighteen dead, Lord Zarek. We have a

further five wounded that are already being tended to outside, but they should survive. I have had our dead set aside for burial. It may help to have the company physician look at that cut across your forehead as well, my lord, lest it become infected."

The man called Gildred I think, had said back after a short pause.

"Tsk. It will be fine, Gildred, Saint Michael will look over me. Besides, I have suffered worse… even if it has been an exceedingly long time since anyone has managed to mark me with a blade. As for the casualties, that is more than I would have liked. This lot put up quite a fight compared to the towns to the south. Did any escape?" The Lord Zarek man had asked.

"It does not appear as such my lord. No one was spotted attempting to flee since our arrival," Gildred said.

"Good. Have the men make certain none have been missed and sort the children out. Decapitate and cremate them, the heads included—you are aware of the usual procedures. See that they are done to the letter."

I knew at the time that he must have meant Matthias and the other kids, tears welled up in my eyes while I listened in darkness from the cupboard. I didn't like Matthias, but I didn't want him hurt either. I had no idea what 'cremate' meant, but I was sure it couldn't be a good thing.

This is like a bad dream I'd thought and curled up in a ball.

"Of course, my lord. Ah, Lord Zarek… May I ask…"

"What is it, Gildred?" Lord Zarek snapped, sounded annoyed at Gildred.

"Well, my lord, we are approaching the last few towns in the area that the recovered texts had indicated. Do you think we finally got the child?" Gildred asked after a pause.

I heard someone sheathing their sword and then a long sigh.

"We can only pray, Gildred. I have my doubts though, I would have expected the child to put up more resistance than this lot. If the historical texts are accurate, and I am sure they are—we might very well be the ones burning, had we encountered the one we were seeking," Lord Zarek said.

"I was thinking the same, my lord."

Neither of the men spoke for a moment.

"How many children did we find here, Gildred?"

"Seven. I believe, my lord."

"Interesting. Our records indicated eight residing in this town. Leave three of the men here to manage the cremations, then have them search the nearby homesteads again for survivors. You are to take the uninjured men and continue to search the surrounding countryside to ensure the child has not escaped. Then I want you to continue to the northeast, set camp for the night along the way, and prepare to cleanse the next settlement, Hiltsten. Await my arrival there after it is done. Our records show it is smaller in population than this town, it should not prove a challenge for you with the remaining troops. I will return and collect the rest of the Order that are camped to the south and be back here in the evening to collect the three you leave behind. And to bury our dead," Lord Zarek had ordered.

"Understood, my lord," Gildred said, followed by the sound of footsteps walking away.

"You three over there! You heard Lord Zarek. You are to stay here and complete the cremations and then search the nearby homesteads again. Our records indicate one child is still unaccounted for, remain here in case they are still here hiding until Lord Zarek returns with the reinforcements tomorrow," Gildred said.

"Understood, sir," a group of men replied.

"The rest of you! Prepare to leave this godforsaken town. We are to search the surrounding area for the missing child before marching northeast to the next cesspit of a town in need of purification," a few voices murmured replies I couldn't understand, and I heard more footsteps leaving the building.

I lay as quiet as a mouse on the cold, dark floor of

my cupboard for what felt like forever, the smell hadn't bothered me anymore, so I just laid there, listening to the sounds of the men that stayed behind dragging things around the hall.

Sometimes they shuffled right by my hiding place, but I stayed quiet, just like Mother had told me too, and they never found me.

****

I don't know how much time passed, but finally someone spoke again and said, "Alright, that's all of them, and the heads too—light it up, Cedric, and let's go search the homesteads again. The flesh will stink this building out, I don't want to be in here while they burn."

"Agreed, if it smells anything like the last lot, I'll be sick. The stench made my gambeson stink like rotting carcass for almost a week. Let's get this done and get out of here," another voice said.

"That's just the way you smell all the time, Bruce," someone said, and they all laughed.

From my dark hiding place, I could make out the sound of a fire start to crackle, and not long after I started to smell smoke. It didn't smell like when Pa started the fireplace at home though. Something was burning, and it smelt horrible, just like the men said it would.

I lay there exhausted when I heard them finally

leave, I was still wondering if Mother might come to get me, 'You are not to come out until I say so' she'd said, and I hoped she still would. She wouldn't leave me, I knew she wouldn't.

Please be alright Mother and Pa, don't forget I'm here, I'd silently prayed.

I remember curling tighter into a ball, still too terrified to open the door and look outside. All the fear had made me exhausted… and a short time later I must have fallen asleep.

I'd been woken up when I heard the sound of footsteps, I held my breath like I'd done before, thinking the bad men must have come back. I could hear someone walking slowly into the building, no one was talking though, maybe they were alone? I'd hoped inside it was Mother finally coming back for me like she promised.

I'd kept as still as I could, it was hard though because my whole body wouldn't stop shaking like I was shivering from being cold, except I wasn't cold. It was sweltering in the closet, and I was very thirsty.

There'd been a sudden, soft thud, like something dropped firmly onto the wooden floor, and then I'd heard a man begin to make soft, quiet whimpering noises, gasping like he was having trouble breathing.

It sounded like he was crying.

I'd been confused, wondering why the bad men would be crying? Unless it wasn't the bad men? Then I wondered, what if it was Pa, and he was crying because he couldn't find me.

I wanted to open the door and see, I didn't want to be alone anymore. I'd needed to see who was out there.

So, I built the courage up to try and slide the wall across like Mother had done but found it wouldn't move! I'd started to panic, growing terrified that they would leave, and I'd be alone again! I pushed it harder, I didn't care if the person heard me anymore, I had to get out of here! Then I heard whoever was on the other side approaching.

I became like a mouse again, quiet and holding my breath, listening, hoping to hear Pa or Mother's voices speak. Praying it was them that had found me again.

When the door slid open, I clutched my sword and waited, the outside light was so bright that I had to use one hand to cover my eyes, peeking through my fingers I made out the tall, outline of a man, taller than Pa, with dark, dried blood all over his face and head. It made his thick, sweaty, brown hair stick to his face and neck. His armour was filthy.

"… Kael?"

The man had spoken my name, his voice had sounded gravelly, like his throat was really dry. He must have been as thirsty as I was at the time.

I'd slowly taken my hand away from my face and looked into his eyes, they were dark and very red where they should've been white, but… I recognised him.

"Lothar!" I had yelled excitedly and hugged him.

"Quiet, boy! You must keep it down. Yes, it's me, we need to get out of here. Are you injured?" he asked me.

"No, I'm…" I had begun to reply, before I noticed all the bodies lying around us.

Everyone was dead, all the villagers that had hidden in the hall… and Mother… oh no… not Mother… there she had lay… not far away… I couldn't help myself and I'd started to cry.

"Stop it, boy! Don't look!" Lothar suddenly grabbed me, and picked me up like I weighed nothing, smothering my face into his chest which had blocked my view.

His chest plate was hard against my forehead, but I was too upset to care. I just kept sobbing.

"We're leaving this place. There is nothing left for us here," he mumbled to me, and carried me outside.

I shut my eyes and didn't look just like he told me to.

***

"Boy. Get up, it's time for us to hit the road," a gruff voice said.

Lothar's voice, he roughly shook me awake. I must have finally fallen asleep and now he had to go and wake me up.

He was such a big oaf.

I yawned and stretched my arms up.

"I'm awake already! You don't have to shake me like that, you could just ask next time you know," I snapped at him, annoyed.

"Mhm," he grunted back.

Mother had always said to me 'You're not a morning person, Kael,' and sometimes, I knew what she meant.

Mother.

I felt sick in my tummy every time I pictured her face.

Thinking about my tummy made me realise how empty it was, and I looked around, then at Lothar.

"I'm hungry, do we have anymore bread?" I asked.

He reached into his satchel and chucked a thick crust down onto my blanket.

"Here. Now get out of there and pack your bedroll up."

I frowned but stood up and began doing like I was told, it wouldn't hurt him to ask a little nicer.

I noticed he already had his sleeping roll and gear packed up and resting by the door, he must have gotten out of bed and done his earlier I realised.

Placing my bread aside on a small set of drawers, I started rolling my bed roll up. I peeked at how Lothar had done his to try and do mine the same, but it was harder than I thought.

He just stood there watching me with a stupid frown on his face. I did get it done eventually but it was a little messy and not as small as his.

"Here, boy. Give it to me," he asked still frowning.

"No. It's fine, I know what I'm doing! Pa showed me already."

His face stiffened a little when I mentioned Pa, but then he just shrugged.

"As you wish. Are you ready?"

"Yes. Where are we going?" I asked while I put my pack on my shoulders and tucked my sword down the back, the same way Lothar was wearing his.

"Hiltsten. We need to make sure they know what's coming their way," he replied, and passed me my bread again from on top of the drawers.

"Eat up. It's a long trek for a child."

I took the bread off him.

Even with all the bad stuff going on right now I couldn't help but feel a little excited when I heard we were going to Hiltsten, I'd never left Drassox before.

Pa always said Hiltsten or Branwick were too far away for a boy my age to walk, but he'd promised to take me when I turned ten.

I guess that won't happen anymore I thought, feeling sad again. I wished he were coming with us now. I wanted to ask Lothar what had happened to him, but I felt like it wasn't a good time. Lothar seemed to be thinking to himself a lot, and I was afraid to hear his answer too.

I missed Pa… and Mother, I missed them both so much already.

CHAPTER 3
AN OMINOUS ENCOUNTER

'He shall ravin as a wolf; in the morning he shall devour the
prey, and at night he shall divide the spoil'

The boy and I had been trekking uneventfully across the long, grassy plains for most of morning, and were now approaching a forested section that marked a little over the halfway point to Hiltsten.

The sun was high in the sky, casting a warm glow over everything it touched and judging from the angle, it appeared to be close to midday. We were making great pace, the boy had surprised me thus far with his endurance.

At this rate, we should arrive in Hiltsten by the late afternoon. Hopefully before sunset anyway, I didn't want to be caught out here after dark. I feared the soldiers that had attacked Drassox would strike Hiltsten next. It was the logical target, I knew they would follow a similar path as the one we were currently trekking, which only reinforced my belief we had to get to our destination before nightfall.

"How much further is it, Lothar? My feet are sore," the boy began to complain for the first time since leaving the cottage.

He'd remained stoic up until now, which was admirable. The lack of food and rest though was taking its toll on his vulnerable frame. It was to be expected, he was too young to leave Drassox yet.

I continued looking forward as I answered him, "That forest ahead is just past halfway. It'll likely slow us down a bit as we pass on through, but we should arrive before sunset."

I was trying to encourage him, but it clearly had the opposite effect.

"Halfway!? But I'm tired! And what are we going to eat? We've had nothing but a bit of stale bread since last night," he moaned, and then started dragging his feet.

I wasn't frustrated by his whining, it stopped my own mind wandering down into the dark of recent events… and kept his own from dwelling on them. His resilience to yesterday's massacre had greatly astounded me. It appeared children recovered well from such things.

They say ignorance is bliss.

"If we're lucky, we might find some berries or mushrooms in the forest," I replied.

I saw him raise his eyebrows just a little, in surprise.

It wasn't a lie, the wet season had only just passed, and the plant life around us was flourishing, everything was a lush green and blooming. I had no doubt we'd find something to eat in the grove ahead.

I was skilled at foraging, unfortunately though, I was unable to hunt at present since I lacked a bow. It was a small matter, we had no time to hunt right now anyway, let alone skin and prepare a kill to roast.

No, I decided, we must rely on whatever we could find and gather quickly, continue moving, and focus on trying to put as much distance between us and the soldiers as possible.

Even with hunting off the table though I still chided myself for not taking that soldiers crossbow when he had dropped dead from… well, whatever the fuck it was that had caused his worthless life to cease.

I still counted it as a stroke of luck, but I wasn't convinced that's what it was.

At least I'd thought to take a sword at the time. It was a decent made weapon too, good quality steel with an even weight, unfortunately it lacked the familiar feel of my own sword which in comparison, had grown to feel like an extension of my own limb.

That blade had seen me through countless battles and many a training session. It had previously belonged to my father, inherited to me a few summers prior to his death. I recall times when I was not much younger than the boy, watching him practicing with it for hours. He'd told me that a true master should hone his craft every day, whether it be blacksmithing, soldiering or even farming. 'Your skills are like this blade, boy. Neglect them and their edge will dull all the same' he would say.

As I grew into a man I'd followed that advice, reciting it like a mantra whenever I didn't feel like training, using it to motivate myself. I had yet to be bested in combat, although I came close more than once. I've killed many men in my life, not always for honourable reasons either, but I'm still alive and they are not. I regret to think that maybe I've let my skills wane a little these later years, maybe things yesterday would've turned out differently had I not. Maybe I would've killed that man, and the people of Drassox would still be alive, maybe not.

Maybe I just thought too much.

"Can we eat these?" The boy asked interrupting my thoughts.

I glanced over to see what he had found, he was pointing to a green bush I recognised, that had small clusters of black berries growing amongst its leaves.

Having just approached the thicket of the forest, I knew we'd find food here, but this particular plant was not it.

"No, boy. That's called Buckthorn. It won't kill you, but it'll make you sick."

He looked at me, frowning, making no effort to hide his disappointment, then resumed walking.

"Well, it looks like blueberries… except black. Blackberries," he mumbled to himself.

"Blackberries don't look like that," I told him, staring ahead.

We continued walking along in silence, the brush had condensed quickly upon entering the thicket, the smell of pine needles filled the air, and the pleasant sounds of birds chirping from the treetops could be heard all around us, it would be considered serene, if not for the dark images occasionally flashing through my head reminding me of yesterday.

I considered using my sword to hack through the worst of thick brush, but that would be too obvious to follow for any pursuers, I had my suspicions our escape wouldn't go unnoticed.

Back in Drassox, before the boy and I had fought our way out, I noticed the corpses of the enemy soldiers had been neatly stacked. I held suspicions that the reason was for burial when the group returned. This was not cause for concern on its own, our lives in Drassox were over… my concerns were the three men

I'd left dead in the town square as the boy and I, had fled the area.

Well, two men. I didn't exactly kill the crossbowman.

Regardless though, those bodies… were not neatly stacked.

They lay butchered, on the very ground where I'd taken their lives, an obvious sign to anyone returning that someone had survived the massacre and fought their way out.

A reason to pursue us if they chose to finish the job.

I'd scolded myself more than once since waking up for not having taken a little time to hide the bodies.

"Lothar… did my Pa die?" The boy said sadly, interrupting my thoughts again.

This time it wasn't such an innocent question and took me by surprise. I knew this would come eventually but I was hoping it wouldn't be this soon, it stung me deeply.

The death of my friend was weighing heavily on my mind.

I paused, partly in shock, and partly to consider my response, trying to decide how to tell him, what I should tell him, and how much. My heart said he had a right to know, but I had no experience in dealing with young children.

I hadn't found time to have any of my own, choosing to focus on my role as Captain of the guard, spending most of my time training the men at arms and assuring the safety of the settlement.

Something I had quite clearly failed at.

I allowed my gaze to fall to the ground while we continued to walk, the boy trudging along behind me patiently, waiting for me to speak.

After a moment I replied softly, "Yes, he did, boy."

That was the best I could come up with? After everything that had happened to us. I scolded myself.

His pace slowed, and we continued forward in silence.

The pain lay thick and heavy in the air between us, the sound of nature around, trickling in and filling the void that had suddenly appeared.

A moment later he spoke again, softly, the sadness evident in his timid voice.

"How?"

God. This was worse than I thought it would be.

Stop it.

You are behaving as a coward would.

The boy deserves to know, and it's fallen upon you to tell him. It's your duty, you owe it to Elias.

Once again, I hesitated before replying and considered what I would say, and how much he needed to know.

Taking a deep breath, I began, "… He was not far from me when it happened. A coward, too weak to face your Pa like a man, fired a crossbow, and he was struck from a distance. There was no way of stopping it."

Liar. If you hadn't antagonised the man, things may have turned out differently. If you'd considered Elias's concerns, he may still be alive. If you'd told him to stay back with the men and approached alone, he would still be alive.

If, if, if.

The boy just nodded his head slowly and kept on walking, his gaze dropped to the ground, and he didn't speak again.

We kept walking into the forest for a while until I decided to break the silence, in an attempt to lighten the mood.

"You know, boy. I knew your Pa a long time before you were born. Even when he was your age. You are just like him."

He looked up at me squinting from the sun, "Why do you say that?"

"Well, I was a bit older than him the first time we spoke. I was out gathering firewood for my father when I stumbled across your Pa, barely a little bit older than you at the time. He was hiding in the woods just out of town," I began.

"Hiding? I never saw Pa get scared of anything. What was he hiding from?" He asked.

The boy's interest piqued now.

"Everyone gets scared, boy. Being brave isn't about the absence of feeling fear—it's feeling terrified, but doing what needs to be done anyway," I paused, letting him ponder this for a moment.

"Your father was young at the time, and some of the other kids from the town wanted to beat him up," I smiled and then continued, "I don't recall the reason why they were after him, but when I found him, he was scared out of his mind."

"What happened next?" He asked.

I stepped over a fallen tree trunk and waited for the boy to do the same before we continued walking.

"And then, they found him. There were three of them, except he wasn't alone anymore. I was there now, and I made them wait their turn as your Pa beat them all up, one after the other. They weren't so tough when they were singled out, and they never bothered your Pa again. I also never saw your Pa run away from anyone again either. He found his bravery that day," I told him.

The boy stopped, looking up at me for a moment, meeting my gaze.

Then without another word, he resumed marching forward, his pace a little faster, his chin held a little higher in the air, and just a little more spring in his step.

He didn't say anything more, he didn't need too.

I smiled to myself. Maybe I can do some things right after all, I thought, as I quickened my pace to match his and we marched in silence.

"Ah, here," I said.

We'd just come into a small clearing, containing a good-sized mushroom patch. I crouched down to the ground alongside it. The boy came scurrying to my side, perhaps a little too eagerly.

"Mushrooms?" He asked excited.

His stomach, along with my own, had been growling in protest for the past hour or more as we trudged along through the forest, the half loaf of bread hadn't been enough to sustain us for long.

"Yes. Pick them, they're fine to eat raw, but we need to move fast. Do you understand? We can't linger here," I said.

He nodded his head in reply, practically licking his lips already.

"Here, place them in this," I said and passed him a small piece of cloth from my pack.

He hurriedly knelt and began quickly picking the mushrooms as though he thought I was going to change my mind if he wasn't fast enough.

I wandered off to the side, leaving him to gather the mushrooms and pushed my way through some thick bushes.

Ahh, there it is.

I knew I could smell something giving off a faint, sweet aroma, and my senses hadn't betrayed me. It was a raspberry bush, tucked just out of sight.

These should keep the boy happy. Well, as happy as one can be after what he's been through.

What we've both been through.

Some raspberries might be a small comfort, but they're the best I can do right now I thought as I began picking them from the bush and placing them in the small leather pouch on my belt as quickly as I could.

"Uhhmmmm, Lothar!" I suddenly heard him yell to me.

For god's sake, why is he yelling? He needs to learn to keep his bloody voice down. I stood back up and angrily spun around, pushing my way back through the thicket, returning to where I'd left him.

"What is it, bo—"

I instantly froze, my jaw dropping in awe at what I was witnessing.

Standing not twenty paces from the boy was a huge, muscular stag. Besides the animal's size, what was perhaps most striking, was its pure white fur and matching antlers. It was spotlessly clean, appearing to almost radiate its own light, as the sunrays reflected off its brilliant, shiny coat.

I'd hunted these forests for most of my life and never witnessed such a magnificent creature as this before. What was even stranger was that it seemed to be focused intently on the boy, curious, as though his presence confused it, frustrated it, angered it.

Its posture was tense.

Hostile.

"Boy. Do not move, whatever you do. You need to listen to me."

"Lothar, I'm scared! Why's it staring at me like that?" He replied, his voice shaking and threatening to break.

"HRRMMPHH!" The creature grunted, slightly lifting and slamming its front hooves down into the ground, as though issuing a challenge to the boy.

"Be still, boy!" I hissed.

What the hell was going on? I've never seen a stag react like this, they're normally peaceful creatures. I know that they can act protective during rutting season, but… this behaviour was different to what I'd seen in the past from these animals.

"Lothar, w—what do I do?" the boy stuttered, becoming increasingly panicked.

"Just hold your ground, boy. Don't move and don't speak anymore, I'm going to come to you," I said slowly.

He was too far away, I needed to get closer. The beast seemed to have no interest in me and was focusing all its energy on the boy. I decided to use this to my advantage and began carefully edging my way towards him, slowly and deliberately, creeping across the forest floor as to not make a sound or sudden movement. I didn't want to provoke the animal in any way.

I was almost close enough. Just a little further and I'd be able to reach him in time.

A powerful creature such as this could kill a man in seconds, the boy would stand no chance if it charged.

"HRRMMMPHHH!" It stomped again feinting slightly forward this time, and the boy began lightly whimpering.

I noticed the sun was no longer shining on us, the forest had become eerie, almost dark as though the canopy above had tightened, now blocking out the glow of the sun.

He was only a short distance away from me now.

"Boy… stay calm, I'm almos—" And then the beast charged.

***

I felt too terrified to look where Lothar was, I was doing my best to do as he told me and not to move at all, but I couldn't stop shaking. I felt just like I did when I was hiding in the closet and the bad men came.

Why couldn't I stop being so scared and just do what needed to be done like Lothar said brave people did when they felt scared? How did him and Pa do it? Why wasn't I like them?

You need to hurry Lothar, it's going to get me.

Please.

He wasn't far away, I could hear him. I just had to hold on, I needed to be brave. He would save me.

My eyes were almost shut when I heard the massive thing in front of me make another loud grunt, louder than the first time. It sounded closer, I had to check.

I slowly opened my eyes to peek, and straight away I made eye contact with it. The stag became perfectly still like it had frozen solid, staring dead straight at me.

And then without any warning it charged.

I heard a sound to my left and saw Lothar start to sprint towards me out of the corner of my eye just as the stag did.

I shut my eyes again and waited.

The next thing I felt was Lothar's strong hands grabbing me and lifting me off of my feet, pulling me in close to his armour like he did when I saw mother's body, lying there on the floor.

He bravely turned his back to the stag so his body was between it and me, I couldn't stop myself from opening my eyes and watching over his shoulder while it galloped towards us.

Suddenly a deep, ferocious, growl thundered through the air, sounding like it had come from a monster. I watched in shock when a large flash of dark fur crashed through the bushes to the side of us and smashed into the white stag as it charged forward.

I couldn't believe my eyes, it was a massive wolf, with fur as black as the night, by far the largest wolf

I've ever seen—and I'd seen a few that Pa had killed with his bow when they tried to steal the chickens and hens from our coop.

Lothar dropped me to the ground and spun around drawing his sword from his back as soon as he heard the deafening growl. Standing behind him, I watched both animals roll around on the ground, fighting.

The stag angrily swung its huge antlers back and forth trying its hardest to hurt the wolf, while the wolf snapped its jaws back and bit the stag all over its body leaving deep wounds.

Eventually the wolf managed to grab its prey on the throat and using its massive neck and jaws, which were almost as thick as me, pinned the white stag to the floor of the forest.

It was so strong, the stag couldn't get up, its hooves kicked all around the dirt making a mess of the mushroom patch while it tried to stand and fight back, blood began to cover its clean white coat as the wolf's razor-sharp teeth bit into it deeply and wouldn't let go.

The great, white stag struggled and thrashed until it slowly began to stop fighting back, tiring itself from struggling so hard against the huge black wolf on top of it.

The wolf's dark eyes looked at us while it held its jaws clamped onto the stag's throat waiting for it to die, steam pouring from its nose as it breathed with a mouthful of white fur.

"Boy, back away slowly. Do not turn around. Go straight into the bushes, now," Lothar quietly whispered, trying not to draw anymore of the wolf's attention.

I did as he said and very slowly backed up being careful to tread as silently as I could, feeling like an ant being so close to such huge animals.

We backed further away and luckily the wolf seemed to ignore us, before it started to drag the almost dead stag the other way, skidding the heavy, dying animal across the dirt, leaving a trail of blood. The stag let out a long, slow moan, as it disappeared from our view.

Even though we couldn't see the wolf anymore we were still scared to turn our backs in its direction, so we kept walking backwards, away into the trees for a bit longer.

"It's time for us to leave this forest, boy," Lothar said, and I agreed.

My heart was beating out of my chest when we turned around, Lothar motioned for me to walk in front of him from now on and we continued through the forest.

Somehow, during everything, I still had the mushrooms I'd collected in the cloth.

What seemed like forever later we finally cleared

the trees and bushes, and a big grassy field lay ahead of us. We hadn't said much since seeing the two animals fight, I was just happy to be away from them, and hoped I'd never see anything like the wolf or the stag again.

I'd eaten all the mushrooms, Lothar didn't want any, he said he wasn't hungry, I'm not sure how. He also surprised me with some raspberries he'd found and not said anything about. Maybe he was planning to keep them for himself and changed his mind because he wasn't hungry anymore. He'd hidden them in his belt pouch, so they were a little squashed from picking me up when the stag charged, but they were still yum.

I don't know how he knew I liked raspberries so much, sometimes he would be nice, and it surprised me.

"That was really crazy, huh? That wolf was massive," I said with a mouthful of raspberries, and kept on walking in front of him waiting for an answer. Sometimes I noticed he didn't answer me straight away, like he was thinking about what to say because I wouldn't understand, but I'm smarter than he thinks.

"Hellooo?" I said again and swallowed.

"Don't talk with your mouth full. And it wasn't a wolf. At least not a regular one."

"Oh, well what was it then?" I asked and again he made me wait for an answer.

"It was a dire wolf… I haven't seen or heard of one being in these parts for a very long time, not since before the Great War. I heard stories that there used to be a lot of them back then, but they were all hunted and killed off," he finally replied.

"A dire wolf? Why'd it save us like that?" I asked looking back at him.

"It didn't save us, boy. We were lucky it had something it wanted more, otherwise we'd be dead. They were known to be very dangerous, that's why they were hunted down and killed."

"Well, it looked like it saved us. That stag was coming straight for me."

"Well, it didn't. Now walk faster, we're almost there," he said sharply.

"Are you scared it will come after us?" I asked feeling a little worried myself.

"No, I'm not. That stag will keep it busy for a while," he said after considering it.

"I'll be happy if we never see one again. I don't know which one was worse, the wolf thing or the big stag," I replied.

"The dire wolf was worse. Now stop thinking about it, that's Hiltsten just up ahead."

I looked where he was looking in the distance, the sun was still in the sky, but low now. Lothar had said we were earlier than he expected but I wasn't surprised, we'd walked pretty damn fast since seeing the wolf and stag so it made sense we would be early.

As we hiked closer, I could start to make out the town of Hiltsten. They had a big wall all the way around the buildings, it was so cool. Drassox didn't have anything like that.

The wall had been made of wooden logs stuck in the ground side by side and there were more of them than I could count. The wall was also really tall, and the tops of the logs looked like they had been cut into sharp points.

We could've used a wall like this when the bad men came.

"Why didn't we have a wall like that around Drassox?" I asked.

He sighed and did his normal make me wait for an answer.

"We've never needed one. For a long while, Hiltsten was constantly being attacked by groups of brigands and that's when they constructed the wall. It took many months to complete, and they needed help while they built it. So, a few summers ago, they requested aide from us in dealing with the brigands. I brought men from Drassox, and we helped the people here clear the area," he told me while staring straight ahead.

"Did my Pa come with you?" I asked.

We were close enough I could make out a set of gates and noticed there was a tall tower on the other side. I thought I could see a man on top, but we were still too far away to be sure.

"Yes, he did, boy," Lothar mumbled in reply.

"I have a name you know. It's Kael. K-A-E-L," I told him annoyed.

"Mhm."

All I got for a reply was a grunt, he could be so grumpy sometimes.

CHAPTER 4
ARRIVAL TO HILTSTEN

'And let them make me a sanctuary; that I dwell among them'

We were finally at Hiltsten. I had not been here in years and if I'm honest, I felt a little trepidation now that we were so close to its gates.

In the back of my mind, I believe it's because I know that they'll ask me questions about Drassox, and even the thought of talking about what happened there still pains me inside.

I'm pretty much certain that it always will.

The guilt.

The dishonour.

The things I saw.

The BURNING.

These are the burdens I must carry with me, the punishments for my failure to protect everyone I cared about.

Regardless how I feel about it, me and the boy will arrive there soon, and I'll need to speak of yesterday's massacre.

And now I've something else to worry about on top of that.

Since the forest, all I could think about was that black wolf and the white stag. I could make no sense of it, a stag behaving that way? The mere appearance of a dire wolf?

It was unheard of.

Nothing made sense these past few days.

What did the soldiers want? Why were they killing children and entire towns of people? Who were they? What happened to that man with the crossbow? What was I even doing here at Hiltsten with the boy?

My entire life was in Drassox, and now it was all gone, swallowed up into the abyss.

I have no answers and no hint what I'll do from here, I have a child with me, yet no idea how to care for one.

Yet…

For some unknown reason I feel compelled to protect him, as though it's my duty to ensure no harm comes to him. It's a feeling I also have no answer for, perhaps he's grown on me in our brief time together, or perhaps it's because he reminds me of Elias, and the grief we share for him.

Either way, I hope I find some answers soon, I need a clear path to follow, I don't enjoy this feeling of hopelessness.

"Lothar!? That you?" A surprised voice called out invading my pondering.

I looked around and realised we had arrived at the gates to Hiltsten. And there, high above, on a roughly constructed guard tower, a familiar figure looked down at us. I stared back at the tall, skinny man for a moment trying to recall his name, before I finally recognised the figure perched up above.

"Ah, Cassian. I see you have changed professions since our last meeting?" I replied, remembering that the last time I was here, he had worked as one of the labourers.

I recalled him helping to construct the wall while we had provided the soldiers to protect the town from further brigand attacks.

He laughed and said, "Yeah, 'ya could say that. A few of us had to step up and fill guard roles after the casualties we suffered when you were 'ere last. 'Twas a rough time, I'm sure you remember though."

I nodded at him, "I remember. Things have changed though, Cassian. Now I'm the one who needs help," I said getting to the point.

I didn't come all this way for small talk with a

gatekeeper, I'm a Captain, and I must warn the Duke so he can begin preparations—not sit here reminiscing on the past about problems long resolved.

"Oh yeah, how's that, Lothar? I can't imagine a fine warrior such as yourself needing our help," he replied gratingly.

Now he was beginning to irritate me, I bit my tongue to stifle the anger I could feel rising inside of me.

He means no harm, he couldn't know what me and the boy have been through. Speaking of the boy, he was standing closer than normal to my side and being quiet for a change.

"With respect, Cassian, I'm not here to exchange pleasantries, I need to speak to the Duke. Now. Open the gates that I made possible for you to build, and let us in. We've had a rough journey, and my purpose here is urgent," I said becoming my authoritative self once again.

I saw him smirk then with a sarcastic tone he retorted, "Oh, sorry your highness, I didn't mean to upset 'ya," which only infuriated me further.

Who the fuck does he think he is speaking to?

I let out a low growl but tried to calm myself by taking a deep breath before giving him an answer.

"Cassian. This is no small matter. The Duke will let me in when he hears I've come, and if you haven't opened the gate within the next few moments, I will tear you in two as soon as he does. I'm not in the mood for childish games."

I hadn't wanted to threaten the man, but my anger and the events of these past days finally got the better of me. Regardless, he got the idea I was serious and responded with a shocked expression muttering "sorry", then began climbing down from his post.

"You wouldn't really tear him in half would you, Lothar?" The boy whispered looking up at me as Cassian disappeared from view.

I grunted and ignored him but noticed he was still standing closely to my side while he fidgeted and adjusted the wooden sword on his back as he stood there.

A few moments later I heard Cassian fumbling with the gate latch on the other side, and a satisfying "click" followed as he slid the bolt across and unlocked the door.

It opened and we were greeted by his boyish face, now wearing a concerned look.

"There, I opened it. I'm sorry, Lothar, I didn't mean to anger you," he quickly apologised, making me almost feel bad for threatening him.

I didn't feel bad though, he hadn't needed to prod at me.

"It's fine, Cassian. We've had a hard few days, I must speak with the Duke, it's extremely urgent. Can you let him know that I've arrived?" I instructed him.

He nodded his head, "Yeah of course, Lothar, I'll go and see him at once. Wait for me in the town square," he replied and took off in a hurry.

I turned my attention back to the boy, "We need to move, boy. Follow me."

It was clear I had not needed to tell him, he didn't appear to want to leave my side, still choosing to invade my personal space, although I didn't mind either.

We started walking through the town, following along a wide dirt road in the direction of the village square.

Hiltsten was a smaller settlement than Drassox with only around forty villagers I believed, at least this was true the last time I was here. They also had less men at arms than Drassox, due to the casualties suffered during the brigand crisis, fortunately the production of the wall had helped in safeguarding their town from outside threat.

Fighting aged men were a hard commodity to come by in small villages such as ours, the towns still needed farmers and labourers to work in the fields and produce crops to feed the people. We made do though as best we could, a lot of people worked multiple roles within the community to do their part.

Branwick was the largest of the three settlements south of the Strunn river, I had not been there for six to seven summers now, and last I was, if my memory serves correct, they had over one hundred villagers and around sixty trained men at arms.

Considerably larger than Hiltsten or Drassox.

They would be our most valuable ally in dealing with the threat that was on its way. Unfortunately though, I believed Hiltsten was out of time.

They would fight this next battle alone, the enemy would arrive here not long after me, I was hoping they would at least wait until morning to begin to approach the settlement, but I couldn't be sure. Assuming had cost me dearly lately, and I would not fall victim to this again.

The boy and I strode passed multiple small wooden homes on either side of us, all were evenly spaced apart.

While we continued our way towards the town square, many of the townspeople stopped what they were doing to stare, it was not often they had visitors here, Drassox had been much the same. I looked around and saw women washing clothes on scrubbing boards, people milled about here and there, and a man was hanging deer skins up for tanning.

The houses were quite simple, cottage style builds, with wooden planks for walls and crude doors. The rooves were made of thin wooden slats and then layered with thatched straw to help hold the heat inside on the chilly wintry nights. Every house had a chimney, some even had two.

Hiltsten was much closer to the Hadrian Ocean to the east than either Drassox or Branwick, and as a result tended to have much colder nights.

"This place doesn't seem much different than home, maybe a bit smaller," the boy said, it was the first words he had spoken since we entered through the town gates.

"It's not all that different. Drassox isn't home now though, best you forget about it, boy," I told him as we walked.

"I don't want to forget—" he started, and I decided to cut him off before he could finish.

"—It's for the best!" I snapped looking at him firmly, and his eyes fell to the ground.

I didn't like to tell him this, but it would do the boy no good to waste his thoughts on something we would never have again.

As we entered the town centre, which was just a large flat area in the middle of a circle of houses, I spotted a group of children playing and watching us a short distance away. Their innocent playing reminded me that the meeting with the Duke I had planned was no place for a child.

He would be better served staying here with the other children. Nor would it do him any good to hear me recount the events that occurred at Drassox. No, I would need to leave him here with someone while I attended the meeting.

With this in mind, I looked around the town centre. A few people were loitering about, but it was a young woman that caught my eye.

She was of medium height for a lady and the way she was watching me and the boy suspiciously from a short distance away, doing her best to pretend she was not curious about our presence, caught my attention the same way we had caught hers.

I decided she had a fairly trustworthy look and began to approach her. As I grew nearer, I realised the woman was quite attractive, likely just shy of thirty summers in age, her simple brown and white dress covered a petite frame, her hair long and black. She had a kind face with emerald, green eyes that while kind, harboured a look of sharp intellect.

She watched us approach with a scrutinising gaze.

"Can I help you?" She called out, seeing we were obviously heading in her direction which only reinforced the thought I had that those emerald eyes did not miss much.

My intention had been to speak first but she hadn't given me much of a chance.

"Greetings ma'am. I'm Lothar, and this is… Kael. We've travelled here from Drassox," the boy glanced at me feigning a look of shock that I had used his name for a change.

"Not a ma'am. Again, how can I help you?" She asked flatly.

I decided it'd be better to get to the point with this woman and not dillydaddle like Cassian had to me at the gate.

Speaking of which, what the hell was taking him so long anyway?

He had better arrive soon or we would be having words privately, my patience had just about worn thin after these past two days, and I was struggling to remain level-headed.

I could constantly feel my anger trying to grow inside from the things I've witnessed as of late. I needed to focus, 'regain control of my reserve' as my father would say.

"I would like to ask a favour if you can be of help, miss…?" I waited for her to introduce herself, she was not making this pleasant.

Truth be told, I had always found women difficult to converse with. Probably the reason I've never taken any vows of matrimony at my age. I've always been much more qualified performing my duty as a Captain.

"The name's Delaney, I prefer just Del." She replied after pausing and looking me up and down.

"Glad to meet you, Del. Listen, I need to attend a meeting with the Duke. Could I ask you to watch the boy for me, just until I return? He does not require much care." I told her.

The boy's head snapped up at me annoyed as he

blurted out, "Grrr! I don't need any care, I'm not a baby, Lothar!"

Del just frowned heavily at me as I had said this.

"The boy?" She said and just stared at me waiting.

"Ah. Kael, I mean." I stammered.

She looked at the boy and winked, making him giggle quietly.

This entire conversation was reminding me why I preferred my duties as Captain of the guard over idle chinwag.

"Yes, Lothar, I'm sure I can handle that. I'll introduce him to the other children, I do have duties to finish before sunset, but I won't be far away. By the way, I like your sword, Kael. I bet you are really good with it, would you like to come with me for a little while?" She said, clearly more proficient with the boy than I was.

"I am, I practice a lot. And yep, I'll come with you." The boy told her, glaring obviously at me as he left my side.

Even though he was feigning to be annoyed at me I could see he was actually a little sad I was leaving him.

That's life, he'll survive.

"I appreciate the help, Del. I'll be heading off now but will return as soon as the meeting is over," I told her again.

She shooed me away and took the boy by the hand as they both wandered off towards the group of children together.

Now that that's sorted, it's time to find that useless fool Cassian.

I looked around and spotted him coming my way, luckily for him. The timing couldn't have worked out better.

I strode towards him angry about having to wait, he sensed it and as I approached, held his hands out defensively.

"Woah, woah, I'm sorry it took so long, Lothar, I spoke to the Duke and he'll see you now. He awaits you at the town hall, if you'd like to follow me, I'll take you?"

"Good. Lead the way, Cassian," I replied, impatiently.

We walked a short way through town and arrived at the hall.

The building itself was smaller and not as well constructed as the town hall in Drassox had been, although to be fair, they did have a wall surrounding the town which added considerable protection.

As we approached the doors, Cassian sped ahead and opened them for me, telling me to enter. He would return to his post atop the guard tower as befit his station, it would be untoward for a simple guard to attend a meeting with the Duke and a Captain, even one that had come from a neighbouring town.

I entered the hall without hesitation, but inside my

heart was beating much faster than usual, my hands felt clammy.

It wouldn't serve me to appear nervous or afraid, the moment I had been dreading had arrived.

"Lothar, welcome."

The Duke's voice echoed towards me from where he sat at the head of a large table in the middle of the hall.

He was ready for my entrance.

I had met Duke Roland in the years previous, a large man, not overly tall but broad, and approaching sixty summers, a ripe age in Blightreach. Most were lucky to survive that long, but Roland still appeared reasonably healthy, aside from his obvious excess intake of food. He'd been powerfully built in his younger years, but his hefty frame carried a lot of extra weight now, perks of being a Duke I suppose. He wore his grey hair short and still had a long thick beard, although it was greyer than I remembered.

I glanced around at those present in the chamber, feeling my nose twitch up as I spotted the Duke's advisor, a soft and unlikeable, fat, red-haired man named Herman. Also seated was the Captain of the guard, a medium built man by the name of Amond, both men nodded to me as I approached and I returned the gesture.

Amond was young and inexperienced to be a Captain, but it was slim pickings since the brigands attacked, the towns previous Captain had been killed in battle.

"Duke Roland, thank you for granting me an audience so soon and unannounced. Unfortunately, I bring terrible news of Drassox," I inform him.

"There's no need for formalities, Lothar. Tell me what's happened that required the Captain of the Drassox guard to travel all this way, alone—and with a child at that," he pressed.

"As you wish, Roland. I'm sure you heard of the reports from the south, groups of armed men attacking towns and murdering the inhabitants," I began.

"Yes, it is most concerning," he said, nodding slowly.

Time was not a commodity I had available, I just had to get to the point.

Just say it.

I took a deep breath and continued.

"They… they attacked Drassox yesterday morning. It was a massacre, Roland, none survived except myself and the boy I came with. They slaughtered everyone and then burned the children in the hall… th—they cut their heads off and burned them in piles," I paused before my voice broke, and everyone present waited in stunned silence for me to continue.

"…I have reason to believe that Hiltsten is their next target. They could be here tonight if they have decided to press on." Herman let out a quiet gasp, and the Duke motioned for me to continue.

"It was a force of fifty soldiers, very well trained and equipped far better than any group I've ever seen. They demanded of us to hand over our children and when we refused, they attacked without mercy. We were outnumbered but managed to kill part of their force, I'm unsure how many wounded they have. I guess the remaining numbers to be under thirty. You need to begin preparations for a defence at once," I looked each man directly in the eye as I spoke.

The Duke began slowly nodding, taking in what I had told him and then turned to Amond without further hesitation.

"Captain Amond, begin preparing the men and defences. Bar the gate, mobilise the guard and arm any of the able men in the town. Put as many of our best archers that can fit atop the watch tower as possible and send Lucas out to scout to the south with orders to report straight back as soon as he finds any signs of this group."

Amond pushed his blonde hair out of his face, picked his helmet up from the table and secured his chinstrap. Then he simply nodded before standing up and exiting the hall to fulfil the Duke's order.

"My lord, we should look to evacuating the town, not ready ourselves for a battle. If Drassox, with its larger force and better trained men could not stop them, what hope do we have!?" Herman exclaimed looking shocked at the Duke's decision.

Fucking gutless coward.

I had never liked Herman, and now I disliked him even more. The type of man to allow others to do the fighting for him while he hid in a hole, only emerging when it was safe.

"We have nowhere to go Herman aside from Branwick, and if Lothar is right, no time to prepare everyone for the journey. Unless you have another idea?" The Duke said and glared at Herman.

Herman gave no response aside from looking like a whipped dog. The Duke satisfied he had made his point, then turned his attention back to me.

"You are an experienced battle leader, Lothar, what do you propose?" He asked me.

I had already considered this during the journey here, Hiltsten had only one choice as I saw it.

"With the women and children slowing us down we'd only be caught in the open plains between here and Branwick—and then slaughtered. We stand no chance in an open field. Our only chance is to mount a defence here, behind the walls of the town. Not long before the attack on Drassox, I sent our fastest scout, a man named Orin, to warn Branwick. I don't know if he made it there safely. But if he did, they may already have aide on the way here since learning Drassox has fallen," I replied.

The Duke looked at the table deep in thought and

then slowly stood, "I remember Orin, a fast scout from memory, we can only pray that he was able to make it to Branwick safely. I agree with your plan, Lothar, like yourself we will not give in to the sick wishes of these tyrants. If battle is what they threaten us with for not bowing to their demands, then battle is what they will receive."

CHAPTER 5

AN ACT OF AGGRESSION

*'Behold, I have given you authority to tread on serpents and
scorpions, and over all the power of your enemies, and
nothing shall hurt you'*

As I walked away holding Del's hand, I couldn't help but feel nervous, and a little sad that Lothar was leaving me. We had been together since… since the bad things happened. I wasn't really mad at him for calling me 'boy' all the time or making it out like I needed to be looked after.

I just didn't want to be away from him, especially in this new place. He could be a little grumpy most of the time, but he was the only person left in the world that I knew, that knew Mother and Pa. I felt safe with him, somehow, I could tell he would never let anyone hurt me.

This new lady Del seemed nice, I liked the way she stuck up for me with Lothar, maybe we would end up friends and then I wouldn't be as alone.

I continued following along behind her, away from Lothar, and past some houses on the edges of the town square. We came to a stop, and she turned then knelt onto her knees, so she was the same height as me.

"Don't worry, Kael, he'll be back for you soon. In the meantime, I'll introduce you to the other children and you can all play together, you might even make some new friends," she said to me, sounding excited.

I raised my eyebrows, maybe she was right, but I really didn't think so.

"The other kids at Drassox used to be mean to me most of the time because I liked to go goblin hunting," I told her and looked away.

"Well, I think this bunch and you will all get along great. Goblin hunting sounds fun! You should ask them if they want to go with you, I'm sure they'll want to. If not, maybe you and I can go when I finish my errands, if 'the man' isn't back by then." She said 'the man' trying her best to sound like Lothar and laughed, which made me laugh as well.

"Come on, let's go over and meet them. Don't worry, I'm the children's tutor, they know to listen to me. I hold classes in the hall sometimes, it keeps them from getting into mischief. I also like to think I teach them a thing or two." She explained with a smirk.

I smiled back, and then we started walking the rest of the way over to the group. I noticed as we approached that there were two boys about my age, they looked kind of similar, like siblings maybe, and both had curly brown hair. Next, there was two blonde girls, one looked a little younger than me and the other a bit older, I think anyway.

The last boy looked about twelve and was very fat, he also didn't look friendly, or happy to see me.

At all.

Great, another Mathias.

They stopped whatever they were talking about when they heard us coming and just stared straight at me, all at once.

I tightened my grip on Del's hand while I looked back at them and then down at my worn, leather shoes. Mother had made me these shoes, I hadn't noticed until now how dirty they had gotten from walking so far the last few days.

Luckily, Del wasn't shy like me. She spoke up straight away, the way she had with Lothar.

"Hello, children! I want you all to meet Kael. He's visiting from Drassox for a little while, I thought it would be nice if I introduce you all to him."

She had said it excitedly, but they all just mumbled or shrugged.

Except the fat one.

He sneered at me, I don't know what I had done wrong to him but he reminded me of even more of Matthias now.

Del must have noticed because she turned to him, and without her happy voice that she had used so far said, "There'll be none of that behaviour, Erik. You're going to be extra nice to Kael here, or you'll be dealing with me, do you understand?"

He instantly looked at the ground, trying to hide from her gaze and replied, "Yes, Miss Delaney. Sorry."

"That's better. The rest of you, introduce yourselves." Del told them and one by one the other kids told me their names.

The two boys were siblings like I had thought, and their names were Marc and Tomas. The younger blonde girl was Mari, and the older one was Samantha. The fat, mean boy, I already knew, was Erik.

"Very good. I have some errands to complete before sundown, you're all to play nice and make Kael feel welcome. I'll come check on you later, Kael. All of you have fun," she told us and then walked off, leaving me on my own to deal with Erik and the other kids.

We all stood there for a moment, no one seemed sure what to say as Del disappeared from our sight.

Then as soon as she was gone, Tomas decided to talk first and asked me, "Why are ya so dirty, don't cha have baths in Drassox?"

Marc and Erik both snickered at that.

I hadn't really noticed how dirty I was, we had been on the road for two days without a bath. I didn't really care enough to answer to him either, I didn't want to talk about home, I just wanted to be left alone. But they weren't going to let me.

Erik stepped forward next, "They don't bathe in the south, they're all dirty because they sleep with the pigs!"

Then he let out a loud laugh.

I hated him.

"No… we don't," I said, clenching my teeth.

Why did he say that, it's not true, Mother always made me bathe. Every night she would spend time warming the water in the pot over the fire while Pa stoked it and bought wood inside, then she would make me wash. And we didn't sleep with the pigs—they slept outside in the paddock. We slept in the house in our beds.

He snorted, "Southern lies. If that was true, you wouldn't stink like you do and walk around so dirty like one of the animals. I bet you haven't washed those clothes in two summers."

Marc and Tomas laughed from behind Erik when he said this.

The girl Samantha stepped forward looking at him and said, "Just leave him alone, Erik. Why do you have to be so mean all the time?"

"Shut up, Samantha, I'm not being mean. Just

pointing out what I can see," Erik said back to her.

He walked closer towards me and started again, "Why aren't ya saying anything, KALEY?"

Why are kids always mean to me? I'm sick of them. I'm sick of everything.

"My name is Kael. K-A-E-L. Not Kaley," I mumbled, still looking at the ground.

Pa wouldn't let other people speak to him like this, he'd beat them all up, just like he did to those mean kids when he was small, Lothar said so.

And Lothar would never let anyone talk bad to him, why can't I be like that?

You SHOULD be like that.

All of a sudden, I was thumped hard in the chest and felt the wind knock out of me. I stumbled back coughing loudly.

Erik was staring at me grinning, he'd just hit me hard with both palms, almost knocking me over.

"Don't ever try tell me how to spell again, KALEY," he said while his two friends, Tomas and Marc kept snickering behind him.

"Erik! Just quit it, he's younger than you and he hasn't done anything wrong. I'm going to tell Miss Del if you don't leave him alone," Samantha yelled, but Erik didn't seem like he cared at all.

He just turned and threatened her, "Shut up, Samantha, or you're gonna be next. I'm the boss here."

She looked at me sadly, her eyes said she was sorry

and then she took a step back before looking away.

Where was Miss Del?

No! Stop being a coward! Pa or Lothar wouldn't need to be saved by anyone! I'm tired of being pushed around!

This time I will be brave! Just like them!

I felt my anger rising inside and I stood up, reaching behind my neck, slowly pulling my sword out and raising it in front of me.

I tried my best to look scary, just like I'd seen Lothar do. My sword might not be a real weapon, but it would still hurt him.

Instead, though, Erik burst out laughing.

"Oh, look everyone the little runt has a stick. Go on then, pig boy, hit me with your toothpick. I dare ya."

That's it. I wasn't waiting to be asked again, I hated Erik, I hated Hiltsten, I hated the people who killed Mother and Pa and everyone back home. I wanted them all to know how much I hated them so I swung my sword as hard as I could, like Lothar did to those bad men in the town square after he rescued me.

It whipped through the air straight for Erik's head.

And then it stopped, right in the middle of my swing. Somehow, he had caught it, grabbed hold, and was holding on firmly while still staring at me with that stupid, ugly grin.

"Is that ya best, pig boy?" I heard him say, but now he was no longer smiling.

I stared at him in shock, how did he do that?

Before I could figure it out, he ripped my sword from my hand and punched me hard in the chest, knocking the wind out of me again. I fell to the ground gasping for air, defeated as I looked up at him.

He looked at my sword, now in his hand, and still wearing that big dumb grin said, "Stupid stick's mine now."

THEN HE SNAPPED IT OVER HIS KNEE.

I don't know how to say what happened next.

All I saw was black and red flashes.

Pa had made that sword for me! It was all I had left to remember him by. I've lost everything and everyone I ever knew and now I've lost my sword Pa made as well.

I wanted to scream, I want to kill Erik, stomp his head like Lothar done to that man til there was nothing left of him, make sure he could never make that stupid grin again.

I hate him!

I realised I was lost in the black and red flashing, it started to swirl together, blocking my vision like a cloud in front of the sun, and then the blackness completely covered the red until only the black was left.

Then I heard a faint sound, that quickly became louder and clearer until I realised it was a deep scary voice. It was speaking of anger, hatred and making

Erik pay.

The voice hurt my ears, it was deafening but it was inside my head. I think it was… me.

I felt my knees hit the ground and my hands pressing to the sides of my head, I couldn't hear or see anything except the vibrating rumble of the voice and the blackness.

And… chanting? It was so faint, but there were definitely other voices. And then, just as fast as it had all started, I saw the sky above me return and the voice and chanting stopped.

My eyes focused and I noticed it looked a little darker than before, like sunset had come, but it was normal.

What wasn't normal I realised, was Erik lying on the ground with blood leaking from his nose and mouth, he wasn't moving and his face looked very red.

I looked around at the other children, Tomas and Marc were pale like Mother said I got when I was sick, Mari looked confused, and Samantha… she just started screaming.

***

I stood there silent next to Del, while she argued back and forth with a small group of other townspeople. A fat round man and woman were being much louder than the rest of the folk.

I could hear Del speaking over the crowd.

"I saw what happened, Erik was pushing Kael around and then Erik hit him, Kael hit Erik back with his wooden stick aside the head and it broke. This wouldn't have happened if your son wasn't always picking on the other kids, Patrice. I've told you about his behaviour to the other children more than once."

The fat man stepped forward angrily pointing his finger at Del.

"You think being pushed, justifies this out-of-town delinquent smacking my son in the head with a lump of wood, Delaney!?" He rudely yelled back, turning his chubby finger to me.

Is that what happened?

I thought Erik snapped my sword over his knee. I'm sure he did. Did I imagine him catching my swing? Did I really hear that voice? I don't know what is going on, I hope Lothar comes back soon. I'm scared, I just want to go home.

"Calm down, Gerald, they're just children. I've checked Erik out and he'll be fine, no harm has been done," I heard Del again.

"That's not the fucking point, Delaney! And what about the others? Tomas and Marc are telling a different story altogether. They swear that boy just looked at Erik, then his eyes rolled back showing the whites, and he started growling like an animal. Then Erik begins convulsing and bleeding! What kind of damned devilry is that!?" Erik's father, the man called

Gerald yelled back at her.

Del just shook her head like what he was saying was ridiculous and put her hand on my shoulder.

"Gerald, I already told you and Patrice that I saw what happened myself. With my own eyes! And you're choosing to believe two young children's fairytale?"

"That's exactly what I'm doing, Delaney, both boys repeated exactly the same story! I don't know why you're lying for that boy, but I'm taking him to the Duke right now," Gerald said as he started marching towards me.

Del stepped forward in front of me to block him just as someone else pushed their way roughly through the crowd, knocking people aside.

It happened in a blur but the next thing, Gerald was grabbed by the throat by Lothar, who had appeared from nowhere, then slammed up against the wall of the closest home.

Lothar was almost lifting him off his feet, so Gerald had to stand on his tiptoes. I watched wide eyed while Lothar leaned in close, so their faces were almost touching.

"If, you lay one finger on that boy. I will end your life," he whispered calmly to Gerald.

Lothar is terrifying when he's angry because he's so calm and it looked like Gerald thought so too because he just closed his eyes and shook like a leaf.

Everyone around us also went silent and didn't say

anything else so they must have agreed.

Lothar stared into his face for a moment longer and then he let go of Gerald turned back to me and Del, my heart was racing.

"If you two need a place to stay, I can put you up for the night?" Del said quickly, looking at Lothar.

He looked down at me, studying me, then looked back at Del. "Thank you. Can we meet you there in a moment? I need to have a word alone with the boy."

"Sure. My house is that one over there, I'll chat to you both when you arrive, dinner will be served shortly. See you soon, Kael," she said scruffing my hair, and then left us alone.

All the townspeople had wandered off now, Erik had awoken and his Mother and Pa had helped him up, a bit wobbly still, then they walked back to their house together down the way.

The two of us stood there watching Del walk away, Lothar seemed even quieter than normal. I started to worry that maybe I was in trouble, or that he was mad at me for fighting with Erik.

It hadn't been my fault though, I didn't start it, so I tried to tell him, "I'm sorry, Lothar, I didn't mean to fight Erik! He was being mean and saying bad things about Mother and Pa and then he pushed me and hit me and—"

"—Be silent and listen to me, boy," he said, cutting me off before I could finish.

I looked up at him and waited, I could tell he was thinking about what to say next.

"I'm not angry at you for hurting the fat boy, I would have done the same thing if I were in your shoes. I'm glad you stuck up for yourself, just like your father did all those summers ago."

I let out a sigh of relief, I felt a little better knowing he wasn't angry at me at least.

"But," he continued.

"I need to know the truth of what happened. The other children were telling a different story, that you just looked at the fat boy, and he collapsed. Is that what happened? Don't lie to me, boy," he stared into my eyes waiting for me to answer.

I thought to myself.

Was it true? Was something wrong with me? What if I tell him the truth and he lets them take me to the Duke and then leaves me here? I don't want to be alone. No, I can't tell him. I have to lie, I'm sorry, Lothar.

"That's not what happened! They're just making lies up to get me in trouble! He punched me and then I hit him with my sword, and he fell down! You can ask the lady Del, she said that she saw it happen!" I yelled.

He stood still listening to me letting me finish, then slowly nodded his head.

"It's fine, boy, I believe you. Come along, let's go have some dinner with this Del, and put this behind us."

That sounded good to me, he seemed calm again too. I felt bad about lying to him, but I wasn't even sure if it was a lie, I wasn't sure about anything.

We began walking towards the house Del had pointed out earlier, her home didn't look much different than any of the other houses nearby. They were all similar size except Del's had some dresses like the ones she was wearing hanging up on a clothing rope against the front wall, but that was the only thing that really made it stand out.

Lothar and I walked up, and he knocked on the wooden door. Del must have been waiting for us because she opened it straight away and invited us in.

"Kael, Lothar, come in. I've made rabbit stew for dinner, there's plenty for all of us," she said, and Lothar motioned for me to walk in before him.

"Thank you, it's much appreciated," I heard Lothar mumble as he walked inside behind me.

***

"Thanks, Del! That was really yum. We haven't had much to eat lately because we've been walking nonstop since Drassox," I told her licking my lips while I used my spoon to scrape up the last of the stew out of the bowl.

I saw Lothar was eating really slowly and hadn't finished his bowl yet, like he wasn't hungry. Well, I'd been starving, I don't know how he couldn't be hungry after all the walking we had been doing, plus my legs were really sore.

"You're welcome, Kael. If you're finished eating, I prepared the tub earlier. Would you like to bathe in the other room?" She asked me.

Would I ever, I kept thinking that I might actually be smelly since Erik had called me pig boy.

"That would be great," I replied to her, feeling a bit happier that I was going to be clean soon.

Del smiled at me and stood up from the table, "I'm just going to show Kael the wash tub and come back. I'd like to speak to you about something if you don't mind?" She said to Lothar.

Lothar looked up at her from his seat and nodded his head once, then Del took me to the other room.

There were only two rooms in the house, one was the cooking and common area and the other was Del's bedroom and wash tub.

The tub was already filled with water, toasty warm just like Mother used to make it.

"I'll leave you to it, Kael, the clothing rack is just there to hang your clothes on. Tomorrow I'll see about cleaning them for you, but for now, I need to talk with Lothar, so take your time and relax," she told me, and then left the room.

I couldn't wait to have a nice warm bath, I thought while I took my clothes off and hung them up on the clothing rack she had shown me. I climbed into that tub feeling the best I had since Drassox, maybe things wouldn't be so bad here after all.

CHAPTER 6
UNCONTROLLED WRATH

*'For you equipped me with strength for the battle; you made
those who rise against me sink under me'*

I sat there at the table staring into my bowl of
stew, it was a good stew, I just currently couldn't
find my appetite.

From where I was seated, I could make out Del,
explaining to the boy where to hang his clothes and
then mention something about cleaning them for him.

A moment later there was a gentle thud as she
closed the door to the other room and returned to her
seat at the table, sitting back down.

I looked up at her from my meal and spoke.

"Thank you for the stew it's great, unfortunately
my hunger has left me. What is it you wanted to talk

about?"

She paused, her eyes mysteriously darting cautiously about the room. When she was satisfied we were alone, she spoke in a hushed tone.

"While you were with the Duke, I noticed Captain Amond outfitting the men and doubling the guard in the tower. I'm guessing the news you brought was not good. Should I be worried?"

I thought on this for a moment looking at Del sitting across from me, waiting patiently.

She had a right to know, but I also didn't want to be responsible for hysteria to spreading through the town, the time for that would come soon enough. This woman had taken me and the boy into her home though, so I did feel it only right that I should give her something in return.

And as of right now, I have nothing else of value to barter.

"What I'm about to tell you, Del, must stay between us," I began, "Although, I'm sure the entire town will know shortly anyway. But until that moment comes this conversation is to remain private, do you understand?" I told her, keeping my voice low while listening to the boy humming to himself from the bath.

Her face became grave, she nodded and replied, "Yes. I understand."

"Good. Early yesterday, not long after sunrise, Drassox was attacked by an unusually large force.

Larger than we could handle. It was a massacre. Everyone was…"

I paused for a second as my mind began to wander back… picturing images of the charred corpses of the children… of Tanya lying there, belly hacked open.

I shook my head, as though it might clear it and Del raised an eyebrow at me.

"Everyone was slaughtered except me and the boy. I believe the group that attacked us are on their way here as we speak. It's unlikely they are far behind us. I don't know who they are, but what I do know is, it's the children they are after but I've not learned why," I looked to her face as I finished speaking.

Puzzled, I took note that she had the most peculiar expression upon it. One that told me she didn't appear to be surprised or shocked for any of this to reach her ears.

Unsure what to make of this, I continued studying her expression while I awaited a reply.

A moment passed and just as I was about to question her reaction a loud knocking at the door interrupted us, followed by a man loudly shouting my name.

"Lothar! Captain Lothar! Are you in there!?"

I had a strong feeling I knew what this meant, my stomach quickly filling with a sense of dread. It would not be good news.

Del looked concernedly at me as I rose out of my

chair and strode toward the entry. Opening the door revealed the panicked eyes of Captain Amond, wide with shock, sweat dripping from his forehead as he began to address me. "Lothar, thank god. My scout Lucas returned with word. The enemy approaches, I need to ask that you accompany me to the town gates—now."

I could see the fear in the man's eyes, he had not been a Captain long enough to deal with a threat such as this, I didn't berate him for it, even I had already failed at the task.

I turned my attention back to Del and said sharply, "Please stay inside and look after the boy for me. I'll return when I'm able. Neither of you are to come outside."

This would be no place for women or children, battle was coming, and I would not fail again.

She looked back at me, her hand covering her mouth while her eyes showed heavy concern that replaced her normally cheerful demeanour she had shown so far.

She nodded and shut the door quietly behind me.

I returned my gaze to Amond.

"Lead the way," I ordered, then followed closely behind him.

We beelined straight across the now empty town square and then down the road the boy and I had travelled earlier this day, enroute back towards the gates and the tower.

I could see up ahead a small force of men had gathered, the town guard I presumed. I counted twenty men, and I was doubtful this would be enough.

"Amond, how many of these men have actual experience in battle?" I questioned my host as we approached.

He looked at me wearily, "Honestly, too few of them, Lothar. We've twelve trained men at arms, I managed to muster and arm another eight men from the town. We also have three archers, including Cassian in the watchtower. Twenty-five men counting myself and you… although from what I remember, you're worth five."

I snorted. Maybe that were once true, but I'm older now, and don't believe I'm the warrior I once was. My dead friends lying in the town square of Drassox were testament of that, the charred childr—

—Bah! It doesn't matter.

These men are not trained as well as the men of Drassox, Amond was as aware of this as I. If the wall is breached, we may not have a chance against a better equipped, superior fighting force.

"Captain Amond!" A man, barely older than a boy yelled as he jogged towards us from the gathering of fighters.

"Lucas! I heard you made it back, I'm glad to see you're not harmed. Did you make it close enough to count enemy numbers!?" Amond replied.

I watched the two men as they spoke.

"I did, Captain, they looked very well armed. Nor did they look like brigands. I counted twenty-five of them," Lucas replied looking terrified.

Amond looked back to me a little more confidently.

"Well, at least we're not outnumbered. Your men must have killed a few of them in Drassox," he said.

"Mhm," I grunted, before giving my reply.

"Listen to me, Amond. We can't afford to allow the wall to be breached at any cost. Order your men to begin constructing platforms along the wall so our archers can stand on them and loose arrows over. If we can thin their numbers down before they break through, we may have a chance of finishing them off when it comes to hand-to-hand combat."

Amond looked to me and then back to his men nodding his head in agreement.

"Right! You heard him! Gather anything you can to make footholds against the wall. Lucas, take two men with you and handout all the longbows we have, ten arrows per bowman and give Lothar one as well."

I watched hopefully as the men set about their tasks.

This might just work.

Maybe we actually can win this and get revenge on those that condemned Drassox.

***

It was pitch black, the sun had long since abandoned us of its purifying light and warmth, replaced with the frigid air and ominous glow of the moonlight casting eerie, distorted shadows, of the soldiers now approaching Hiltsten.

Eight men were in position standing atop the wooden platforms, they'd been hastily constructed using anything the men could get their hands on. I counted among them. We all held longbows, with ten arrows stuck in the dirt next to us.

The remaining fighters were in formation at the gate led by Amond, prepared and ready to meet the enemy head on, if and when necessary.

We waited in deathly silence, nothing but each other and lingering doubt to keep us company, but even that was drowned out by our own thumping heartbeats. Gradually I began to hear the steady rhythm of footsteps becoming clearer, as the marching brought the enemy soldiers closer.

Closer to my chance for revenge, for redemption, and atonement. I was ready.

I didn't feel any fear for myself, only fear of failing these people, failing the boy. There would be no words spoken this time. I wouldn't allow them to dictate the initiation of the battle again. When they came within range, we would spring our ambush and slaughter them with arrows, cowards such as these do not deserve a fair fight.

It wouldn't be long now, out in the field I could make out four rows of men, six abreast… And one extra.

Was it him? The one I fought in Drassox?

It was hard to tell in the moonlight, the armour looked different though, and I couldn't be certain.

They came to a halt, barely out of range on the road to the southwest. The one that had been leading stepped forward, wisely still out of range, and shouted out.

"People of Hiltsten! I am Cleric Gildred, of the Order of St Michael! I know you are watching! You may think you are safe behind the walls, but you are not! Open the gates, I give you my word most of you will not be harmed! We have come for one purpose. You have until the count of ten! Deny me and face the same fate as your neighbours!"

From the sound of his voice, I knew this was not the man I had fought with in Drassox, but likely, one of his underlings.

It didn't matter, he would die all the same.

"10… 9… 8…!" The man, calling himself Cleric Gildred began to count down.

I glanced over to Amond, he returned my stare with a furrowed brow and shook his head, we had already discussed this.

Duke Roland had made it clear to us, just as Duke

Edmond had, that no deal nor bargain would be struck, even after that coward Herman had tried to convince Roland to just hand over the children. I wouldn't think twice to rid the world of his kind absent consequence.

Who was this Order of St Michael? I had never heard it before.

At least now however, I had a name for those that were responsible for the attacks thus far.

"7... 6... 5... 4...!" Gildred continued counting down.

Staying low as to not give away my position I readied my longbow, drawing an arrow from the ground next to me and notching it in place, in my peripheral I could see the other archers doing the same.

The inevitable was about to begin, and after it was over all those on one of our sides would cease to live.

"3... 2... 1. So be it! Order, advancing shield formation!"

When I heard this, I raised my height enough to glance over the wall and made out the enemy company tightening ranks and interlocking shields.

I recognised their tactic straight away, a standard strategy. They would move forward as a single armoured unit until they were close enough to attack the gates and create an entry point. While obvious to spot, it was effective and what I would have done also.

I looked to those around me and addressed them as one.

"Aim for the men on the sides, they're sides are exposed, we need to force them to cluster."

Shifting my attention above I yelled, "You three in the watchtower! As they cluster together, rain arrows from above into the rear columns!"

I received several nods of agreement in return, everyone now had their orders.

We began to loose arrows at the advancing force, their defence was tight and very few shots found home. I witnessed two men fall at the rear due to overhead arrows from the watchtower, the men rolled around on the field in agony, clutching wounds as their brethren continued advancing forward, leaving them exposed to be finished off in the next volley of fire.

"Pffffft! Pfffffft! Pffffft!"

The whiplash of bowstrings being released sounded off repeatedly around me and an opposing soldier on the left flank fell to the ground, I saw the silhouette of an arrow protruding from his face.

So far, the plan was working flawlessly, the enemy's advance was slow. It almost appeared as if they had stopped.

Or they had stopped?

Why would they stop? Were they about to retreat?

Don't be a fool, I told myself. We wouldn't be that

lucky.

I held my arrow for a moment trying to decipher what was happening out in the moonlit field when I saw an orange glow appear out of nowhere in the centre of the group, behind the protection of their shield wall.

I squinted trying to focus on it. What is that? It almost looked like a glowing ember.

Suddenly, a gap appeared in the shields and a man emerged holding a large crossbow, the glowing stone sat at the tip of the weapon attached to a bolt.

Though I had never seen one in person, I recognised what it was. Something my father had only told me stories about from his time in the Great War. A weapon that was capable of destroying stone fortifications or obliterating entire units.

My blood ran cold as I remembered its name.

Blast stone.

Before I could alert Amond and his men, the bolt was let loose toward the gates, the enemy closed the gap in their shield wall only barely in time before the blast stone struck.

What followed was a deafening sound I do not have the words to describe accompanied by a tremendous blast which threw me from the platform I was standing upon.

Shards and splinters of fiery wood rained down from the sky and a putrid smelling smoke clouded my vision, causing my eyes to water.

As I lay there, on the ground my head spinning, I heard a loud cheer erupt from outside the shattered gates and I forced myself back to my feet.

All those around me had been knocked to their feet as I had but were luckily, also unharmed.

"Gather your wits men! Draw your swords and follow me! We need to reinforce those at the gate now!" I yelled drawing my own sword from its sheathe and running towards the gate that no longer existed.

I could see men lying on the ground among the lightly flaming wreckage. Somehow, most were slowly rising and helping others up around them. A good sign.

"Amond, Captain Amond!" I called looking around the debris.

"I'm here!" Came a reply from a face blackened with soot, and he began coughing.

"They're about to charge! We need to form the men up and bottleneck the advance here, at the hole!" I shouted frantically.

They were almost upon us, I could hear the rhythmic beating of shields and the rattle of chainmail as they marched forward, there was no time to catch our breath.

"Everyone get the fuck up now! I don't give two shits if you are hurt! Form up and prepare to meet these mongrels!" Amond screamed.

Men began scrambling around and forming up into lines at the broken opening like they were told.

At least they listen I thought as I took place front and centre with Amond stood next to me. Through some divine grace we hadn't suffered any casualties in the blast, I couldn't believe it. Many of the men were blackened and bleeding from scorch wounds though.

The man to my left had lost half his beard and eyebrows, now replaced by pinkish, weeping flesh, it looked incredibly painful but he didn't complain.

I heard voices up above me and looked up spotting Cassian and two other archers in the tower.

"Cassian! When they charge, have those with you loose your arrows down upon them—and don't hit us for fucks sake!" I yelled to up to him, he shouted back that he understood.

And then without any further warning a great cry broke out and the enemy charged into our lines.

They appeared through the cloud of smoke, I halted an advancing soldier's charge with a hard push kick into his shield, sending him careening backwards and knocking down two men behind him.

The two forces clashed on either side of me, and I took a step back into the safety formation of my own side. For a brief moment the lines held in a stalemate while the second columns attacked over the first columns shields. Men were caught with wild stray attacks that opened up terrible wounds on any exposed flesh. I stabbed my own weapon forward as an opponent's unguarded face appeared before me, the tip of the blade striking the man square in the mouth, shattering his teeth as it penetrated deep into his oesophagus, I heard air escaping with a wet gurgling sound from the hole it had created when I tugged it free, twisting my wrist as I did so to inflict as much damage as possible.

The man to my left fell as a heavy overhanded swing of a mace landed squarely on his head, caving his skull in and flinging bits of brain matter onto my cheek. I grabbed hold of the mace handle before the foe could retract it and drove my blade back where his arm was coming from until I felt the tip plunge into soft flesh and he released a shrill, blood curdling scream.

Men were falling on both sides, but the odds appeared to be swaying in our favour. I could hear arrows whistling down from above, followed by wet thuds as they found their targets.

All of a sudden, I heard dissention coming from the enemy ranks, through the mass of bodies I saw a man at the rear of the enemy ranks fall, dropping his sword to reach behind and clutch at his back before he collapsed.

And shortly after, another similarly fell.

"Someone is firing arrows from behind them!" I

heard Cassian yell down to us.

To my knowledge Amond nor Roland, had sent anyone outside the wall prior to the battle aside from Lucas, and he'd already returned. It was someone else.

Whether it was a friend, or another group looking to use the situation to their advantage remained to be seen.

Regardless, this newfound attacker was causing the enemy force to panic. I could see the man named Gildred, looking frantically around realising he was trapped, and then a couple of men at his rear began to turn and flee, as is the nature of cowards.

Gildred screamed at them to stop but his lines were now breaking, their morale had been shattered. Those that continued to try to flee were fatally silenced forever by arrows, slung from the darkness.

Those that didn't, begun to fall quickly now that they were outnumbered and being assaulted from both sides.

What remained of their defensive line finally crumbled, and so, we abandoned formation and pressed the attack. I charged forward releasing the most ferocious battle-roar I could muster, raising my sword as I did so to block a blow from a man in front of me while deftly drawing my dagger. I rammed it up into the unarmoured gap of his armpit.

He let out a childlike squeal and slid to the dirt, his lung and possibly heart, punctured. His eyes bloodshot with pain.

Only four attackers remained upright now, including Gildred. He was cowering behind them like a cur, the terror clear on his panic-stricken face, his remaining men charged forward and were quickly overwhelmed and cut down.

I walked towards him with pure, uncontrollable wrath, burning upon my eyes. I was not surprised when he dropped his weapon and ran. I moved to give chase, but he didn't get very far before an arrow cut through the night, and found a home in his ass cheek, sending him tumbling to the floor.

That was the last of them, no more enemies were left standing.

"FORM UP SHIELDS, ON ME!!" I screamed loudly to the men around me, not forgetting someone was out there in the darkness, expertly placing arrows into bodies.

The men, to their credit did as they were told swiftly once more, one of which was Amond.

In total eight of us had survived the melee that I could count.

"Captain Lothar!" A voice cut through the air from the surrounding blackness.

"Who goes there!?" I shouted back, my eyes darting around trying to pinpoint the origin of the voice.

I peered ahead and saw three men stand up from a

nearby ridge to the west, not sixty paces away.

"It's me, Orin!" The man yelled back and started jogging towards us.

"Orin? I can't believe it!" I replied feeling relief as he approached, accompanied by two other men. We embraced when I saw with my own eyes it really was him.

"Orin, before we speak, I have something I need to see to. Help the men gather the wounded… and finish any of these surviving vermin off," I told him, with deathly inclinations hanging from my tone.

He nodded grimly, and all of the men including Amond, began pacing back to the field of dead and wounded.

I watched them go and turned away, I had someone I needed to have a little discussion with.

Not far ahead, on the dirt in front of me, a figure slowly, pitifully crawled along. His fingers clawing in the dirt, trying desperately to widen the ground between us, squirming and wriggling along like a wounded animal did when it had been caught by a hunter's arrow.

I took my time as I approached, watching him crawl along the ground like a slug, knowing the man couldn't escape.

My eyes glanced over the blood trail as I closed the distance.

It was thick, the claret had a dark tone to it, I knew

this meant he wouldn't survive, his life force was leaking out, only stifled by the arrow currently embedded deeply in his behind.

Odd that the thing killing him was also extending his worthless life. Well, not for much longer.

My ears had blocked out all sound besides his laboured breathing and painful moaning. He glanced back over his shoulder, and upon realising I was almost upon him tried to quicken his grub-like escape.

Fitting, I thought and quickened to close the gap, then rammed my sword down firmly through his lower calf muscle, his shin bone offering scant resistance apart from a wet crunch and crackling, before the blade slid smoothly down into the dirt, pinning him in place.

"AAAARRRRGGGGHHHHHHHH!!!" He screamed in agony.

A soothing sound to my ears.

"Sorry about that, I just wanted to have a word with you before you left," I told him, my voice devoid of any emotion.

He lay there gasping, sucking in deep heaving goblets of air.

"You don't have long, Gildred. So much to my dismay, we must make this quick," I began.

He whimpered in response.

"Who is the Order of Saint Michael? And why do you think you have the right to go from town-to-town murdering whoever you please. Murdering… CHILDREN?" I hissed and lightly twisted the handle of my sword causing him to let out another shrill squeal.

He lay there trying to catch his breath while I waited for his reply to come.

"You fucking dumb peon! You have no idea what you are preventing us from accomplishing… when Lord Zarek arrives with the main force you are all dead! He… will wipe this shit stain of a town… from the earth!" He said back to me, loud enough for all around to hear.

His breath was becoming shorter, I needed to hurry.

I stood on his pinned leg and leaned my weight forward causing another outburst of profanity from my helpless guest. "So, that's his name. Tell me why, Gildred—Now."

"We… are trying… to prevent… HIS… return…" came his reply, his breaths becoming increasingly shorter.

He'd nearly bled out, and that was too good a death for a child killer, sadly I wouldn't get the answers I wanted today.

"Right. Well, it looks like we've almost ran out of time, Gildred. And you don't deserve to die peacefully—not after the sins you've committed. Every man must be held accountable for the severity of his crimes. And yours were… most severe," I whispered to him while I carefully drew my dagger from its sheathe.

Kneeling, I grabbed a fistful of his hair and wrenched his head back towards me, causing him to elicit a weak defeated groan.

Then I placed the edge of my blade against his throat and slowly began sawing through his vocal cords and windpipe, he gurgled and squirmed as I did so, but I held him firm with my knee on his back and continued sawing, being sure to take my time and extend his suffering as long as possible.

I watched the last of his life leak out, turning the sand red while little puffs of air made claret bubbles as he struggled to breathe through his open throat.

And then Gildred, made his last gurgle and died.

A fitting end for the man.

I felt absolutely nothing when I wiped my dagger clean on his white surcoat, staining the clean fabric, then replaced it into its sheathe. As I did so, a leather pouch on the backside of his waist caught my eye.

I reached down and unclasped the buckles holding the flap in place, opening the satchel revealed a small, weathered book. Blood had managed to soak in from the wound to his buttocks, but it was not completely damaged.

If luck was on my side, it may hold answers to who this group was, so I pocketed it in my own pouch. Then reached down again to unclip his dagger belt, removing it, and clasping it around my own waist. It was a fine weapon, and I knew someone who needed it more than he did now.

I stood up, pulling my sword free from his lifeless limb, before returning it to its sheathe on my back, then began the walk back to the men.

As I returned, a few of the men gave me sideways glances, refusing to meet my gaze, before shifting their eyes away to continue scouring the field of bodies.

"I take it your business with that man is concluded then Captain?" Orin asked me, pulling his sword free from a downed foe with a wet sucking sound.

Beside him stood two men, dressed in leather armour holding longbows, quivers slung on their backs.

I paused to scan the area, quickly counting the dead men from Hiltsten, eleven from what I could see, which meant three wounded had been taken away. The men had held up much better than I had expected but still, if it were not for Orin's ambush, I fear we would all be lying dead in the dirt right now.

"It was inevitable, one of your arrows saw to that. Who are your companions Orin?" I asked, looking between the two of them.

One of the men stepped forward before he could reply.

"My name is Tobias sir, and this is my cousin, Ezekiel. We came from Branwick with Orin."

Both of the men appeared young, slimly built, with chestnut hair and similar features. *So, this is as much aid as Branwick was willing to send* I thought.

I went to reply but Amond appeared and interrupted, holding out his hand to the men.

"Thank you both for your help, I'm Amond, Captain of the guard here at Hiltsten. We owe you a great debt."

The two men shook his hand.

"You're both welcome to stay the night, I can have quarters prepared for you if you like?" Amond finished.

They looked to each other and then to Orin before Tobias replied with a hesitant look upon his face.

"We appreciate the offer, but we overheard Captain Lothar's interrogation of that man," he said nodding in my direction, "We need to return to Branwick at once with the information that a larger force may be headed this way."

"So soon?" Orin asked surprised.

Tobias nodded, "This news can't be delayed, Orin."

With that, they shook my hand and then Orin's, he thanked them for their help and they both left as quickly as they arrived, back into the night.

I looked to Amond after the men had departed.

"Amond, I need to return to the boy and have Orin fill me in on his journey thus far. I would suggest having the men repair the wall as best as they're able, then have the bodies of the enemy stacked outside for burning. They'll bring disease if left too long."

He nodded in agreement and turned away without another word, returning to his surviving men.

"Follow me, Orin," I croaked, my throat suddenly feeling dry from the smoke of the earlier blast.

***

A short walk later and we were back at Del's home, my weary body was beginning to feel the fatigue of battle as I opened the door to her abode, Orin trailed closely behind me.

The door creaked loudly as it swung on its rusted hinges, opening to reveal the startled faces of Del and the boy.

A look of relief flashed over both of their faces as our eyes met, the boy immediately breaking into a smirk.

"You came back?" He said hesitantly.

Del looked at Orin, and then back to me, waiting for me to speak.

"Of course I came back, boy. I have something for you too." I replied and reached down, unclasping Gildred's dagger from my belt.

"This is to replace the one that the fat boy broke. I'll teach you how to use it when I have time," I said and handed him the dagger and its belt sheathe.

His eyes lit up, he seemed happy with the gift and

took it from my grip. I realised it was the size of a short sword in his small hands.

Del eyed me suspiciously but didn't say anything.

"This dagger isn't a toy like your last one, handle it carefully until I give you proper instruction on how to use it. Are we clear?" I said.

He looked up and nodded.

"Good. Now, I need to speak to Orin in private. Del, can you take the boy into your room for a moment?"

She nodded to me and ushered the boy along and they both disappeared from my view as she closed the door.

Finally, I turned to Orin next to me and motioned for him to take a seat at the table, he scooted around so he was on the opposite side to me.

When he was seated, I looked to him and said, "Tell me everything that happened after Lord Edmund sent you to Branwick."

He stared back at me gravely then began speaking.

"I left to the north as planned, Lothar, but it wasn't long before sundown when I looked behind me and saw the smoke coming from Drassox. I raced back as fast as I could fearing the worst, but I was too late, everyone was already dead."

I poured two mugs of water from the pitcher on the table and passed him one of the mugs inviting him to go on.

"Your presence wouldn't have changed that, Orin," I told him calmly.

He took a swig and continued. "There were soldiers everywhere, Lothar, at least a hundred men. I had to hide in between a stack of hay bales and hope they didn't set fire to them with me inside. A group of men were looking at a body on the ground in the town square, one of the men they addressed as Lord Zarek - the same name your friend outside mentioned. This Zarek fellow was curious about the way the corpse had died, he said the death was unnatural, that an unholy force had caused the man's blood to leak out. I overheard him say that it had to be the child they were seeking, that the child must have escaped with whoever had killed two other men that lay nearby."

I listened to this intently, unsure what to make of it.

Orin looked from his mug to me and spoke grimly.

"Lothar, if no one else survived the massacre, then they were talking about you and Elias's boy."

"Mhm, maybe," I grunted, still pondering what he had just told me.

I didn't know what else to say. Why the boy?

My mind wandered back to our escape from the town square, and the man with the crossbow that had suddenly collapsed after I killed those two soldiers.

Could the boy have caused this?

Some strange events had occurred around him

sure, but nothing that couldn't be easily explained or put down to coincidence.

He just appeared to be a typical child.

Orin went on, "I heard Zarek say Hiltsten was their next target and his second in command was already on his way there. He was furious that they must find the two that had escaped, I waited for my chance to slip out unnoticed, while they were digging graves to bury their dead from the battle. I ran all through the night as fast as I could to Branwick. When I arrived the people there argued amongst themselves. They refused to send aide, Lothar, but Tobias and Ezekiel offered to join me and scout the situation in Hiltsten. That's when we stumbled upon the battle taking place and decided to set up an ambush, just like you taught me in training."

"You've done well Orin, thank you. A hundred men won't travel as fast as you or I did, I wouldn't expect them to arrive until the early hours of dawn at best. We need to convince the Duke to evacuate the town and join forces with Branwick," I replied now feeling the exhaustion setting in.

I was even more confused now. How could they justify murdering entire settlements over one child?

I needed answers. And then I remembered I still had the book, I had meant to read it later after I had rested, but I was curious that it might be able to explain some of what I had learnt so I went to reach down to open my satchel but a heavy knock on the door stayed my hand.

I don't get a bloody chance to breathe around here anymore, I thought as I went to answer the knock.

CHAPTER 7
FOR THE GOOD OF THE PEOPLE

*'See the hour is at hand, and the son of man is betrayed into
the hands of sinners'*

I sat on Del's bed looking at the sword Lothar had given me, he had called it a dagger but to me it was a sword.

My first real sword, I felt like an actual knight.

It was heavy, heavier than I thought it would be. The blade was polished and shiny, the handle had a golden coloured hilt, and the grip was wrapped with black leather.

Dragon-skin leather.

The sheathe was also made of the same fancy leather but it had squiggly patterns carved into it.

I traced them with my finger while I sat there, I

didn't know what they meant but I liked how they looked and felt, the leather was smooth to touch.

I stood up from the bed and put the belt strap over my shoulder and clasped the two halves together diagonally over my chest, so the sword hung on my back.

I noticed Del had been there, leaning with her head against the door watching me the whole time. She had a strange look on her face, like she was thinking about something important.

I was about to ask her what she was thinking when a loud knock thumped and made me jump.

Del jumped startled, then snapped out of whatever she was thinking.

"Wait here, Kael," she said and then left the room, leaving me alone again.

I could hear Lothar's deep voice talking to someone, but it was too muffled to make out what he was saying.

It was making me a bit angry, I wanted to see what is going on. I'm tired of being left out and treated like a baby, I can help with whatever it is too, if he would just give me a chance.

Maybe I need to show him that I can help.

Yep, that's it. I'm going to see who is out there and what all the fuss is about I decided.

So, wanting to prove myself I opened the door and barged out loudly, making sure everyone could hear me.

I saw Lothar, his friend, Del, and another three men standing inside, they all turned their heads at once and looked at me. It was a lot more people than I pictured and now I didn't feel as confident as I had in the room.

"I told you to stay down the back, boy," Lothar said frowning at me.

Del surprised me by immediately stepping forward and glaring at him.

"Excuse me? This is my home, you don't make the rules here, Lothar—and you can stop acting like you do. I told Kael he could come out."

I watched them both. she was always sticking up for me, which I liked… but I did feel like I was being naughty right now for disobeying Lothar.

"Mhm," he grunted and ignored her, still frowning at me.

I felt like I needed to say something, everyone was staring.

"Are you leaving again?" I finally asked, feeling a bit embarrassed with all of them watching.

He looked at Del and then to me and said, "Yes. I need to attend another meeting, but I won't be long. Stay here and rest, boy. We'll likely be travelling again soon."

I sighed and nodded my head, arguing wouldn't do any good. Lothar was stubborn like the old mule we used to have at home. I don't know what made that mule stubborn, but Pa always said he was.

"Good. And remember what I said about not using that blade until I show you how to handle it," Lothar continued, noticing I wore it on my back now.

I nodded again but didn't say anything else.

"We need to get a move on, Lothar, the Duke is waiting," one of the men interrupted rudely.

Lothar's eyes snapped to the man, and he looked angry for a moment, but his expression quickly became normal again.

"Learning a little patience wouldn't hurt the man, Amond. Regardless, I'm ready to go anyway, but Orin will accompany us. He has firsthand accounts of the enemy."

The rude man called Amond seemed pleased at this and then looked at Lothar's friend Orin.

"The Duke would like to hear it. We're short on time, both of you, give Raymon here your swords and he'll have the town smith hone them. Your armour could use repairs too, Lothar, you can drop it in with him after we speak to the Duke."

That's nice of him I thought, Lothar's armour was filthy, he might even have a bath if he takes it off for once. I hadn't seen him remove it yet, even when we slept at the cottage. He looked gross with all the blood on him.

"My armour is fine, but the edge of this blade

could use some work, I scavenged it off a dead soldier in Drassox after mine broke. But have the smith do it quick, Amond, we need to be prepared to leave this place," Lothar replied, and removed his sword belt, handing it over to a short man with no hair. Raymon, I guessed.

"My blade is still sharp—it never saw use in the battle." Orin told Amond.

"Suit yourself. Anyway, let's move," Amond ordered, and all the men walked out of Del's home shutting the door behind them.

I watched them go feeling left out, I wanted to go to the meeting too, it wasn't fair.

Del turned to me, still deep in thought about something and said, "How many summers have passed since your birth, Kael?"

That seemed like a strange question right now I thought, sometimes adults just didn't make sense to me.

"I'm almost nine. My Pa always said he would bring me here when I was ten and big enough to make the trip. But I guess that won't be happening anymore…" I replied and stared down at my feet, noticing my dirty shoes again.

I missed Mother and Pa so much, lately it felt like everything I looked at reminded me of them.

"Do you know exactly when the day of your birth is?" She asked.

I looked back up at her confused, raising one of my eyebrows wondering why it mattered.

"Well, I'm not really sure. Mother kept track of things like that. I know it's really soon though. Why?" I questioned her back.

Her eyes seemed to widen when I mentioned Mother.

"No special reason, Kael, I just want to get to know you since we are spending so much time together. What was your mother's name?"

Well, I guess that does make sense I thought to myself, Lothar is leaving me with her a lot and I'm a stranger in her home.

"Her name was Catherine… but she wasn't my real mother. My real Mother died when I was born and then Catherine and Elias—my Pa, took me in because Catherine was friends with my real mother," I told her.

Her eyes seemed to light up even more when I told her this, like she had figured out what she was thinking about.

She became excited and looked quickly around the room almost like she was searching for something, she was acting kind of funny.

"Kael, I want you to go to my room and rest like Lothar said. I need to head out for a short while, but I'll be back very soon. Please don't go anywhere, it's not safe outside tonight."

Great now she is leaving me alone as well, what is

with adults being so busy all the time?

"Fine…" I grumbled back to her.

She reached out and pulled me towards her giving me a hug and said softly, "Trust me, Kael, I won't be long, I promise. We'll chat when I return, I even have a secret to tell you."

She winked at me, and then walked away leaving me alone, shutting the door behind her.

I turned and looked around her common area, the chairs were still pushed out from the table where Lothar and his friend had sat, a mug of water was at each end, and a ceramic pitcher where Lothar had sat.

I fiddled with my sheathe strap. I was annoyed they had left me alone again! I'm not a baby that can't leave the house, I made it all the way here when Pa said I needed to be ten to do it, I even had my own sword now. A real one.

Like a knight. I could protect myself, and others too.

Lothar was a knight, and so was Pa.

They would never stay home because someone told them to.

I decided right there and then that I was going to that meeting with the Duke as well.

Me and Lothar had travelled all this way together, I deserve to know what it's about too.

So carefully I crept over and opened the front door trying my best to do it quietly, but it was a creaky damn thing.

Pa used to wipe some left-over oil from Mother's cooking on our door hinges when they creaked and it fixed them, I would need to show Del how to do it when I saw her next. Maybe then she would forget to be mad about me sneaking out.

Probably not though, I would definitely be in trouble for this.

But I don't care.

I slipped out through the door gap and slowly closed it behind me, so it didn't swing shut and make a bang. It felt like I was taking too long already, I had only just made it outside.

I'm going to need to move faster, or the meeting will be over before I arrive!

I crept out onto the town square and began walking along, past the rows of homes. Luckily it was dark, and everyone was hiding inside like they had been told to by the Duke's soldiers earlier.

Well, everyone except me at least. I had a secret mission.

Now that I was outside, I realised I didn't know which way the hall was. I had seen the direction Lothar, and the other men had headed though, so I figured I would just go that way, which also led towards the gates I remembered from earlier.

I skulked through the shadows, close to the houses lining the town square so their shadows would help hide me, and back towards the main road Lothar and I had come in on.

So far so good, no one had heard me or came out to investigate yet.

This was easier than I thought it would be, I'm better at this than I expected I thought and smirked to myself.

I turned right onto the main road and continued sneaking along in the dark, I imagined I was one of the street cats we used to have around town, Mother would feed them sometimes. It used to scare me the way their eyes would glow yellow and green in the pitch black.

Once I went fishing with Pa at night and saw heaps of red eyes in the water, he said it was from the fish. I thought it was even more terrifying than the cat eyes.

As I crept along further, I began to hear loud noises coming from up ahead, in the direction of the gates. I could make out torches over there as well and it sounded like lots of people were working, there was tapping and banging going on like they were building something maybe.

I decided I would need to find another way, they might see me if I got too close and I'd get caught.

I quickly crossed over to the other side of the road where it was darker, most of the homes had the bed-candles snuffed out now, which made it much easier for me to move along unnoticed and I relaxed a little.

I passed two more homes and spotted another road turning off the main one I was on, not much further ahead of that I made out the shape of a large building, much larger than the homes so far anyway.

That must be the town hall I thought and felt my heartbeat faster with excitement. I was almost there! I could see light coming from inside, through the slim window openings.

I started to quicken my pace and closed in, now I could see where I needed to be. My plan was working perfectly.

As I grew nearer, I made out someone standing in front of the double doors, a guard maybe?

Yep. So, I was definitely in the right place.

They must have posted a guard to stop anyone listening in on their secret meeting. Well, he wouldn't stop me.

I just had to sneak around him and get over to one of the windows around the back where no one would see me.

I hugged close to the last home on the side road that led to the hall doors, all the lights were out inside this one as well which was exactly what I needed to get closer.

As I passed a window covered by a straw shutter, my heart nearly skipped a beat. I heard a noise and froze to listen, but it was someone snoring loudly.

I let myself breathe normally again.

Calm down Kael, snoring is good it means they are fast asleep. I continued tiptoeing around the home, taking care to be extra quiet. I didn't want to wake the snorer up.

I neared the back wall of the house and turned to look over at the guard, he was standing almost side on to me from here, all I had to do was cross the empty space and I'd be safe against the hall and out of his view.

But… the problem was it looked like a VERY long way now I was actually here about to do it and I started having doubts.

What if he sees me? What if he takes me to the gaol?

No, he won't see you. It's so dark tonight with only a half-moon, he won't be able to see you from this far.

You just need to do it, you're a knight and knights aren't scared of anything.

I crouched there and watched him, holding my breath and waited for my moment.

Then I saw him turn his head away from me.

It was now or never.

I sprinted across the dark gap as fast and quietly as I could and it felt like it took forever, the whole time I was terrified to look in the guard's direction even for a moment, so I just kept my eyes dead ahead and ran the fastest I've ever ran.

The next thing I realised I was pressed up against

the hall, puffing with my heart racing, I had actually made it!

Huddling there I held my celebration and listened, expecting him to come charging around the corner at any moment to grab me and drag me to the gaol.

I waited, but he didn't come. I had really made it!

Alright, that's the hard part done. Now, I just need to sneak around the back, and I'll be able to see inside through one of the window slits.

This should be easy from here, I hoped anyway.

Don't count your chickens before they hatch, Kael. That's what mother would say.

Hugging close to the building I slowly made my way along the side wall, ducking under the two windows I passed on the way, the light inside shone over my head. I wanted to look through, but I could hear voices, and they sounded very close, so I just stayed low.

I was so scared they would look and catch me if I peeked, and I had no Idea what they would do with me then.

It would be safer around the back for sure.

Finally, I made it to the corner of the building and stuck my head around before turning it to make sure the coast was clear, and they hadn't posted another guard.

Which they hadn't, silly adults. I was in luck tonight.

I snuck the rest of the way confidently, I was good at this, like a secret spy. But also, a knight. And definitely not a baby who needs care.

I came to a stop under the window slit, I was still too nervous to look, so I stopped moving and listened again.

I heard a man talking, it could've been Lothar's friend Orin, it kind of sounded like him.

"… that was when I heard this Zarek character say that Hiltsten was their next target."

There was a bit of a pause, and then a reply came from a voice I hadn't heard before.

"A hundred men you say. And you overheard nothing that would hint at why they are travelling from town to town, murdering and pillaging as they please?" It said.

"Nothing at all, sir, it doesn't make any sense. I made my escape while they were busy burying their dead from the battle and ran straight to Branwick for aide. Then I came here as fast as I could, with the two men I was able to enlist," the man, I think was Orin replied.

Another voice I recognised as Lothar spoke next.

"As I said, Roland, they appear to be interested in the children, but we have no idea why. It's imperative we evacuate the town with the remaining men and head for Branwick to join forces. It may still not be enough, but we can at least, decide a plan together with them."

Building my courage, I slowly raised my head and peeked through the slit. Inside I could make out Lothar and Orin standing a short distance away and a large, old man with a big beard was seated in a cushioned chair across a large table from them both. I guessed that he must be the Duke.

I saw the rude Amond man was sitting on his left and then another chubby man on his right I didn't know. There was also four other men that seemed to be guards, standing behind Lothar and Orin.

My heart was pounding while I spied on them, I would be in so much trouble if I was caught, but dang it was exciting though!

The man on the Duke's right knelt and whispered something into the Duke's ear that I couldn't hear.

The Duke looked up and took a deep sigh.

"I don't think either of you are being completely honest with me right now, is there anything more you would like to share?" He asked and began to glare at Lothar.

I wondered what he meant by that. Lothar was an honest man, I know Pa trusted him more than anyone he knew.

"What on this earth are you talking about, Roland!?" Lothar shot back, starting to look annoyed.

I noticed the four guards behind Lothar and Orin slowly moved a little closer to them both.

What did he mean they weren't being honest with him?

I kept watching while Lothar waited for an answer from the Duke.

"I've heard a different version of events, Lothar. Herman, tell us what you said you overheard these two talking about when they were in Delaney's home," he said looking to the fat, redhaired man on his right.

Herman nodded and stood up from his seat.

"Like I said, my lord, I overheard Orin here, say this 'Zarek' fellow was certain the one they were looking for was 'the child that escaped Drassox' and that this meant it must be the boy Lothar came with since 'no one else survived'. Then he said this 'Zarek', was furious the boy had escaped. It is my belief that if we give him what he wants, he will leave us alone." Herman said matter of factly.

Wait, he wanted to give me to them? Lothar wouldn't allow this, there's no way!

I saw Orin glance at Lothar with a look of concern.

"What do you have to say against these allegations?" The Duke asked, looking back to Lothar and Orin.

"I say Herman is a fucking snake, Roland. You think Zarek will just leave you alone after we slaughtered all his men? For one young boy?" Lothar shot back.

I could see he was getting very angry fast.

Herman turned to the Duke raising his eyebrows, and I saw the Duke gently nod. Herman turned back to Lothar and Orin smirking, and then he answered Lothar instead of the Duke.

"Yes, I do, Lothar, and according to the townspeople, this boy has exhibited some rather strange behaviour already in his short time with us. I was told he almost killed another boy without even laying a finger on him. Black magic and devilry they called it!" He began to shout as he spoke.

I realised he was talking about me and Erik.

Had I really done some kind of magic? I don't know any spells, why is he saying this, it's not true!

"You would condemn a young boy over childish rumours?" Lothar scoffed back.

Orin began to fidget, his hand inching closer to the handle of his sword. I noticed Lothar was unarmed except for his dagger.

"Yes, I wou—" Herman started to reply, and Lothar cut him off.

"—I'm not talking to you! SNAKE!" He shouted and looked to the Duke for an answer.

The Duke looked back, meeting his gaze and paused, thinking.

Then he said softly, "I would, Lothar, if it will save this town. Please just hand over the boy."

Lothar looked shocked then became angry again as he replied.

"Roland, I respect you, but I can't do that. What makes you think this Zarek will be satisfied by that anyway, we slaughtered his men! He is going to demand retribution, we mustn't give in to this tyrant!"

Everyone became silent, and then I saw the Duke look almost sad for a split second as he turned his eyes to Herman and barely nodded his head.

Herman stepped forward, a smug look on his face.

"Because, Lothar, we have what he wants. And we will also hand him the man who tortured and murdered this Gildred character—his 'second in command' as I overheard Orin call him."

The moment Herman said this Lothar immediately reached to draw his dagger but the three guards near him grabbed his arms from behind while the fourth guard went for Orin.

Orin managed to wrestle his way free and draw his sword. Lothar struggled to break against the men, but he was overpowered.

"Roland! What is the meaning of this!? Tell them to release me now, this is insanity! We have known each other since I was a boy!" He yelled at the Duke.

I noticed Amond had also drawn his sword and was approaching Orin to back up the fourth guard.

No! What were they doing!?

"I'm sorry, Lothar, but you should have taken that man prisoner instead of torturing him. We could have used him to barter but now, you and the boy are all we have. A small cost for the good of the people of this entire town. Order your man to stand down and he may live. If he does not, he will be struck down," The Duke said, although he didn't look at Lothar at all when he spoke.

Lothar looked at Orin frantically while still struggling.

I could see the worry in his eyes.

What was happening right now! I need to do something!

"You fucking cowards!! Orin, just lay down your arms. You don't have to die for me. That's the last order I give you as your Captain," Lothar said.

Orin looked between the men approaching him and Lothar and started shaking his head.

"Sorry, Captain. I'm gonna have to ignore your order this time. Drassox looks after its own."

Then he smiled and gave Lothar a small nod and attacked the guard closest to him. Their swords clashed together with a sharp ring that echoed loudly in the hall, and the two of them started fighting.

Lothar began struggling violently, like the stag had done trying to break free from the wolf in the forest, trying his absolute hardest to break free so he could help Orin.

I couldn't do anything but watch, there was just too many of them and my body felt frozen.

"Roland!! Stop this madness now before it goes too

far!" Lothar screamed as he fought, but the three men managed to wrestle him to the ground.

Amond closed in and started attacking Orin together with the fourth guard, Orin was fighting bravely but even I could see he was being overwhelmed.

I watched as he blocked a high attack from the guard, and as he had his sword held high Amond attacked, stabbing his sword hard into Orin's chest, thrusting cleanly through his leather armour and out through his back.

Lothar roared like a beast, I saw the rage and pain on his face.

I opened my mouth to scream when suddenly a hand reached around from behind and grabbed me tightly, pulling me back and covering my lips so I couldn't get it out.

The guard from the front of the building has found me!

I panicked and struggled while I tried to thrash my way free, but he was much too strong.

A rage began burning inside of me.

Speaking to me.

The same voice I had heard when Erik was bullying me.

It was telling me to fight, to draw my sword and slaughter whoever had dared to grab me and then kill anyone else that dared stand in my path.

Red and black flashes filled my vision just like when I had been pushed to the ground by Erik and I heard the same chanting echoing faintly in my head.

Then a soft female voice whispered in my ear and snapped me out of it.

"Kael, calm down! It's me, Del!"

I stopped struggling and looked back as she released her grip on me.

"Del…?"

It really was her!

But she was dressed differently now, and had her hair tied back. Gone was her simple brown and white dress, replaced by a leather outfit that kind of looked like armour but fit her tightly, and it was dyed black. I noticed she also had a dagger strapped to her waist.

"Yes, I told you it's me, Kael. We need to leave, you must come with me now," she replied grabbing my arm.

I heard Lothar yelling and more struggling inside the hall as she started to pull me with her and I shook her off, ripping my arm back.

"No! I need to help Lothar! And what are you doing dressed like that?" I argued with her.

I was not going to leave Lothar, he's my friend.

"Lothar has been captured, you need to come with me! I knew your mother, Kael, your real mother! Her and I were very close, I promised her I would help you. Please, we need to escape this town," she pleaded with me.

She knew my mother. How?

That doesn't matter right now Kael! Lothar is in trouble!

I peeked inside the window slit again, and I saw him being dragged away, his hands tied behind his back and a hessian sack had been placed over his head so he couldn't see.

He needed help.

My help, he had no one else anymore just like me, we had to look after each other.

I was a knight now too, and knights always save their friends, just like Lothar, and Pa, and all the men in Drassox that tried to save the town.

I turned sharply back to Del, "NO. I won't leave him, we'll all leave here together when I rescue him. He would never leave me, and I won't leave him either," I said back to her firmly, meaning every word I said.

I wasn't going to let anyone else close to me die. I might be small, but I would rescue him somehow.

Del looked at me pleadingly, but I glared back at her and eventually she nodded. I think she realised she wasn't going to change my mind.

"Alright, Kael, but you need to let me free him. I know the town and the people, much better than you do. Plus, you heard them, it's you they are looking for and two of us sneaking around is also much easier to notice. You need to hide while I rescue him, and I know the perfect spot they won't look. Deal?"

I frowned, I wanted to help, but she did have a good point. They were looking for me and I hadn't even been sure where the hall was when I snuck out, how would I find where they took Lothar? I didn't even have any idea where to start.

"Fine. But you need to promise me that you will come back for me…" I said sadly remembering how Mother hadn't.

"I promise I'll come back for you, no matter what happens," she whispered, looking me straight in the eyes.

"Alright… show me this hiding spot then," I replied to her.

I wanted so much to believe her, but I couldn't help feeling scared that I would lose her too.

"Follow me," she said, looking around quickly, and then began sneaking away, with me following closely behind.

CHAPTER 8

WHO ARE YOU STRANGER?

'You shall treat the stranger who sojourns with you as the native among you and you shall love they as thyself'

I had thrashed and fought as hard as I could to free myself from my bonds, but all it had achieved was me being beaten mercilessly for my efforts as my captors dragged me away.

The gash on my head I'd suffered in the battle at Drassox had reopened and now I could feel the blood dripping down my face while I sat there tied to a chair.

I didn't know exactly where I was, but I'd been here for at least a couple of hours. I couldn't see much, apart from blurry shapes and shadows through the damn hessian sack they had placed over my head before dragging me here.

The trip from the hall had been rather short, so I knew it couldn't be far from there. Wherever it was, it stunk of animal shit like a barn. The floor was dirt too, and the air felt frigidly cold, so a barn was a good guess I figured.

Why had that young fool not surrendered like I had ordered him to? Damn his loyalty.

I wanted to murder them all for what they did to Orin, if it weren't for him bringing aide to us in the battle, this entire bloody town would be six feet under already. That rodent Amond had attacked and slain him like a coward as I watched.

Whilst I cursed Orin for a fool in my head, in my heart I felt deep pride for his actions. He had done what I would've done and faced his end like a warrior.

What I should've done anyway.

The only fool was myself for letting those guards get the jump on me. It was my fault he was dead, it was my fault everyone was dead. I botched the defence of Drassox, and now I'd allowed myself to be captured while Orin was murdered.

I couldn't allow myself to fail the boy as well. I WOULD NOT.

I overheard my other captors say they were going to help the others search for him when I was taken here and that he had not been found at Del's home.

Nor had she, which was good news.

Still, I needed to get out of here to help them, and

right now I couldn't see a solution to my current situation, hell, I couldn't see a fucking thing with this bag on my head.

I tried once more to struggle against my bonds and received another sharp blow to the head in return like I had more than a few times thus far. I could feel numerous lumps on my skull beginning to take form and it pissed me off.

"Don't try that again! How many times do I have to tell you, you're bringing this on yourself," an unknown voice yelled at me.

This voice was the only one I had heard since some of the guards had left to look for the boy, I hoped that meant there was only the one man watching over me.

It would make it easier when the time came, all I needed was for him to give me one slither of an opportunity, and I would tear his windpipe out with my bare hands.

This town would've been finished long ago had Drassox not come to its aide during the brigand attacks, they should be praising us like gods right now, not betraying us!

These past few days had been filled with nothing but battle and death. And now betrayal to top it off.

Everyone I once knew and trusted was dead.

I was having a difficult time accepting it as I sat here trickling blood, all of the events of late weighing heavily on my mind.

The boy is the last one left.

I owe it to Elias to protect him… and although I don't like to admit it, he's grown on me lately.

I must rescue him, I won't let him die too.

"How does it feel betraying those who helped save you and your entire town?" I said at whoever was in the room with me, my tone laced with venom.

I was antagonising whoever was here to speak, I needed to know if he was alone. I heard the shuffling of someone's feet, as though they were pacing about.

And then a reply came.

"I'm just doing as I'm told. My family live here, Lothar, I'll do what I need to protect them, I know you understand that, you aren't stupid."

"Oh yeah, by taking orders from a snake like Herman and betraying those that have saved you in the past?" I spat back, feeling myself fill with rage again.

I wanted to squeeze the life from Herman. He deserved to die, he was nothing but a cockroach.

Silence followed and then more pacing, before the man replied back to me again.

"Yes, Lothar, if betraying you and that boy means that this town, and my family, can live and not end up like Drassox did, then that's what I'll do. Now, just quit your moaning and don't speak to me again, or I'll give you something to moan about."

I couldn't believe the nerve of this wretched scum,

real tough guy while I was tied up.

"You'd piss your pants if I broke free from these ropes right now," I said to him, which was pointless as all it got me was another crack in the side of the head, harder than the last.

My skull was throbbing, I could feel blood dripping from my nose as well now, no doubt broken. It wasn't the first broken nose I've suffered but that didn't make me feel any better about it.

I continued to sit there now in silence, my entire body complained of soreness, aches and exhaustion. I realised I hadn't rested since the night me and the boy spent in the abandoned cabin.

What I would do for a nice cosy bed right now, and the warmth of a tender, female body lying next to me. I might not have taken vows of matrimony in my life, but I did see a lady in Drassox from time to time, Joan.

She had been widowed a couple of summers back, losing her husband to sickness. She was a good sort, and pretty too.

We spent a few nights together when I had the time, but I was always too busy to commit to her, which was what she had wanted. We'd spoken of it once, she grew upset when I'd explained I was too busy with my role for that.

I never saw her body, but I presume she is dead now too, lying somewhere in the town hall with everyone else no doubt. Her beautiful green eyes forever closed, hidden from the world.

Battle takes a toll on a man, physically and mentally.

But it pales in comparison next to true betrayal. Duke. Roland.

A man I'd known since I was a boy, a man who knew my father. Both Roland and Amond deserved to pay for their betrayal, and especially Herman.

I could feel my strength leaving me as exhaustion and the beatings began to set in when a sudden creak, followed by a light thud snapped me awake.

A person had just entered the building I was in.

I heard my captor turn suddenly and call out to whoever it was, "You! What are you doing here? They're looking everywhere for you!"

Oh no, don't tell me the boy is here.

I held my breath listening for a response when a familiar female voice broke my trepidation.

"I came to hand myself in! I'm terrified Frederick! I haven't done anything wrong please don't let them hurt me! I—I'm so scared…" She broke out into heavy sobs and whimpers.

It only took me a second to recognise who it was.

Del. If she is alive and here, then where is the boy?

"Calm down. No one is going to hurt you, Del, they just want the boy, Kael. Do you know where he is?" Frederick asked.

I heard Del sniffling trying to compose herself.

"I don't know, I left him and went to take water to the men rebuilding the gates, then when I returned, he was gone! I looked everywhere for him! And then I saw Amond and some other guards, and they shouted and chased me, they had their weapons out! I didn't know why they were chasing me so I ran to hide, I was so scared! And then I saw you… I knew you would help me Frederick…" she continued, sobbing again.

I stayed silent, biting my tongue to stop myself screaming at her and kept listening.

I had ordered her to look after the boy.

What the fuck did she mean she had left him?

"Of course I'll help you, Del. Come on, don't cry, it'll be alright I promise," Frederick said back to her softly.

"Oh, thank you, Frederick. I always knew you were a good man… such a strong man, a protective man," she whispered seductively.

I tried my best to peer through the fabric of the bag, it looked like the two shapes were touching, like they were embracing.

If this bitch is a traitor as well, I'm going to kill her too I swear.

"I've always liked you, Frederick, I've seen you watching me in the square. You like me too, don't you? You don't have to hide it." Del said to him, her voice sounding even more seductive.

"Well, I… wait—you have?" He asked surprised.

"Yes, Frederick. Always." She spoke softly, innocently.

I was straining my eyes to make out what was going on, it looked as though they were starting to kiss each other.

"Del, no… we can't do this right now, I—I need to watch him," Frederick mumbled hesitantly.

"No, he's not going anywhere, he's tied up. Don't fight it, Frederick, I want you to protect me," Del said, and I could hear her kissing him.

What the fuck was going on here? Was I invisible?

Damn it all to hell. This is my moment, I'll take them both while they're occupied with whatever this shit was.

I'll charge into them with my chair and smash it apart to free myself, hopefully. Then end them both before they can react.

Sorry Frederick but today is not going to be your lucky day.

I held my breath, tensing my body, preparing my legs to spring up powerfully and charge into the two shapes.

"Thwack, thwack, thwack, thwack!"

Suddenly a noise I knew all too well began in rapid succession and froze me from following through with my charge.

It was the unmistakable sound of blade piercing flesh, I could make out small blurry movements in front of me, accompanied by both male and female grunts.

And then a thud as a body collapsed.

"Thwack, thwack, thwack, thwack!"

Several more puncture sounds reached my ears, followed by a slow, weak gurgling, as the last of someone's life force slipped from their lungs.

That sick fuck has just murdered Del! I could see a blurred shadow of him hunched over her corpse still stabbing it in a mad frenzy.

"Thwack, thwack, thwack!"

It was now or never.

I sprang into action and barged clumsily towards him, still tied to the chair intending to ram him senseless, but it had looked better in my head and he swiftly stepped out of the way. My feet kicked Del's body making me trip, falling awkwardly and landing painfully on my face, unable to break my fall because of my bonds. I felt my teeth chip when they smacked together and the pain on my broken nose shot through my face.

"Ooof!" I groaned loudly and struggled to recover my footing.

I had to get up before that maggot used his blade on me, I thrashed about on the floor blindly, trying desperately to stand but failing.

At any moment I expected to feel the plunge of icy cold steel penetrate my body and strike one of my internal organs.

And then, looming above me and closing in I started to make out a dark shape, reaching towards me intending to snuff my life out next.

"Stop thrashing about!" A voice said to me.

Like fuck you spineless cur! You think I'll make this easy for you? I'm going to make you work for your kill and hopefully drag you to hell with me!

"Lothar, I'm here to help, stop! Kael sent me!" The same voice yelled, frantic now.

Feminine.

Familiar.

"Del…?" I asked tilting my head, straining to see through the shapes features through the sack.

"Yes, it's me you idiot. Don't move, I'm going to take your hood off and cut your hands free," she replied.

I felt a hand scrunch the top of the sack and start to pull it off, yanking my hair painfully with it.

I winced and closed my eyes as the material tugged past my twisted, bent nose, sticking to it because of the dried blood, before sliding away from my head, revealing Del's face, dagger in hand.

She looked strangely different now, gone was her cheerful demeanour from earlier seemingly replaced with a cold, calculated look. Her black hair was tied back, and she was wearing a tight-fitting black leather outfit, resembling something a thief might wear. It wouldn't do much to stop a blade but would definitely make her harder to spot in the dark.

"What're you doing here?" I asked, staring at her groggily.

"Shh! There's no time for chatting right now, roll over so I can cut your bonds. We have to hurry back to Kael, he's hidden, but I don't know for how long," she said while helping me roll over.

It was difficult with the chair still attached to me.

"Why the fuck did you leave him alone to come for me!? I told you to look after him!" I growled.

I felt my arms release as she cut my bonds and then I flinched as a slap to the back of my head stunned.

"You ungrateful sack of shit! I would've left you in a heartbeat! Kael begged me to save you, if I hadn't, he was going to try himself!" She scolded me.

I mumbled sorry, maybe what I said was a bit uncalled for I thought as I stood to my feet rubbing my head. The relief to my hands was instant as they were freed and the feeling started to return to them.

Glancing around the room I felt a tiny bit impressed with myself, I'd been correct in my earlier assumption, it was a barn. Catching my attention though, laying on the ground near me was the brutally stabbed up corpse of Frederick.

He had a vicious slash, parallel across his face that passed from forehead to lower cheek. The incision travelled through one of his eyes, splitting it, and had caused the eye to resemble a punctured, runny egg yolk.

His throat had also been crudely, and savagely cut, almost gouged open. Not in the neat, controlled manner in which I had dispatched Gildred.

This looked even more violent… chaotic.

I glanced cautiously at the woman before me, this act didn't line up with the petite, chirpy person, I'd met up until this point.

"Who are you, woman?" I asked, studying her, taking in her leather clothing and change of demeanour.

"There'll be time for chit-chat after we've escaped, Lothar. Right now, we have to get back to Kael. Grab Frederick's weapons, he won't be needing them anymore," she replied and cast a cold glare at his corpse.

She did have a point.

I bent down, still feeling a tad unstable from the beating I'd received and began unclasping the dead man's dagger and sword.

How kind of him to replace what they'd taken from me I thought to myself as I slid the sword into the sheathe on my back and put the dagger into the belt around my waist.

Not the finest steel but they would do, I've killed men with much less. I would kill Amond with my bare hands if given half a chance I thought, seething with anger as I pictured him driving his sword through Orin.

Pray I don't stumble across you in my escape Amond. Pray.

"Alright, I'm ready. Take me to the boy," I said to her when I was finished adjusting myself.

"Stay close, and don't speak. The guards are out everywhere looking for us," she replied to me, and began moving out.

The woman traversed through the town in a fast, fluid, yet silent manner, further enforcing my belief she was or had at least been a thief or cutpurse at some point in her life.

The ruthless way she had killed that man Frederick though, appearing completely unbothered by her actions, well that hinted at something more than just a common criminal.

The remaining guards were scouring the town looking for us, we'd heard a shout of alarm not long after leaving the barn, most likely made by someone finding Frederick's corpse.

Right now, we seemed to be undetected, with the guards going from home to home behind us searching the settlement.

We came to a halt in an isolated, corner of the town. It was into the very early hours of the morning now, still dark but I could see the sun was close to rising, it'd be light soon and we needed to be gone before we lost the cover of darkness.

"Do you see that group of bushes up there, on that ridge near the wall?" Del whispered to me calmly.

I looked where she was pointing and nodded.

"Yes. What of it?"

It was hardly a hiding spot, and I couldn't make out any small, huddled forms amongst the brush.

"That's where we're going," came her reply, and once again she began expertly skulking through the night, blending in like a shadow in her dark leather outfit.

I watched her move, studying her briefly and then continued to follow along behind, far less inconspicuously in my dirty yet still somewhat shiny plate mail, and together we arrived at the thicket of bushes.

I took a quick glance around, but I could see no one nor any sign the boy had ever even been here, and I snapped.

"Where the hell is he!?"

I should never have left him alone—he was far too young. What the hell had she been thinking?

I need to find him now.

Del appeared unconcerned however, ignoring me and kneeling down, ruffling around on the dirt floor as though she was searching for something.

I held my tongue and watched as she lift the grass up and it flopped over back onto the ground, like a trapdoor.

Exactly like a trapdoor, because that's what it was.

The boy's scared face appeared, staring back at me from a shallow pit, his expression quickly changed to a look of relief as he realised it was us.

"Lothar, you escaped! And, Del, you rescued him and came back just like you promised!" He shouted, a little too loudly.

Del went to reply but I cut in before she could.

"Shush, boy! Keep your caterwauling down and get out of the hole, we need to move. Now."

It got me a glare from the woman, but I didn't care. We had bigger problems right now. She reached down and helped the boy climb from his hiding spot.

He walked over and stood next to me while Del reached back into the hole and removed a knapsack, slinging it over her shoulder, and then dragged a sheepskin that was covering the floor of the pit out.

"We need to get over the wall, it's high but possible if you help boost us over. We can lay this over the spiked tops for protection," she began to explain, showing me the sheepskin.

I glanced at the wall for a moment, the plan would work, and I couldn't see any other options right now. There would be guards posted at the gates without a doubt so exiting from there was out. The only problem with this plan was that I wasn't sure I could get myself over the wall on my own in my armour. No way I was leaving here without it though, I'd need to remove my breastplate and lob it to the other side, then retrieve it once I got myself over.

I'd manage. It was high but not impossible.

"That's as good a plan as any. I'll boost you first, Del, and then the boy, so you can help him down from the top," I told her, and then moved into position against the wall, spreading my legs to brace for her weight and clasped my hands together to create a stepping platform.

"Obviously," she remarked in a snarky tone.

Hell, this woman was quite a handful to deal with sometimes.

"I can get down myself easily, I don't need any help," the boy said, giving both of us an annoyed look.

Great, now he's going to start giving me attitude as well.

I was about to reply when the faint sound of voices began to reach my ears from somewhere back towards the homes.

It was the guards, and they were not far away.

We needed to leave now, especially as the sun was beginning to rise, I could see it barely lighting the horizon. Shortly the three of us would be much easier to spot and that was not going to be good at all.

Del heard the voices when I did and shot me a look of panic, I motioned for her to hurry up and she began to step onto my hands whilst using my shoulders to help balance herself.

The moment she was stable I hoisted her petite frame up with ease and she threw the sheepskin over the wooden spikes, then began to clamber gracefully over.

Well, that was easy, now the boy's turn.

"You're up, boy. Listen to me, it's high so lose the attitude, let Del help you down the other side. We can't afford to have you breaking your ankle," I ordered him, receiving a grumble in reply.

He approached the wall and this time I stood behind him so I could lift him straight up from his hips, he grabbed the top and thrashed as he tried to lift himself onto the sheep skin. Eventually he got there but not before his foot connected with my freshly broken nose causing me to wince and muffle a painful groan.

I'm sure I heard a giggle as he disappeared over the other side. The little bastard did that on purpose.

With my eyes now watering and fresh blood dripping down my upper lip I began to undo my breastplate clasps. I could still hear the voices behind me, they may have sounded slightly closer, but it was difficult to tell.

Better not linger either way.

It didn't take me long to remove my chest piece, having done it a thousand times before. I instantly felt much lighter.

"Watch out over there, I'm throwing my breast plate over," I whispered hoping they could hear.

A falling breastplate from eight feet could do some damage especially if it landed on that little shit.

Well, here it goes.

I lobbed it over, and heard it land with a thud. Neither of them cried out in pain which was a good sign.

Now, it was time to get this old, thrashed body over.

Ten summers ago, I'd have bounced over with ease, nowadays I'd lost some of my nimbleness and the recent beatings paired with complete exhaustion weren't helping at all either.

I jumped high and grabbed for the top, my hands however failed to find purchase on the spikes through the sheep skin, and my feet landed back to the ground with a heavy thud.

Fuck that was pitiful. Try again old man.

I got as close to the wall as I could and prepared to give it another go, then stopped. I held my breath and listened. The voices were definitely louder now, had they heard me land? I didn't want to wait to find out. I need to get over now.

Beginning to feel panic setting in, I jumped again, managing to find a grip this time, but I struggled to lift myself, my feet slipping when I tried to use them to help me lift my body up.

I slipped and dropped to the ground again. Damn this! I need to try something else, I frantically looked around for anything I could use but there was nothing that would help.

Think Lothar, think.

Then I had an idea that might just work, it may make a little noise, but I didn't have many choices right now.

I drew my sword and began inspecting the wall before me. The way the posts fit tightly together side by side, a simple design, each post nailed to the next as they were placed.

It didn't take long and I saw what I was looking for, a tiny gap between two posts, enough to ram and wedge my sword between. I took the tip and poked it into the gap and then pushed hard, hitting the pummel with my palm to drive it in deeper, forcing it to wedge itself halfway between the posts at roughly waist height.

A foothold.

I drew my dagger next, I would need it to create a handhold to balance myself as I stepped up onto the blade. I wedged the dagger in as high as I could reach and decided to go for it.

I gingerly put one foot on the sword edge and used it to step up, grabbing the handle of the dagger as I rose to full height, now able to easily reach the top of the wall. I lifted myself onto the sheepskin feeling the sword slip and fall out of the gap as I used it to push off.

Unarmed once again, but free at least.

Well almost unarmed, I thought before I reached down and pried the dagger free, then slipped over the wall making sure to drag the sheep skin with me.

I landed on my feet with a thud and quickly looked around before spotting Del and the boy, who was holding my breastplate, waiting for me nearby.

I began to approach the pair, eyeballing him.

"Give me that, boy," I snapped, snatching my breastplate back as we started to walk away.

I was still annoyed about him kicking me in the nose, which was, as of this moment, still throbbing painfully.

"DING! DING! DING!"

"DING! DING! DING!"

A bell rang loudly from the other side of the wall as we began to make our escape, now free from the settlement.

Not good.

Surely they hadn't seen me as I climbed over? I knew they were close by, but I felt sure I had made it without being spotted.

There wasn't any time to wait and find out, I spurred Del and the boy along. We needed to put distance between us and the town before they made their way over the fence behind us. It was still dark enough that they wouldn't be able to see us if we got far enough away first.

We moved as fast as we could while trying to remain silent for a good distance before I noticed the boy was struggling to keep up, I turned back to grab him, intending to carry him. That was when I saw the torches, way back in the distance approaching the town.

Coming from the direction of Drassox…

I estimated at least a hundred of them, far too many to be the men from Hiltsten. I realised that this had been the reason the bells had rung, not our escape.

There was no question as to who this was.

Zarek had arrived with his main force.

***

We had continued in silence for hours after seeing Zarek's force approaching, trying to get as far away from his army as possible.

It wasn't long though before a loud blast made Del and the boy jump, echoing across the field from the direction we had just marched from.

I knew instantly what it was.

Another blast stone.

No doubt blowing the gates apart like Gildred had done so this time Zarek's men could storm the town and murder everyone, just as he had done to mine and the boy's home.

Even more deaths to carry on my conscience, were mine and the boy's lives worth more than an entire town?

Should I have just let them hand us over and end this?

No, I must find a way to stop Zarek killing anyone else.

We'd been heading in the direction of Branwick, choosing to stay off the road for obvious reasons.

I couldn't think of anywhere else to go. I was praying the Duke there, Lord Gerard, would already be hatching a plan on how to deal with Zarek's force.

Branwick had a decent sized force of its own, with the right preparation it was possible we could stop him. If they find out it's the boy he's after though, they may betray us as well.

"We need to stop, Lothar. Kael's tired, and so am I. We haven't stopped for hours, and none of us has slept all night," I heard Del say, interrupting my thoughts.

The boy didn't say anything, he looked as though he was about to pass out on his feet, admittedly I felt the same. I could no longer recall walking the last few hours, I just know that we had.

I did a quick scan of the area we were in, an hour or two here would be fine. It was flat grassy fields for as far as I could see, which meant I could see anyone else coming a long way off.

I'd been planning for us to stop and rest soon

anyway.

"Fine, but only for a couple of hours and then we move again. We'll find somewhere safer to sleep for the night," I replied, motioning for them both to stop walking, and sit down on the long grass.

It felt like heaven on my tired limbs to finally stop and relax as I stretched out and lay back on the soft foliage.

"Here, I have some bread and water in my pack," Del said and passed the boy a full waterskin made from goat pelt.

He took a big swig and then passed it to me, I was completely parched and thankful for it. I thirstily took a large scull myself and passed it back to Del, next she tore chunks of bread off and handed some to each of us.

We sat there for a short time eating in silence and passing the waterskin around to quench our thirst, the boy eventually fell asleep using the sheep skin I'd retrieved from the wall as a makeshift bed, he snored softly.

I looked to Del, she had lain back on the grass bed and was staring at the midday sky. I wouldn't sleep until tonight, as tired as I was I needed to remain awake and keep watch, it was also time to get some answers from her.

I chewed the inside of my gum thinking what to say for a bit, and then just decided to come out and ask the question that had been gnawing at me.

"Who are you really, Del?" I said, breaking the silence.

She continued looking at the sky for a moment, then sat upright and looked at the boy, still fast asleep.

"… I knew Kael's mother. His real mother," she began softly, while staring at him, as though her mind was somewhere else.

I sat there quietly, waiting for her to go on.

"Her name was Mirella. From a very young age Mirella had shown signs she wasn't normal, signs that she had… powers." Her eyes still not leaving him as she spoke.

"Go on," I said, urging her to continue.

"Mirella was able to heal the sick, her parents believed it to be a gift from God. But as she approached womanhood and began to bleed… her gifts attracted other attention. Something dark, something evil. It wanted what she had."

She paused again and looked at me this time.

"It was Lucifer himself, Lothar. Or rather, his spirit. He invaded her dreams, tormenting her… telling her she must bear a child for him, to use as his vessel so he can return to the world."

Del stopped and took a sip from the waterskin before speaking again and I waited.

"Mirella arrived one day to the holy commune that I called home, a place high in the mountains, she was fourteen at the time. Her parents begged my people to help her, and the priests agreed. She was left there with us, and it was decided she would live in the church, where she would be safe from Lucifer's grasp. She was forbidden to ever venture outside where he could get to her, our priests tried everything to break Lucifer's hold on her. But ultimately, they failed. Not long before her seventeenth summer, upset at being locked up all the time she chose to sneak out to explore the mountains… She thought he was gone. But he had been patient, he got to her that day and raped her from within. Still our Priests believed they could exorcise the infant and cleanse its spirit as it entered this world. But the Prince of Treachery's influence was far stronger now his vessel grew within her belly, he ravaged and twisted Mirella's mind, convincing her our priests were planning to murder her child. She panicked believing his lies and ran…" Del stopped to take another sip of water before passing me the waterskin.

I grabbed it, taking a quick gulp.

"And then what?"

She glanced again at the boy to make sure he was still asleep then spoke once more.

"And then we lost track of her. My commune sent four volunteers out to live in the towns to the south, to try to locate the child and return them both if we came across the pair. We had no idea where Lucifer had convinced her to hide, so we spread out, living in different towns, waiting for a sign of the child or Mirella. I was one of these people, I took the role as tutor so I could keep an eye on the children. That was almost nine summers ago now. Our ancient texts say that as punishment for his past sins to God, Lucifer's mind and body were split in two. His consciousness, sent to Limbo in the first circle of Hell, while his body lay dormant in the ninth circle, within the frozen lake Cocytus awaiting his return. As each summer has passed of the child's life, Lucifer's mind has crossed through one more circle of Hell. From Limbo, to Lust, to Gluttony, Greed, Anger, Heresy, Violence, Fraud… and finally Treachery where his body waits. When the ninth circle is eventually broken, Lucifer will reunite with his body and take full possession of the child and all their inherited powers. Then he'll use them to ravage the mortal world.

Her expression grew grim.

"Lothar, I have no doubt that Kael, is Mirella's child."

I stared at her unsure what to say. That was quite the tale. I lay there on the grass considering everything she had just told me while studying her, I was convinced this woman had clearly lost her mind, what she just told me was ridiculous.

She's a god damned cult member, although it explained a lot about our current situation, nothing I had seen thus far led me to believe the boy was possessed by a demon.

Lucifer himself at that. It was preposterous and I didn't believe any of it, not for a second, which must have been obvious to her as she watched me processing what she'd just told me.

"You don't believe me, do you?" She asked, visibly annoyed.

"I believe that you believe it, that is enough. Do you know who the men are chasing us?" I replied with a shrug.

She paused and thought for a moment, probably deciding whether or not she would tell me anymore, before she finally gave in and answered me.

"Yes, I do. They're called the Order of St Michael, a group of fanatics that believe the only way to rid the child of Lucifer's grasp is to kill him and allow his soul to pass to God for forgiveness. They're wrong in this, and they MUST NOT succeed, Lothar. What the Order don't realise is that with Lucifer's consciousness this close to crossing the final circle, Kael's death would only allow the Prince of Treachery to completely possess Kael. Kael's mind is the only thing holding him back now, he's too close to being reunited with his body. The only way to stop the cycle is to cleanse Kael's soul."

I listened to her talk, then looked at the boy. He lay there not far from me fast asleep. Whether I believed this bedtime story or not didn't matter to me, I had firmly decided I wasn't going to let anyone harm him.

I'll find a way to stop and kill this Zarek. He'll pay with his life for the evil he's done to the world.

CHAPTER 9

THE NIGHTMARES

'When we wake afraid, may a prayer of trust in you be the first thing upon our lips. You are our refuge and safe place'

I looked around me into the darkness, everything was pitch black and I couldn't see anything at all.

Where was I? Where had Lothar and Del gone?

There was no way they would both leave me alone.

I went to walk, but my feet felt funny, like I weighed the same as a feather.

Actually, everything felt funny. When my foot touched the ground, I noticed it didn't make any sound as I walked either.

What is going on right now? Am I dreaming?

I tilted my head down to the floor to try and figure

out where I was but there was nothing there to look at.

Nothing except blackness, like the ground had disappeared.

Had I slept through until nightfall? Why didn't Lothar wake me?

Everything was so dark I couldn't even make out my own feet below me. My heart was thumping, I didn't like this, whatever was happening didn't feel right. It didn't feel right at all, kind of like a dream, but a lot more real than any dream I'd ever had before. I felt awake not asleep.

Lothar and Del must be here somewhere, maybe they're lost too and looking for me.

"Lothar…? Del? Is anyone there? I can't see anything," I called out, but my voice made no sound at all.

I was sure I was talking, but I couldn't hear anything, there was no sound as the words left my mouth.

Had I gone deaf? I started to panic, something was really wrong. I had a strong feeling something very bad was happening right now.

"Lothar!!! WHERE ARE YOU!?" I tried again, yelling as loud as I could.

But like the first time I tried, no sound came out.

I didn't even hear a whisper.

My breathing started to get heavy, my chest felt tight, but I realised I could still hear myself puffing, so

I knew I wasn't deaf which was a relief.

But why wasn't my voice working? Had I lost it? My throat didn't feel sore like that time Pa said I lost my voice and it hurt to swallow. And I could still speak then, my voice was just a bit croaky.

Oh no, please don't leave me alone out here Lothar.

I started to whimper quietly and huddled there feeling helpless, this has to be a nightmare, it isn't real.

Why do bad things keep happening to me.

Don't panic, stay calm. It's just a nightmare, everything will be fine and you'll wake up soon, it's just the night terrors again.

I took a deep breath and stopped myself crying.

Yes, night terrors.

This past two summers I had begun to have nightmares a lot, that something was after me. I never saw what it was, but I could just feel that it wanted me and that wouldn't be good if it caught me. Mother had said it was just night terrors and Pa had helped me carve my sword so I could use it to keep me safe when I slept, he'd told me he had put a magic spell on the wood to make it stronger in my dreams.

I wished I had it now.

Then I remembered I had the sword Lothar had given me, I reach behind my back to grab it, but I couldn't feel it.

My hand grabbed nothing, like I was made of air.

This made my heart start to beat even faster, I

began to panic again but I heard something that made me freeze.

What was that?

A soft chanting… ever so faintly, somewhere not far away. It was the same chanting I had heard when Erik pushed me over and when Del had grabbed me behind the town hall in Hiltsten. Why did I keep hearing it?

I couldn't pinpoint where it was coming from, so I quickly looked everywhere around me for a sign, but I couldn't see anything but blackness all around. Suddenly the chanting became a little louder, and a tiny bit clearer.

I held my breath so I could listen, trying my best to make out what it was saying, but it was still too quiet. I couldn't catch the words over the thumping in my chest.

A flicker somewhere to the side caught my eye and I turned my head to see what it was. A dim red light had appeared, far off in the darkness, it was a long way from me, but it was there. It was easy to make out, glowing like a flaming torch and was the only thing I could see around me apart from pure black.

I stared at it, trying to make out what it was, it seemed to have a shape inside, the darkness flickered around it, like shadows near a fireplace.

And then it looked like it was beginning to move towards me, very slowly.

The chanting grew louder again, but I was still unable to make the words out. I was so close to understanding them now, if it got any louder, I would be able to.

But instead I became terrified, it washed over me like a pale of water, like my heart was telling me I didn't want to be here when the orange glow arrived. A bad thing was coming, I needed to get away.

Hide.

So I turned and started to run, my feet feeling as though they were stuck in mud, making it almost hard to run. I looked back and saw the light was gaining on me, and the chanting grew louder again, closer.

I opened my mouth to scream for someone to help.

***

"Get up, boy. It's time to go."

I opened my eyes, and Lothar was hunched over me, roughly shaking me awake, his familiar face making me feel safe again.

I sat up, still exhausted but feeling so glad he had woken me up from the nightmare. I was terrified when I wondered what might have happened if he hadn't.

What had that chanting been saying? I was so close to making it out. Another few seconds and I would've known…

Maybe it was best I hadn't, I don't want to dream like that ever again.

I yawned and began getting up from the sheepskin I was using for a mattress, I noticed Del was watching me strangely again.

"Did you sleep well, Kael?" She asked when she saw me catch her staring.

"Kind of, I had a night terror. It was really scary, I'm glad I'm awake now," I replied to her, rubbing the sleep from my eyes.

She looked at Lothar, and he just grunted, not interested in whatever she was looking at him for.

"Roll that sheepskin up, boy. We need to get moving," he said to me.

Del suddenly looked annoyed for some reason and then said, "Where are we going and what makes you think you get to decide? I seem to recall being the one to rescue you."

I watched the two of them quietly, I had seen Mother and Pa argue before and I could always tell when it was going to happen, Pa would say 'Calm down Cat' and then Mother would get even angrier. Which made no sense to me, it seemed like good advice.

Del seemed ready to argue right now, I hoped Lothar didn't tell her to calm down, I'd never seen it work on Mother before.

"We're going to Branwick. There's nowhere else we will be safe," Lothar said and began walking.

I started to follow him and Del ran in front of him.

"Did you not listen to a word I told you!? We need to head to the mountains, to the commune I grew up in!" She shouted in his face.

Lothar didn't really react, I stood just behind him watching, waiting for him to respond. When he did, he was very calm.

"We're going to Branwick to see what aide they can offer us. It's on the way, we'll discuss this further in private once we arrive," he said back waiting for her to move out of his way.

Great, grownup secrets again.

Just like Lothar and his secret meetings with the Duke.

The mountains sounded fun though, but I'd like to see Branwick too, and if it was on the way, then I thought we should head there first.

Del looked at him frowning, and turned her eyes to me and asked, "Kael, what would you like to do?"

I heard Lothar let out a big sigh and turn to me as well.

Were they really going to let me decide? I've never even left Drassox before yesterday! I don't want to make the decisions I just like to know what's going on.

"Well, I guess I would like to see Branwick because I've never been there, and Lothar says it's on the way so…" I told her looking down to the ground feeling embarrassed.

I hope she didn't get angry at me as well for not

saying the mountains.

She went to reply, but Lothar cut in first, "Good. It's settled. We were going there regardless though, boy. Now let's continue west and stop wasting daylight. We still need to find somewhere to sleep tonight, there should be farmsteads along the way."

Del looked at me and nodded, she didn't seem angry which I was glad about. I smiled back at her and then we all continued to walk in the opposite direction that we had come from, away from Hiltsten.

Lothar led the way for the next few hours while me and Del followed behind him, it was rough walking because of the long grass, some of it was as tall as my chest and that made it hard for me to trample like Lothar was doing to it. He said we had to avoid the road in case the bad men were searching for us.

Del at least, seemed to agree with him about that.

She also seemed to prefer walking with me than with Lothar, they hadn't spoken since they had their little argument earlier. I don't think that bothered him, he didn't like to talk much anyway, he was always thinking about things. I liked to try and guess what he was thinking about sometimes.

So far since walking, we hadn't come across any of the homesteads Lothar said we'd find, it wasn't dark yet, but the sun was getting lower on the horizon, it was feeling colder too, so I'd wrapped the sheepskin around myself to keep warm.

I was glad to have a little bit more energy after my short nap and felt much better than I had when we left Hiltsten. Lothar still hadn't slept at all though, he must be really tired, I don't know how he managed to never complain, I want to be like that one day.

Not long after I had woken up earlier, we'd spotted smoke rising from behind us, back in the direction of Hiltsten.

Something was burning, Lothar had stopped and watched it for a while as the smoke grew thicker and blacker in the sky, it had seemed to bother him a lot, but he didn't say anything about it. He just stood there silently, staring into the distance for a bit, then he'd turned and carried on walking, looking ahead at nothing. He seemed sad, like something was on his mind. I think he felt guilty about leaving the people behind, he had known some of them and I'm sure they weren't all bad.

Still, I didn't understand why the Duke had betrayed us, I thought he was Lothar's friend, he shouldn't have done that it was mean.

As we continued along struggling through the tall grass, I couldn't stop thinking about what I'd heard that fat man Herman say, that the bad men were after me, I wondered what I'd done that made them want me. I just wish they would leave us alone, I don't know why they have to be so mean.

"Did your parents ever speak of your real mother,

Kael?" Del suddenly asked as she walked next to me.

Lothar cocked his head to listen as she spoke, but he didn't slow his pace at all.

"No, not really, they said they'd tell me about her when I was old enough to understand. Whatever that means," I replied quietly, concentrating on trampling the grass in front of me.

That won't ever happen now, they're dead.

Everyone is dead.

You and Lothar aren't though. You aren't alone yet, and I have Del now too.

"… Did you really know her?" I asked after a moment.

I had wanted to ask her for a while, but I was scared she would say she had just made it up to make me come with her, I don't know why I thought that.

She put her hand on my shoulder and helped me clear some thick grass that was in my way.

"Yes, I really did, Kael. We met when she was fourteen, I was one summer older than her at the time. Her name was Mirella," she said.

I was busy trying to follow Lothar's path that he had trampled through the thicket, but it was difficult.

Wait she said Mirella?

"Are you sure? My mother and pa told me her name was Lucy," I said looking up at her confused.

I'm not sure why they would've made a name up, maybe Del was thinking of someone else and didn't really know my mother.

Or she was confused. I hoped not though.

I noticed Lothar slowed down and then waited until we were next to him before he started walking again, matching mine and Del's pace, he looked like he was thinking of saying something and then, he finally did.

"Your Pa and I found your real mother while we were out on patrol one day. She'd been running for a long time when we came across her and was exhausted. She told us her name was Lucy," he finally said, without looking at me.

Del jerked her head up and spoke before I could reply.

"What else did she say, Lothar?"

He kept walking, making us wait like he always did. He was so hard to get to talk sometimes it was really rude.

Finally, when he felt like it, he continued.

"She told us that there were people chasing her and she needed help. We decided to let her stay in the town and told everyone her name was Lucy, she went into labour a few nights later. As she gave birth, Catherine couldn't stop her from bleeding… before she passed out, 'Lucy' revealed to Catherine that her name was actually Mirella and begged her to care for her child. The only ones that knew the truth were myself, Edmund, Catherine and Elias. After she died, Elias and

Catherine raised the boy as their own."

So, Del really did know my mother.

I was a bit annoyed to hear I had been lied to, why did it matter if I knew my mother's real name. It seemed like a silly thing to lie about to me.

I glanced at Del and saw she was glaring at Lothar, he didn't seem too interested in asking her why though. Eventually she got tired of waiting.

"And you STILL don't believe me?" She said sounding like she was angry again.

Believe her about what?

What had I missed when I was sleeping?

I was getting sick of this, they shouldn't be keeping secrets from me about my mother.

"I believe that she came from your commune, Del. That is enough. Now stop talking, there's a homestead up ahead," Lothar shushed her.

He sure was brave sometimes.

I looked up ahead where he was staring and saw a home through the grass, a short distance from us. It looked really old, the wood was rotting in parts and the straw roof looked like it could use some thatching done, it must leak a lot.

I'd watched Pa fix our roof back home a couple of times, he never let me on there to help though, he said I might fall. I bet I could've done it though, I'd climbed up there once when he was away and didn't fall, Mother yelled at me but she didn't tell Pa, luckily.

Lothar signalled with his hand for us to slow down as we got close to it, and then he crouched, motioning for us to join him.

Hidden by the long grass, we stopped and huddled close together.

"Alright, I'm going to see if anyone's home. Be quiet and let me do the talking, people here don't normally get many friendly visitors," he said to us, and when no one replied he nodded, then stood back to his feet.

Me and Del followed behind him towards the front door, I saw there was a chicken coop on one side of the house with two chickens inside and a small vegetable patch with carrots, potatoes, and some other things.

It was beginning to get dark now, we were lucky to find this place, it even had food by the looks of things.

When we were almost at the door, it suddenly swung open and we were greeted by a very old man with a pipe in his mouth, smoking something that smelt funny. Rupert our town smith used to smoke a tobacco pipe, but this smelt different.

The old man's eyes looked odd, they were just white with no colour, he was completely bald, and the wrinkliest person I've ever seen.

He stared past me, like he was looking at the field behind us and then started to speak.

"I don't 'ave much. But 'ye free 'ta take what 'ye want. All's I ask is 'ye leave a blind old man 'ta live out his final years in peace," his voice was dry and croaky.

I realised his eyes must be white because he was blind, it would be hard not being able to see. I wonder who looks after his veggie patch and the chickens.

"No one here means you any harm, old timer. All we need is a place to shelter from the night. We'll be gone by the early morning, before dawn," Lothar said to him in a soft voice that I wasn't used to from him.

The old man slowly nodded.

"That ye can 'ave. How many are 'ye, 'an where 'ye headed?" He asked staring straight through us.

"There are three of us. A woman and a boy accompany me, our destination is our own business," Lothar replied, although he said the last bit less softly than before.

"Alright, alright, I never meant 'ta pry. Step inside, it'll be a chilly one tonight. I 'ave the fire 'goin 'an a pot 'o veg stew on the boil," the old man said and stepped back out of the doorway, making room so we could enter.

He was right, it was getting colder, I could feel it through the sheepskin now. I was happy we would have somewhere to sleep, and warm stew sounded amazing. My feet were sore from walking and my stomach had been rumbling since I woke up from my nap earlier.

I followed Lothar in and then looked behind me at Del, she stepped inside last and shut the door after us.

She hadn't spoken for a while now, I think she was annoyed we weren't going straight to the mountains, and she was probably also worried the bad men might catch us too. I was as well, but Lothar seemed sure they wouldn't find us this far from the road, I really hoped he was right.

***

We sat around the old man's table eating our stew in silence, no one was talking because we were so hungry and too busy eating, the stew was so good, but it could've used some meat in it, like one of the chickens from outside.

While we'd waited for dinner, I had learned that the man's name was Hank, and he'd lived here for as long as he could remember, which must have been a very long time since he was so old.

He told us he lost his ability to see a couple of summers back, one day his eyes just started to get blurry and eventually, they stopped working altogether. His wife had died last summer, and his sons had all moved on, heading to Branwick to start new lives.

I asked him how he looked after his veggies and chickens when he couldn't see, and he told me that when you lose your sight your other senses are heightened, he stared at me for a long time after he said this. I'm not sure what he was looking at since he was blind, but it looked like he could see something.

It kind of freaked me out a little.

I finished my bowl of stew and looked around, everyone else had emptied their bowls as well, even Lothar. Hank stood up with a groan and his knees made cracking sounds, it sounded painful.

"Well, an old man must get ta' sleep. Feel free 'ta sleep where ye can find the room, I don't 'ave much in the way 'o spare bedding I'm sorry," he said.

Del stood up and replied, "Thank you for your help, we'll manage, good night."

Me and Lothar told him goodnight and then Hank shuffled off to his bedroom at the back of the house leaving us alone.

I watched him as he went, trying to figure out how he knew where to go, maybe his other senses really had heightened.

Lothar reached over and picked the water pitcher up and poured some into his cup, he looked at me and glanced at my mug, I shook my head. I wasn't thirsty, I was very tired though.

"I'm going to go to sleep too, my legs are sore and I'm falling asleep," I said to him and Del.

Del looked at me and said, "That's a good idea, Kael, we have a long way to go and need to be up early."

Lothar nodded at me and spoke next, "Grab the sheepskin and set yourself a bed up near the fire, boy.

It'll get cold tonight."

That sounded like a good idea, I stood up from my chair and grabbed the sheepskin, carrying it over to the floor near the fire and laid it out, then sat myself down and said goodnight to them both.

I lay there for a bit quietly, and then I heard them start talking to each other. Maybe they thought I'd fallen asleep or couldn't hear them. I'm not sure, but I laid there and listened anyway.

"You need to believe me, Lothar, Kael needs the help of my people. We must cross the Strunn and head for the mountains," I heard Del say.

I wondered why she thought I needed help, I feel just fine.

I heard Lothar put his mug on the table.

"I've told you, Del, we're going to Branwick first. It's not up for discussion," he said sounding very tired and not in the mood to argue.

I can't believe he was still awake, he must be exhausted.

I heard Del sigh loudly.

"How do you know Zarek won't find us here?" She said next.

Lothar didn't speak for a bit, I had my eyes shut pretending I was asleep. I pictured he was sitting there, staring at the table choosing when he would reply, like he did to me all the time.

"Because we are far off the main road, and his men

walked all the way from Drassox. Then they massacred the people of Hiltsten… they'll need to stop to rest as well. They won't risk travelling in the dark. We're safe for tonight, Del," he finally said.

"You better be right. We can't allow the Order to get their hands on him, Lothar. I know you don't believe me, but it will be the end of everything. He's too important," I heard Del say.

Why did she think I was so important, is it because of my mother? I wish they'd tell me more instead of whispering to each other when they think I can't hear them.

"Look, I'm too tired to discuss this right now, Del. I'm going to get some sleep, you should too. We're leaving before dawn," Lothar replied, and then I heard his chair scrape across the floor as he stood up.

Del started to say something back when suddenly a very loud howl cut her off.

"AAAAARRRROOOOOOOOOOOOOOOO!!"

I sat straight up from my bed and looked at Lothar and Del, Lothar glanced back at me listening but didn't say anything, he put his finger to his lips, telling me to stay quiet.

And then we heard it again, closer this time, and went for longer, but it was still a good distance away.

"AAAAARRRROOOOOOOOOOOOOOOOOOOO!!
"

"Lothar, what was that?" Del whispered looking

scared.

I had a feeling I knew what it was, it sounded like a wolf.

But much louder, like a very big wolf. A black one. A dire wolf.

The old man's bedroom door opened, and he stood in the doorway.

"Keep it down you lot, it's just a lone wolf. Get 'em all the time out here, he'll go away," he mumbled to us, and then shut his door again.

Me and Del looked at each other, then to Lothar, whose eyes were fixed on the front door.

"Stay here with the boy. I'll be back shortly," Lothar replied to her.

I watched him push his chair back in, then grab a torch from the wall before walking over to the fire to light it. Without a word he walked to the door, stood at it and paused for a moment to draw his dagger, before opening it and leaving me and Del alone inside.

CHAPTER 10
ARRIVAL TO BRANWICK

'Bad people get what they deserve. Good people will be rewarded for their deeds. A fool will believe anything; smart people will watch their step'

I shut the door to the old man's house as gently as possible behind me, the soft thud sounded louder than it actually was in the eerie silence of the night.

Silent except for the loud howls we'd just heard.

I had my suspicions as to what had made the call, and it worried me. The half-rotted home wouldn't be enough to stop a hungry dire wolf, not even close.

I scanned the fields of tall grass around the dwelling, holding my torch out in front of me trying to cast the light further out to the surroundings. It helped, but I still couldn't see much.

My heart thumped loudly in my chest, I expected at any moment the long grass to part and the giant black wolf from the forest to emerge and attack me. I only had a dagger to protect myself, I would've felt better with a sword, or even better yet, a spear.

A low growl somewhere nearby ignited my fears further, I turned sharply in the direction of the sound and what I saw made my blood run cold.

Not thirty paces away, lying low in the thicket were two glowing red orbs. They were eyes obviously, enshrouded in darkness and radiating an aura of death. I froze, but stood my ground and glared back at them, if the creature wished to attack, I wouldn't back down.

One of us, or both would die tonight.

We stared at each other for what felt like an age, my grip so tight around my dagger that my fingers began to hurt, the beast was deathly still, watching me and issuing a low growl.

Then it stood, broke eye contact with me and sprinted off, disappearing into the grass back to whatever hell it had come from. If its appearance had been meant as a challenge, I'd been the victor this time.

I let my breath out in a sigh of relief, realising I had been holding it and then allowed my grip to loosen on my dagger before turning away myself and re-entering the home, making sure the door was bolted behind me.

For what good it would do if the beast returned anyway.

"What was it? Did you see it?" Del asked sounding panicked.

The boy, and the old man, now out of his room again, both stood next to her staring at me waiting for me to answer.

"It was nothing, a lone wolf was passing by like you said, old man. I scared it away," I lied.

Hank seemed satisfied and returned to his room shutting the door behind him, the boy lay back down but Del was still eyeing me suspiciously.

I ignored her and walked over to a spot on the floor and sat myself down, it was a good a spot as any to rest.

As I sat, I felt something in my belt pouch dig into my side. Annoyedly I grabbed at it, trying to feel what it was.

I realised it the book I'd scavenged from Gildred, in the drama I'd forgotten all about it with so much occurring since the battle. I decided to remove it out of the pouch and take a look before I went to sleep, I may not get another chance for a while. I opened the leather cover, blood soaked the pages, but luckily the blank text was still legible.

Using the light of the fire I began to read.

It appeared to be Gildred's personal travel journal.

Year of our Lord, 1256, Maius 20th',
This eve' we depart the halls of the Grand Septum,
leaving only a few to watch over our Sanctuary. Lord Zarek
himself has been chosen to lead us in our Holy Crusade.
Every man among us has been preparing all his life for this
moment, to stop the return of the Prince of Treachery and
allow good to triumph over evil.

We will not fail God in our duty.

St Michael watch over us.

'Year of our Lord, 1256, Juniius 10th'
We have crossed a great distance already, yet still have a
long way left to travel to reach the location our historians
indicate Lucifer's vessel is residing in, I pray their
interpretation of the holy texts is accurate. Lord Zarek
believes we will approach the first town in the area by the eve
of this month.

'Year of our Lord, 1256, Juniius 24th',
It has been over one month since we set out on our holy
crusade to find the possessed child and free his soul from
Lucifer's grasp. The journey has been long and arduous but
we are making great progress. The Priests of our Order

believe the era of judgement is fast approaching, and time is running out. As such, Lord Zarek forces the men to make haste, our destination, a local populace named Arman, the first town on our journey North.

'Year of our Lord, 1256, Juniius 31st',
Yesterday we arrived at Arman, the people refused to hand over the children as Lord Zarek commanded. We slaughtered them to the last, then beheaded the children and burnt their remains in a holy fire to cleanse their souls.

Lord Zarek does not believe the child was here. Some of the men questioned the orders, so Lord Zarek had them flogged for their impotence as an example to the rest of the Order that his commands are not to be questioned and his word is law.

He made it clear that we must not shy from our duties to God.

'Year of our Lord, 1256, Quintillis 5th',
We have continued to the North in our search, Lord Zarek grows more concerned each day about our inability thus far to find the one we seek. The ninth year is fast approaching, after that he will be too powerful. We must stop

him. Time is against us.

'Year of our Lord, 1256, Quintillis 11th',

Today we cleansed two small settlements residing close to each other, Ridgewood and Marlot. They both refused to hand over the children, as Arman before them had, so Lord Zarek ordered them all to be put to death. I wish they had just listened.

The inhabitants of Ridgewood managed to kill a small number of our Order which sent Lord Zarek into a rage, he commanded the men to flay the perpetrators alive and leave them for the ravens as warning to the next towns so it is known that any that harm the soldiers of God, can join the Devil in Hell.

'Year of our Lord, 1256, Quintillis 13th',

This morn' we came upon a large waterbody, the maps indicate it is named Lake Roe. In two days trek we will approach the next town, Drassox. Our sources indicate they are defended by a small, town guard led by a somewhat competent Captain, a man known throughout the area for his battle prowess. Lord Zarek and I will speed ahead with one third of the men. Some of our Order do not agree with the methods we used in the previous town of Ridgewood, Lord Zarek decreed any man that speaks of it and causes dissension among our ranks is to be flogged and then executed.

'Year of our Lord, 1256, Quintillis 15th',
The town of Drassox were far fiercer than we had expected, 18 of our Order lie dead and a further 5 wounded, even Lord Zarek himself was injured. Again, it appears the child is not here either. Lord Zarek believes a child escaped and has commanded me to venture forth with a detachment of men and cleanse the next town, a small but fortified settlement called Hiltsten. It should not put up much resistance, I believe Lord Zarek has sent me ahead alone, to test my commitment to our cause. He himself will return to collect the main force and meet me there in a days time, I will not fail him. He has displayed an unforgiving demeanour of late, the men fear him, and I share their concerns.

'Year of our Lord, 1256, Quintillis 16th',
This evening, we approach Hiltsten, my plan is to attack in the dark of night. The villagers hide behind a crudely built wall but I am not concerned, our Blast stones will make short work of it. Now that Lord Zarek is not with us, some of my

detachment have voiced concerns in our past methods,

believing that our actions may damn our souls to the fires of

the nine hells. I spent a great deal of time reminding them that

our cause is just. Although in my own mind, I have wondered

the same at times.

I am glad Lord Zarek is not here, I have no doubt he

would have executed a number of the men as traitors to our

cause for their words. He has grown increasingly ruthless as

our journey has progressed, I understand his concern, but I

dare not cross him.

His dedication to the mission is absolute. As it must be.

We are running out of time. The Prince of Treachery is

coming.

By the time I finished reading the final entry in the journal I felt consumed with rage and sadness.

These people had pillaged and massacred five entire towns over an insane belief, and they were so blinded that they dared to call it a 'holy crusade'.

This Zarek, sounded like the devil he was trying to prevent returning, and according to Gildred even some of his own men were weary of their cause, yet still they followed him.

The weakness of men was something I would never understand. I put the journal away, closing my eyes and trying my best to shut the images out of my mind, to forget the burning.

***

A few hours later, I rose and woke the boy. It was the early morning, just before dawn by the look of things and I saw Del already lie awake. My sleep had been troublesome and broken, with concerns of the dire wolf crashing through the front door and tearing us to pieces while we slept.

Still, I felt much less exhausted than I had last night, and I would take what little victories I could at this point.

As we finished packing up and went to leave, I turned to the old man one last time.

"Are you sure you don't want us to take you to Branwick, you might see your sons there."

He shook his head and replied, "Nay, I'll be fine. My Rosie is buried here, and I intend 'ta live out my days close 'ta her, I don't 'ave much longer on this green earth anyway. My boys will understand."

I nodded then reached out and shook his hand, "Good luck old man, and thank you for your help," I told him.

He nodded back then turned his milky dead eyes to the boy, as though he could see him standing there next to me.

"Take care, young one. 'An remember, in the

darkest 'o times, trust in the light. Do not lose hope. God will save 'ye 'afore the end," he said with a grimace, his blank stare fixated on the boy.

The boy looked up at me confused and I just grunted in reply, God had not helped us thus far. I wasn't a religious man, but if he existed, it appeared to me that he'd abandoned us completely.

Del thanked him for his help next and we departed, starting our journey not long before the sun had begun to rise, just as we'd planned.

I still held concerns that the dire wolf may be out here, but I kept them to myself. We couldn't allow what 'may' be, to dictate over what 'was'.

Zarek was coming, that much was a certainty.

After reading the journal, seeing the lengths the Order had already gone to, I realised that this would not end until they killed the boy or I killed Zarek, there would be no middle ground, no reasoning.

The only way to end this was with more death.

We travelled fast, I intended to put some more space between us and Zarek before we reached Branwick. It would take us the better part of the daylight to cross the remaining distance to the town, our pursuers would likely want to search the homesteads scattered along the way to make sure they didn't pass us by which would help us gain more of a lead. I was hoping that meant they would need to camp somewhere before reaching Branwick or risk travelling by darkness.

I felt some guilt, the old man Hank should've come with us, and I shouldn't have left him. I'm also worried that he knows where we're headed, and I don't think it will take much persuasion for Zarek to get him talking.

"My legs are sore. How much further is it, Lothar?" The boy complained, as usual.

I looked back at him, he was using a stick Del had given him to help him trek, she carried one herself and looked at me waiting for an answer as well. This seemed to be becoming common, one of them asked a question and they both waited for an answer. I squinted ahead, the sun was bright, it looked like it had just passed midday.

"A couple more hours. We should be able to see it soon," I replied.

In truth, I was unsure how much further it was, I hadn't been to Branwick in over four summers, and I'd always stuck to the road.

"How can you be sure?" Del prodded.

I noticed she had a suspicious tone to her voice.

I didn't slow my pace while I thought up my reply, it was obvious she was going to dissect my reasoning.

"Because I am," I said after failing to come up with a suitable explanation, better to give her nothing than a lie I figured.

Surprisingly, she just sighed and started speaking to the boy instead.

"How are you feeling, Kael?" She asked him.

From somewhere behind me I heard him reply.

"I'm alright, it's a long way though huh?"

She laughed loudly.

"Yep, it sure is. I haven't travelled this way in almost nine summers, since before you were born! It's nice to be on the road again though."

It just struck me that she had not once appeared concerned for the people of Hiltsten—her people—even when we saw the smoke rising.

She seems to be heavily interested in the boy though and has taken quite a liking to him. Perhaps it's because of how close his mother and her were, regardless the reason, it's a good thing. It appears to be keeping his mind from dwelling on the loss of Elias and Catherine, and I'm untrained in how to consol a child on such matters. A woman's companionship is what he needs right now, not an angry old mans.

The two of them continued to chat behind me while we slogged through the tall grass, she was asking him about his night terrors and how long he'd been having them. I ignored the discussion as I thought about what I would say when I met with Duke Gerard, I prayed that Orin hadn't said anything to the two scouts that'd accompanied him from Branwick that may have indicated that Kael was the one the Order sought. Our reception and possibly our safety, would depend on it.

"Lothar, is that Branwick!?" The boy shouted and came running to my side.

I really needed to teach him to keep his voice down when he got excited, it was going to get us killed one day.

We'd just crested a small hill, Del came trotting to catch up to join us in taking a look. I squinted ahead into the distance to where he was staring, my sight wasn't what it once used to be, the boy's is obviously much sharper, but I still managed to make out the smudge in the distance he was referring to.

It was indeed Branwick, the largest town south of the Strunn.

And we would arrive before dark, thankfully. It was not that far in the distance at all.

"Yes, it is, boy. Keep your voice down though, let's pick up the pace," I said and began to descend down into the valley before us.

***

We covered the remaining distance to the town quickly and without incident, it was mostly downhill and the long grass had begun to thin out, which made for much easier trekking.

The dire wolf hadn't made an appearance since last night and I could make out no signs of our pursuers, nor had the boy complained further since he spotted our destination.

All good things.

Glancing at the sun I could see we still had a few hours of sunlight left, I was eager to meet with Duke Gerard to inform him of the fate of Hiltsten, and to find out what preparations he was making.

I had met him twice in the past, once several summers back and once with my father when I was a boy. I had found him to be a competent leader and fair.

We passed several homes on the outskirts of the settlement, yet no one came out to greet us.

This wasn't odd as such, but I had expected someone to at least stick their head out to enquire about our presence or offer some kind of assistance.

"Where is everyone, Lothar?" Del asked, the absence of people clearly not lost on her either.

Hiltsten was much smaller and people were always out in the streets there.

I glanced at her and shrugged, it'd piqued my curiosity also though so I decided to find out and approached the door to the next home we were about to pass.

When I got to the door I knocked without hesitation, then waited. But no one came or called out, so I knocked again a little louder, the metal plates of my gauntlets magnifying the sound, yet still no one answered the door. Nor could I make out the sounds of anyone moving about inside.

Now things were becoming slightly odd.

"They probably have a town meeting on right now. Let's make our way to the hall and find out," I said.

Del didn't look convinced and raised her eyebrows back at me.

I had an eerie feeling in my gut, although I couldn't place why, there were many reasons people weren't outside right now.

It would make sense with everything going on, for the Duke to have called a town meeting. I imagined as soon as Ezekiel and Tobias had returned and briefed him, that it would've been the first step, to meet with the townsfolk after discussing the situation amongst his advisors.

"Well, I hope they have some food, I'm starving," the boy said. Again!? It amazed me how he was so small yet always hungry.

I snorted at him.

"You'll live. Let's not linger around, we need to get a move on."

As I turned around, I heard Del mimic my voice thinking I couldn't hear her, and the boy tried to keep his laughter quiet.

"I don't sound like that," I growled without turning around.

They both snickered quietly, and I ignored it.

As we continued to walk, the houses grew closer together, and eventually the road widened and became more obvious. This was clearly the main road which led to the town square and the hall itself, I faintly recalled it from my earlier visits in the summers prior.

"The houses here look different than home, and even than the ones in Hiltsten," the boy stated.

"That's because they are made different, you'll see why if we end up heading further north towards the river," I replied.

"Can't you just tell me why?" He nagged me and I ignored him, it wouldn't hurt him to learn patience.

The boy wasn't wrong in his observation though, while the houses of Hiltsten, and even Drassox were built using lumber for the walls and frame, then straw thatching for the rooves, the homes in Branwick were constructed with stone blocks, even the rooves used stone slates.

This was due to them having a stone quarry, located just to the north, which supplied the town with an abundance of material.

This had in part, been the reason Branwick had grown into the largest town south of the Strunn.

They were always looking for workers to help mine the quarry, the other reason was because of its close proximity to the Strunn itself, which provided a great food source in the way of fish, to all the people in town, it also provided jobs for the locals as fishermen. Because of all this, people were generally more well off in Branwick.

"That looks like the town hall up ahead," Del

stated, clearly even her eyesight was superior to my own.

"It sure does," I replied squinting into the distance.

"So why does it look empty then?" She replied, sarcastically.

We were still not close enough that I could see if it were empty or not, but I knew the population of Branwick was far too big to fit inside the hall all at once and I couldn't make out anyone standing outside the building.

At all. And that was concerning.

"Just wait until we get there first before jumping to conclusions," I said, trying to sound confident.

"I don't know, Lothar, it looks pretty empty to me too. This place is huge, and I haven't seen anyone at all yet," the boy said, backing her up.

"Be quiet, boy. I didn't ask you," I snapped.

The boy mimicked me this time causing Del to laugh.

I didn't laugh, but he did sound funny—not that I planned on letting him know that though.

I ignored the pair of them and increased my pace to the hall.

All the houses we continued to pass along the way appeared vacant, window shutters were down, and every door was closed tight. No one peeked out to see who we were, it was like a ghost town.

Where the hell was everybody?

After passing a few more houses with nary a soul in sight, we finally arrived at the town hall, the doors were shut tight, just as all the houses we'd passed thus far.

"Well look at that! Looks empty to me," Del scoffed.

Thank you for stating the obvious woman.

Looking around the area, I could see an unusually large amount of people had walked through the area recently. It was becoming clear that the people of Branwick had abandoned the town but where they had gone was what I wanted to know.

I crouched down and looked at the footprints in the dirt, they clearly led north, towards the Strunn.

"Hello there!" A voice from behind called out, snapping me from my thoughts.

The three of us spun around, I instinctively brought my hand to the hilt of my dagger as I saw a man exiting from a nearby home but relaxed when I realised he was alone.

Finally, someone who might be able to give us some answers I thought, while I observed the man before me.

He was young, perhaps the woman's age, with an unkempt beard and long hair, pockmarks scarred his face. He looked as though he hadn't bathed for a while, his clothing was as dirty as he was. At a guess, I'd say he was one of the quarry workers.

"Greetings. Where is everyone?" I said back.

Del eyed him suspiciously and the boy moved behind me as I spoke. The man came closer, stepping off the porch of the home he'd just walked out of.

"They all left yesterday, headed north towards the bridge. What brings you lot 'ere?" He replied bluntly, inspecting my armour and then glancing around with distrust in his eyes.

I'd be distrustful in his position as well, I thought and to be honest, the feeling is mutual.

"We're seeking refuge, we fled from Drassox when it was attacked. Then we escaped Hiltsten when the same group razed it to the ground," I answered truthfully, trying my best to shut out the faces of the innocent people I'd left behind to die there.

He continued to study us, appearing slightly surprised, likely deciding if he believed our story or not. I noticed his eyes lingered on Del for a moment, looking her up and down before his eyes returned back to me.

"Well, like I said, everyone's left. But you're free 'ta stay, plenty 'o room now," he let out a raspy laugh after he spoke.

I looked at Del, she shrugged but didn't seem completely keen on hanging around.

It was getting dark now though, we wouldn't make it to the bridge tonight. Plus, we'd been marching all day, the boy was tired, and I was concerned the dire wolf could be tracking us. The absolute last thing I wanted was to run into that beast at night with no shelter.

Fuck that, it'd be better to take our chances here.

I turned my attention to the man again, he was biting at the sin on his thumb staring at Del.

"What was your name?"

He spat some skin on the ground next to him.

"Paxton. Lived 'ere me 'ole life, just right there," he said motioning to the home he'd just came from, and holding his hand out towards me for me to shake.

"Lothar," I replied, reaching back and firmly grasp his hand.

He had a strong grip, likely earned from breaking stone daily at the quarry. Something seemed off about his character though, I couldn't quite place it, maybe I was just paranoid.

"Why'd you not flee with the rest of the townspeople, Paxton?" Del asked him curiously, beating me to my next question.

His eyes flickered from me to her, and then to the boy cowering behind me.

His face now showed a hint of predatory gaze.

"Because we decided we like this town… and we like the look of you too, bitch!" A new voice yelled loudly from nearby, causing me to spin in the direction it came from catching sight of four more men approaching.

Fucking brigands!

"THUD!"

My vision blacked for just a second as Paxton struck me heavily to the back of the head from behind, causing me to stumble forward, almost dropping to the ground as the world spun around me. Dazed but still standing I instinctively drew my dagger and turned back to him raising my forearm and successfully blocking the next blow of the cudgel he had just cracked me with.

The cudgel slipped from his grasp and then he grabbed my dagger hand to try stop me from driving it into his liver and we began to wrestle. I was shaken badly, my legs struggled to hold me up and the concept of time felt warped while I desperately tried to recover from the blow to my already wounded head.

Out of the corner of my eye I saw Del draw her dagger defensively with terror on her face, she was staring at something passed me, I couldn't spare the time to look what it was.

A moment later I found out as I was ruthlessly set upon by the other men who'd rapidly closed the distance between us.

"Kael, RUN!!" I heard Del scream, while I was assaulted from all sides with heavy wooden cudgels like Paxton had held.

The dagger was quickly knocked from my hand when I tried to ward off the blows. I stumbled to the ground succumbing quickly to the onslaught of strikes, even with my armour taking the brunt of the attack.

From the dirt I kicked my foot out blindly, managing to trip one of my attackers up.

He landed in a cloud of dust on the ground next to me and I began punching into his body with my mailed fist.

But the blows wouldn't stop coming, and my last-ditch attack just increased the ferocity of the blows until I was forced to curl into a ball to protect myself from the damage.

"Quick, grab the whore! Don't let her get away I wanna fuck her tonight!" Someone yelled and I felt the frequency of the assault wane just a little as some of the men gave chase to Del.

I desperately tried to stand once more but another blow to the head shut my lights out.

***

When I awoke sometime later my mouth was filled with the copper tang taste of blood and it was nighttime. As soon as I gathered my senses I realised I was tied up on the floor inside the town hall. The rope bit sharply into my wrists, my head throbbed, and the cold air stung my broken nose as I struggled to breathe through it thanks to the rag tied that was stuffed in my mouth. My vision was still blurry, but I could make out two of the men that had attacked us, standing around me.

I could hear the sounds of a man grunting, mixed with a woman letting out muffled whimpers.

My heart sank, oh fuck Del. I knew what this meant, I needed to get free now.

Where was the boy? Please let him be alright.

Fuck! I need to stop this. I'm going to kill these pricks!

"Oh, look, Raza. This fella has finally woken up, got a bit of a headache there 'ave ya fella?" A voice above me said and someone snickered.

"He's woken just in time to listen to me have my turn with his pretty wench," someone else, I assume Raza, replied.

"I wish Jed would hurry up in there!" The other man yelled.

"Yeah, he sure is taking a while, hoggin all the fun."

They were interrupted by the sound of doors swinging open, I turned my head and saw the blurry image of two men walking in the hall, carrying something.

"Oh, ya finally got the little fucker! Where was he hiding?" Raza called out.

"Fuckin' little prick tried to stab me with this. I swear, I'm gonna bleed him real slow. Where's Jed?" One of the men said as they approached.

I noticed he was holding the dagger I'd given the

boy and blood dripped from a small wound on his hand.

The other man, the one carrying the boy with his hand clamped over his mouth was Paxton.

I began struggling at the sight of him, trying to break free in a fit of rage and was kicked hard in the chest plate by Raza.

"He's in there with the whore. And I'm up next so don't get any ideas and waitcha turn!" Raza growled.

"Quiet! Here he comes," someone said.

I could see the boy trying to struggle and squirm his way free, pure fear in his teary eyes. But… also a hint of something else, something that looked out of place on a child so young.

I wasn't mistaken, it was rage. He had murder in his eyes.

I turned my head to look behind and saw another man walking towards the group, a smug smile on his face from ear to ear as he fiddled with his belt buckle.

"Goddam, boys—she's a wild one!" He said grinning broadly.

The rest of the group laughed.

I was going to kill this man. Somehow, I swear.

"I found the little shit boss, he was hiding in a house down the street," Paxton said proudly, and I wanted to kill him too.

I want to kill all of them, all I need is one chance and I vow to God they will all pay.

The boy had stopped struggling now, but his eyes no longer showed any fear at all as he gazed into Jed's eyes, like he was trying to bore holes in Jed's head.

The stare held nothing but murder.

Somehow, he no longer looked like the innocent child I'd been travelling with, the whites of his eyes almost appeared to have turned completely black. I could FEEL his rage in the air.

It can't be true…

"Ya think that pissant stare scares me, kid? I'll cut ya fuckin lips off and make ya eat 'em if ya keep it up, ya hear me?" Jed said.

His tone now icy cold as the grin melted from his face and he matched the boy's stare with the eyes of a stone-cold killer.

The boy was unfazed and didn't look away though, I'm not sure he even seemed like a boy anymore.

Something else was staring out of his eyes.

Something… inhuman.

"Right, give me that dagger. I'm gonna cut those eyes out and stick them in your arse, ya cheeky 'lil bastard," Jed snapped, snatching the dagger from the man near him.

NO! Please no, I need to stop this! I can't fail anyone else!

I frantically started fighting against my bonds again with all my strength, trying desperately to break the rope that bound me, watching as Jed turned towards the boy.

I could feel the aura of hatred filling the air around me, growing thicker by the moment.

And then the boy began to speak. In a voice that was clearly not his own.

"Audes minari vas Luciferis?" His words strained out through clenched teeth, it was a jagged sharp tongue that felt harsh on my ears and causing a shudder to run down my spine.

I was no expert on it, but I recognised the latin tongue… and I could guess at the meaning of the word Luciferis.

All the men in the room stopped and looked at the boy in shock, the smiles melting off their faces one by one.

Jed scoffed, looking around at his companions confidently, and then kept walking towards the boy.

Then the boy spoke again, loudly in the terrible voice.

"Animas vestras in inferno per aeternITAEM DEVORABO!!!"

It felt as though it could cut through ice and caused my head to throb painfully.

I know not what it said, but immediately Jed's posture became erratic, as though any movement was causing him great pain. He managed two awkward steps before suddenly, without warning he froze altogether. His body stiffened, the veins in his neck bulged and his face grew red like a beetroot.

I watched in awe as all five men in front of me reacted in a similar way, their bodies becoming rigid, veins bulging, and extreme pain evident among their swollen faces.

Their eyes begged the boy for mercy, on frozen expressions, and one by one blood began to trickle from their noses.

Then, their ears and eyes also began to trickle, the still expressions contorted into unfathomable anguish before they all collapsed simultaneously to the floor with a symphony of thuds.

Paxton was the last to fall while he still clutched the boy, and then the boy fell motionless with him.

I lay there in complete shock, the throbbing pain in my skull subsiding as I became aware my own twisted nose had also begun to trickle a small amount of blood, as though I had narrowly escaped becoming a victim myself.

Looking at the scene around me I wondered what in the hells I'd just witnessed. I tried to make it make sense in a logical way, but what had just occurred could not be explained, nor ignored.

Del was right. The Order was right.

The boy housed a demon within his mind.

The very soul of Lucifer himself.

Never mind that you fool! Free yourself and your companions!

I rolled over and saw lying almost next to me, was the dagger I'd given the boy, it had fallen when Jed had collapsed.

I started dragging my aching, beaten body over to where it lay, wriggling across the floor as a worm would do and began fumbling around with it for a moment before managing to use the sharp blade to cut my restraints.

Finally free once more, I stood up, still holding the blade and glanced over at the boy, lying there on top of the man he'd killed. He was unconscious, looking like any other innocent sleeping child again.

But… I'd seen with my own eyes what was inside of him, what it was capable of. Was I doing the right thing protecting him? What if the Order was right, and killing him was the only way to prevent the demon's return?

Part of me inside wondered if I should end it now and stop this madness, my grip tightened on the handle of the dagger as I looked down at his sleeping form.

He appeared innocent right now but how long would he stay that way?

A muffled whimper from somewhere deeper in the hall startled me getting my attention.

Fuck, how could I forget the woman I scolded myself.

I turned from the boy and started walking towards

a room off the side of the hall, I could see the door was shut and I feared what I may find inside.

I slowly pushed it open and saw that Del was there. Tied to a table… with her pants crudely pulled down.

It was clear what had occurred.

"Del, it's me, Lothar. You're safe now, I'm going to cut you free… you must hold still though," I whispered tenderly as I walked up to her.

I didn't know what I could say that would make this any better.

She sobbed a reply through the gag tied around her mouth that I couldn't understand. I reached out and carefully cut her bonds, as soon as she was free, she quickly reached down to pull her pants back up.

Then she turned and slapped me hard across the face, making pain shoot through my broken nose and my already throbbing head that was adorned with numerous cuts and splits from the beatings I'd been given the last few days.

"I said we shouldn't come here you bastard!! I told you!" She began to scream at me and beat on my chest plate with her palms.

I was thankful she didn't strike my head again, it pained me to admit it but I was struggling to stay upright as it was, another blow from her and I might just pass out.

Still, she was right, but how could I have known

this would happen? And we needed to come here to gather supplies for the journey either way.

I grabbed her and wrapped my arms around her, firstly to provide some measure of comfort to her after what she'd just endured, and secondly to stop her striking me further.

She sobbed for a moment and began to settle down then looked up frantically.

"Wait. Where's Kael!? Is he alright!?" She asked, pushing herself free of my arms.

"Relax, Del, the boy's fine. Well, fine considering…" My voice trailed off. I wasn't sure what to say.

Concern flooded her face.

"Where is he, Lothar, and what happened?"

So, I began to tell her exactly what I'd witnessed as I led her back to him. When we returned he was still lying asleep, exactly where he'd been when I left him.

***

"So, you finally believe me then?" She asked as I finished telling her what I'd seen.

I took a quick glance around us at the lifeless corpses of the brigands, now sitting in large red puddles as though the entirety of their blood had leaked out their orifices.

"Yes. I believe you, Del," I replied deep in thought, still unsure what all of this meant.

"Then you must help me get him to my commune in the mountains, Lothar, they're the only ones that can help him now. The Order mustn't get their hands on him, it would mean the end for all of us," she urged.

I chewed my gum. One thing was still gnawing at me.

"You told me that Mirella was able to use her powers to heal the sick and injured, why hasn't the boy shown any signs like that?" I asked.

She frowned at me in disbelief looking almost disappointed.

"Isn't it obvious? Lucifer's influence is corrupting his soul and twisting his powers, Lothar. Kael alone wouldn't be capable of killing these men, he's just a child. One with no idea how to use his abilities. I don't think he even knows he has them. Mirella was fourteen by the time she was brought to us."

I nodded slowly, it did make sense.

"Alright, but back in Drassox, a man pointed a crossbow at me, aiming to end my life and then he dropped dead like this lot. Why would Lucifer save me, Del? The boy was under no threat at the time. Why wouldn't he just let someone kill the boy so he could be free?"

She thought about this for a moment before replying.

"You still aren't getting it. He wants Kael's power, Lothar, saving you, ensured Kael's survival. His mind has crossed all but the final circle of hell, Kael is special, an extremely powerful vessel. He is more powerful to Lucifer alive."

She made good points, but something still didn't seem right, I couldn't place my finger upon it though.

Time would tell I suppose.

"Alright, I believe you, Del. We need to gather supplies and head to the river crossing, Zarek won't be far behind us now. From there we will make for your commune."

CHAPTER 11

JOURNEY TO THE RIVER THUNN

'Be strong and courageous. Do not be afraid or terrified because of them, for the Lord your God goes with you; he will never leave you nor forsake you'

Where am I? It's so dark, I can't see a thing. Am I dreaming again? I looked around me but it was impossible to make anything out. Please don't let me be alone again, I don't want to be on my own.

"Lothar? Del…? Are you guys there?" I called out into the darkness, but like last time my voice didn't make a sound.

I took a deep breath and swallowed, I must be dreaming, just try to stay calm and be brave.

The last thing I can remember was Del screaming

at me to run, and Lothar fighting with a man. I done exactly like she told me and ran as fast as I could to a house down the road while the other men chased her and Lothar.

I remembered hiding in the closet trying to be as quiet as I could, but the men came, and they found me.

They grabbed me… but then?

The next thing I knew, I was here.

I took another look around me, but it was just so black I could hardly even see my own hands, let alone anything else.

I was getting frustrated.

And then I heard it. Something like… chanting, again?

It was really faint just like last time, but it was definitely there and it worried me.

I don't want to be here!

I want to be back safe with Lothar and Del…

I hope they're alright, that man had hit Lothar so hard, I don't know how he stayed on his feet. He was really tough, I wouldn't like to be hit like that.

The chanting became louder, so I looked around again and saw a faint orange glow was starting to appear in the distance again, just like the last nightmare I'd had. Everything seemed exactly the same.

I tried my best to listen to the chanting and realised that this time it was even clearer, I could finally make out the words.

"… Vessel of treachery… relinquish the light… accept the darkness and aid his plight… Vessel of treachery… relinquish the light… accept the darkness and aid his plight…"

It just continued saying the same thing over and over, it sounded like lots of voices together and they were getting louder as the glow came closer. My heart began to beat faster.

What's a vessel of treachery?

I don't know why but something inside of me was telling me I didn't want to find out either, so I started to run the other way.

I ran as fast as mother had made us run to the town hall that day the bad men came to Drassox.

It seemed no matter how hard I pushed my legs the chanting kept getting louder, like I couldn't escape it.

I looked over my shoulder and saw the orange glow was catching up to me, chasing me.

Again, I made out a dark figure inside of it, but this time I could see it had a face, and it wasn't human… it was a monster.

The thing had thick, curly horns, coming from its head like one of the rams we'd kept in our pens, and a huge muscular body, even bigger than Lothar. It was much taller than he was too.

I became absolutely terrified and tried forcing myself to run even faster, but my legs started to feel weak.

I was so tired I was gasping to breathe, the voices were all around me.

"… the light… accept the darkness and aid his plight… vessel of treachery… relinquish THE LIGHT…" The chanting was becoming deafening now, as though it was right behind me.

As tired as I felt, I didn't let myself stop running, my chest ached from puffing so hard and my calves felt like they were on fire. I knew I couldn't keep this up for much longer, I wanted to scream for help.

And then, I felt something grab my ankle.

Its nails dug sharply into my skin and I tripped. I was falling face first into the blackness, being swallowed by it.

I opened my mouth to scream for Lothar, but no sound came out and then I heard a deep rumble come from behind.

It sounded like the growl I'd heard the dire wolf make in the forest, as though it came from the same animal.

The voices screamed into my ears.

"RELINQUISH THE LIGHT!! ACCEPT THE DARKNESS AND AID HIS PLIGHT!!" They grew louder, faster, and angrier.

So loud I couldn't hear or even think about anything else.

"Lothar!! Del!!" I yelled as loud as I could, but I

couldn't even tell if I made a sound this time over the deafening chant.

I looked over my shoulder once more and saw the glow standing over me, the monster inside of it staring straight at me, its eyes burning and looking like hot coals in a fireplace.

A putrid sharp smell filled my nostrils as its mouth opened into a wide smile, revealing rows of long sharp fangs and its hot breath hit me in the face.

"… RELINQUISH THE LIGHT!!! ACCEPT THE DARKNESS!!!" The voices continued to scream in my ears as a dark, clawed hand, reached out of the glow to grab hold of me.

And then, right as it was about to touch me, a blinding bright white light cut through the darkness, lighting up everything around me.

I squeezed my eyes shut as I was blinded by it, I held my breathe, expecting to feel the sharp nails cut into me at any moment.

I tried to open my eyes, squinting and I realised that I was outside somewhere, and the dark had disappeared.

I could see blurry shapes all around me.

Wait, I felt myself bobbing up and down.

Something is carrying me, and it stunk like blood and sweat.

Oh no! The monster has me, it wasn't a dream!

I started thrashing about trying to break free from

its hold, but it squeezed me tighter, it was so much stronger than me.

I need my sword! Someone help I don't want to die!

"Lothar!!! Help!!!" I screamed loudly, terrified realising I couldn't break free, but still I kept trying.

"Calm down, boy! It's me!" A voice growled.

Lothar's voice.

I stopped thrashing and opened my eyes a little more, the bright light was the sun, the blurry shapes were the trees and grass, and the smelly monster carrying me was Lothar.

Now I felt a little embarrassed for struggling and screaming out for help like I had.

"Oh. Well, can you put me down? I can walk myself." I said shyly and turned my face from him.

He grunted and lowered me down, as I felt my feet touch the ground, I realised my legs were still tired from running—but I didn't let him see that.

"I was having a nightmare, something was chasing me and there were voices all around. I… I couldn't get away" I said.

My heart was still racing when I pictured the monster's face with the horns and its clawed hand reaching for me.

"Well, you're awake now, boy. And safe." Lothar told me.

I looked up, my eyes getting used to the bright sun

now I wasn't blind anymore which I was thankful for.

I saw Del was standing next to Lothar, not far from me. Her eyes were red like she'd been crying and her hair was messed up a little from when I saw her last.

"Del! You're alright!" I said, happy to see her.

She looked at me and smiled but it seemed like she was putting it on.

"Yes, I'm alright, Kael. It's good to see you're awake again. You had quite the nap."

Had I? I realised I didn't even know how long I had been asleep for, or where we were.

"Where are we now?" I asked them both looking around.

Lothar answered first which was a surprise.

"We're on the road, north of Branwick. We should be nearing the quarry soon."

I was shocked he didn't just tell me to 'be quiet' or 'you'll see soon' like he usually would. And did he just say a quarry? I've never heard of one of those before.

"What's a quarry?" I asked, pushing my luck to see if I could get some more answers out of him for once.

He motioned with his head for me to move and started walking again, Del followed behind.

"A quarry is a place where stone is mined. Remember when I told you that you would see the reason the houses were different in Branwick?" He said, scanning ahead of us while we walked.

I did remember him saying that.

"Yep, I remember," I replied, waiting for him to tell me more.

Del walked behind me, she seemed quieter and less cheery than she normally was, and I also noticed Lothar was walking funny, kind of holding his side, like he was in pain.

"Well, that's because of the quarry. They chip and break the stone there, then shape it so they can use it to build homes and other things," he told me.

"How the heck do you break stone?" I asked him, my legs were starting to feel less tired now that I was using them again.

He spit to the side, and I noticed it was red. Actually, his brown hair looked kind of red now too.

"With big hammers. You hit it really hard, and it breaks."

He was starting to sound bored.

"That'd be fun," I replied stepping over a large rock that was in my way.

I imagined what it would look to smack it with a big hammer and break it in half.

Lothar looked back at me frowning and shook his head, "No, it's not fun, boy. It's hard work, now keep walking, we'll be there shortly."

I smirked and looked up at Del to see if she was going to do his voice again, but she didn't seem like she was even listening to us anymore. Her eyes stared straight ahead at nothing, and it seemed like she didn't want to talk right now so I left her alone and kept following Lothar.

***

It was getting hot, the sun was high in the sky, Lothar had said earlier it was almost midday. I could hear all the different birds talking to each other in the trees, it reminded me of when I used to go goblin hunting near home and the birds would talk and sing songs to each other too.

Things were so much different now, it made me think of Mother and Pa and I realised how much I missed them and our home that I'd never see again.

I was sad, I wished they were with us now, I wished there was a way to go back and change it all.

I felt my shoulders slump and I looked down at the ground while I walked, I listened to the sound of the dried leaves crunch under my feet and thought of how much things had changed since I left home, I felt a lot older now and it'd only been a few days.

Earlier, Del had passed some more bread rolls around with a little dried meat for us to eat and some water. She told me that her and Lothar had taken it from Branwick while I was asleep, to prepare us for the trip to the mountains.

I hadn't realised how hungry I was until the food came out and even though I was feeling down, I was excited to go to the mountains and see the home my real mother was from.

I've never seen mountains before, Del told me it would be very cold on the journey there, so she'd given me a knapsack to carry that had a wool blanket and some thicker clothes inside. Lothar carried a knapsack too now, and Del had the one she'd taken with her from Hiltsten.

She was still being really quiet, I hadn't heard her and Lothar talk to each other at all since I woke up. Something was going on between them, she was upset, I think.

"This is the quarry, boy," Lothar suddenly said, making me look up.

In front of me was a huge wall of rock, it was all jagged and sharp like it had been cut at, there was smaller bits of stone on the ground all around it and some tools were lying about. I could see big hammers that looked so heavy I didn't think I could even pick one up, there was also a tool that had a long-curved point on it that I didn't know what it was used for.

"It's so big! And what's that thing?" I asked him pointing at the curved tool.

"That's a pickaxe, it's used to chip chunks of stone off so they can be broken into smaller pieces," he replied, stopping to let me see.

I walked closer to take a better look, I saw there was a cave, it went straight into the rock wall.

It was so dark I couldn't see anything inside.

Dark, just like in my dreams I thought and shuddered.

I hope that isn't where we need to go, I didn't want to go in there at all. It looked like somewhere a dragon would live… or something that had sharp teeth, horns like a ram… and claws for fingernails…

"We aren't going in there, are we?" I asked staring into the darkness, feeling terrified.

I looked back at Lothar, and he spit on the ground again, I saw it was still red and I noticed that both of his eyes had dark black rings around them. He looked like one of the raccoons Pa brought home for supper sometimes.

"No, we aren't going in there, boy. That's the mine, where they take the stone from, it's of no use to us. Anyway, we need to keep moving," he replied, and this time I realised how tired and worn out he looked.

"Yes. We need to stop dawdling—both of you," Del said in an annoyed tone.

I had never heard her talk like that. Well, she always spoke to Lothar like that, but not at me.

I thought Lothar might say something back to her, but he just ignored it and turned to me pulling something from his belt.

"Before I forget, here's your weapon back, boy," he said handing me my sword.

I hadn't even realised I didn't have it on me anymore, I reached out and took it from him and slid it back into its sheathe. I saw he also had his back in his belt again too.

"Thanks, I didn't even know I'd dropped it," I said.

"My father used to say, a warrior should never forget the weapons he has at his disposal. Don't lose it again," he replied, and started walking again.

I nodded and followed him, but stayed near Del. I wanted to know why she was being grumpy, maybe she'd tell me if I stayed close to her.

Well, I hoped so at least.

I looked behind me and took one last look at the dark cave, expecting to see glowing orange eyes staring back at me from inside. But there was nothing there, just darkness. No clawed hand was reaching out to drag me inside. I still felt glad to see it getting further and further away from us though.

"The quarry was really neat, have you ever seen one before?" I asked Del, trying to get her to talk.

"Yes, it is, Kael. And yes, I've seen quarries before. We have one at my commune, that we used to build the church," she said without looking at me.

"I bet that one's neat too, I can't wait to see it," I replied to her.

"It sure is. We need to hurry though, it's not safe here," she mumbled back.

I sighed and focused on walking. Maybe the cave scared her too, I don't know, but I didn't feel safe near it and I was happy to hurry if that meant we got further away from it.

The only bad thing was that all this walking we were doing was really tough as well though, and it didn't help that I couldn't stop thinking about the face I had seen in my dream. It felt like every time I closed my eyes I saw it.

As though it just kept flashing into my head on its own.

I could still hear the chanting too, it was very quiet, but it wouldn't shut up, and it was making it kind of hard for me to concentrate. I was doing my best to ignore it all and imagine what the mountains would look like.

Del had said earlier that there'd be snow which was what happened when it got so cold that rain froze. Lothar said it wasn't cold enough in Drassox for it to happen and that's why I'd never heard about it before.

We walked for a while without anyone speaking, I'd stopped paying attention to anything except the music the birds were making. Lothar seemed tired and Del still wasn't her normal self when Lothar suddenly stopped in his tracks and spun around to look at me.

"What'd you just say?" He demanded, like I was in trouble.

I froze, and then realised I'd been mumbling the chant to myself out loud without meaning to.

"Um. Nothing, it's just a rhyme," I answered, fiddling nervously with the leather strap of my sword sheathe.

I noticed Del was staring at me as well.

She put her hand on my shoulder and knelt next to me, so we were face to face.

"You're not in trouble, Kael, I promise. But can you repeat the rhyme for us please?" She asked softly.

I didn't want to say it out loud, I was sick of hearing it over and over, but she was finally talking to me, and I didn't want her to get upset again by saying no, so slowly I repeated the chant back to her.

"Well… it goes like this. Vessel of treachery, relinquish the light, accept the darkness and aid his plight," I finished.

Still fiddling with my bag strap and looking at my shoes, I could feel her and Lothar staring at me.

"What's a vessel of treachery?" I asked.

Del looked worriedly at Lothar.

"Where did you hear that, boy?" He growled.

They hadn't stopped staring at me and were waiting for an answer, it was making me nervous, my palms started to feel sweaty.

So, I told them all about my nightmares, about being lost in the darkness, the glowing orange light I could see and the chanting that kept getting louder. Then I finally told them about the monster that was chasing me.

When I finished talking neither of them said anything at first, they just kind of glanced at each other and then back at me.

Del went to say something, but I saw Lothar suddenly cock his head, his eyes widened, and then he cut her off before she could get the words out.

"Someone is coming. Get off the road now," he growled at us, quickly changing and sounding very scary.

Del quickly grabbed my hand and started dragging me off the road into the bushes. I looked back and saw that Lothar wasn't following us, he just stood there, in the middle of the road waiting, with a deep angry frown on his face and his hand resting on the hilt of his dagger.

"Del, stop pulling me! Why isn't Lothar following us?" I snapped at her angrily and pulled my hand free as we reached the bushes.

I glared at her, who does she think she is grabbing me like that!

Wait, why was I so angry? Del's my friend she is only trying to help.

"I'm sorry, Kael, please just do as Lothar said and stay here. Someone is coming up the road," she said pleading to me, and I felt bad for snapping at her.

I didn't even know why I'd snapped like that. It was like I had just gotten angry really fast and couldn't help it.

I crouched down low next to her and peeked through the tall grass that was hiding us, two men were walking up the road towards Lothar, they had white cloth over shiny armour and straight away I recognised the black cross symbol on it.

It was the same men that had attacked us in Drassox.

I hated them! I was going to help this time, I wouldn't just watch again, this is my chance to be strong for once.

I reached over my shoulder feeling for the handle of my sword and felt Del put her hand on mine, stopping me. I frowned at her, but then saw she was trembling.

She shook her head and put her finger to her lips begging me to stop. The men were saying something to Lothar, still peeking through the grass I saw him reply but I couldn't understand what was being said.

My heart was pounding, I wanted to get closer but Del looked so scared that I didn't want to leave her alone either.

Suddenly a painful grunt came from the road and a man cursed loudly making me look back there again.

"Let him go, you unholy blasphemous cunt!"

I saw that Lothar had his hand under one of the men's chins, as though he was holding him up. The man's arms were hanging weakly at his sides, but for some reason he wasn't fighting back or trying to get Lothar to let him go.

The other man had his sword out and was trying to

move around his friend to attack Lothar, but Lothar was using the first man like a shield between them.

I saw red. I wasn't going to watch this happen.

I would kill this wretched filth.

Wait what? Filth?

There's no time. Kill him, drive your blade through his heart.

Yes, I had to hurry. Lothar needs me.

I drew my sword and ripped myself away from Del jumping to my feet. The man was faced away from me, looking at Lothar when I began to sprint towards him. Picking up speed I could see on his back the spot I would put my sword.

And then I felt my foot hook a tree root, and I fell flat on my chest knocking the wind out of my me, causing the man to turn towards the noise.

Lothar reacted in a blur.

He ripped his hand down and I saw in it, his dagger slide out of the man's chin and realised that was how he'd been holding him up. Then he stepped around the man as he started to fall, I watched as the point of his blade popped through the other man's armour and the metal tip pointed straight at me through his chest.

The white cloth turned red, and the tip disappeared as Lothar tugged it free and both of the men hit the ground almost at the same time. Everything happened so fast I could just lay there and stare.

"Kael!" Del yelled and caught up to me.

"Are you hurt? Can you get up?" She asked looking over me.

I didn't know what to say, why'd I think those things and run off like that? It was like I couldn't stop myself, my mind felt all fuzzy.

"Kael, answer me!" Del yelled again.

Her yelling cleared my head a little and I nodded then she helped me stand back up. We walked back to Lothar, when we got there, he was holding the man's sword, inspecting the edge. He seemed happy with it and slid it into the sheathe on his back then turned to us.

"Boy. Don't disobey me like that again," he mumbled sounding very serious.

"But I was trying to help!" I yelled back stamping my foot.

Why couldn't he see that?

"I don't need your help!" He shouted loudly, making me flinch. He'd never yelled at me like that before.

He paused and took a breath then spoke softer.

"You need to listen to me from now on, alright?"

I nodded and looked away. Why did I have to trip over? He wouldn't have been angry if I had saved him, I bet.

"These two were forward scouts—Zarek's force

won't be far behind. We double our pace and make for the bridge," he said looking at Del and she nodded looking worried.

CHAPTER 12
TURBULENT CROSSINGS

'When you pass through the waters, I will be with you; and through rivers, they will not overflow you; stand strong in the face of adversity'

We would be arriving at the bridge soon, it was clear from the tracks that the people of Branwick had gone this way, they'd made no attempt to hide it and had obviously travelled quickly.

As we trudged along the road the sun began to drop behind us, casting dimming rays through the leaves of the canopy above. I was still confused about what I'd witnessed back in Branwick and how I'd not connected the events up to this point.

The man with the crossbow, the fat boy in Hiltsten. Even Elias himself had told me of a time a dog had suffered a similar fate a few summers back when it chased the boy.

And then there was the appearance of the dire wolf, I no longer believed that beast's continued presence was one of coincidence, nor our apparent spout of misfortunes. I couldn't imagine travelling with the Devil himself gave one good luck, if such a thing as luck existed.

It was the voice I heard that terrified me the most though, words can't describe the effect it had upon me. I feel like I should lay dead with those men, as though the magic was intended to harm me as well.

Somehow, I was saved though.

I glanced at the woman, a bruise had begun to show on her cheek that I hadn't noticed earlier, she'd barely spoken a word to me since back in the town.

The horrors she suffered while I was unconscious were clearly taking their toll on her, although I think all of us were suffering in some way. The boy seemed a bit out of character too, maybe it was due to the things he'd witnessed… or maybe it was the dark force residing within him.

I didn't know. I only knew we had to stay ahead of Zarek.

The road we followed was starting to thin as the trees grew in on either side and the dirt was becoming moist and muddy, making it stick to our boots. A good sign we were nearing water.

"How're you feeling?" I asked Del, attempting to break the silence.

She shifted her eyes to me without turning her head.

"I'll manage," She answered bluntly, and then directed her eyes forward again.

She was clearly not managing, but I wasn't going to push the issue, if she didn't want to talk about it then we wouldn't.

"That's good. The bridge is just at the next clearing," I told her, and almost on cue, I heard the unmistakable sound of moving water.

Although I'd only been here a few times in my life, I knew the Strunn flowed notoriously fast, inland towards the feet of the mountains, especially at this time of the year.

Many summers ago, my father had taken me fishing here, it was one of the rare times of leisure he spent with me, unless you counted training for combat as leisure.

The boy jogged up next to me, he'd been trailing a short distance behind us, clearly getting tired again.

"What's that sound?" He asked catching his breath.

"It's the river, boy," I replied peering ahead as the trees opened up into a large clearing revealing the narrow stone bridge that provided crossing over the turbulent waters.

Our path.

However, it wasn't the water nor the bridge that caught my attention. It was the many brown tents and large force encamped in plain view on the opposite side, apparently guarding the crossing.

All the people of Branwick were here and it was clear they were preparing for a fight. I could see chest high wooden barricades lining the far riverbank, which also blocked entry off the bridge. Men holding longbows stood guard behind the barriers, dressed in identical brown leather armour, I counted at least twenty of them.

The bridge itself was constructed of stone, mined from the quarry many years ago, it was wide enough for only five men to walk abreast and would provide an excellent ambush point.

So, Duke Gerard had a plan then.

"Lothar, who're all those people?" The boy asked nervously.

I ignored him as I continued surveying the encampment, this could work. Zarek would still outnumber us, but the narrow bridge would hinder his ability to advance, attempting to cross would be very difficult without considerable casualties.

The boy hit me in the back, startling me and I spun around angrily. What had gotten in to him lately, even the woman looked as shocked as I was.

"Who are they!?" He demanded, I noticed immediately that his voice had taken a slightly deeper tone than it usually had.

I glared at him, trying to discern if this was still the boy I knew, or something darker taking hold.

"The people from Branwick, who do you think it is?" I snapped back.

"Stop it you two, we need to cross now. We have no idea how close behind us the Order is," Del interrupted.

I nodded to her, "I know the Duke here, he was a friend of my father. Stay behind me."

It wasn't a lie, almost everyone south of the Strunn knew and respected my father, he was one of the few men that returned south after the Great War. Most journeyed north, to more prosperous settlements seeking a better life, few returned to the harsh lifestyle the south offered.

Leading the way, I stepped out into the clearing and approached the bridge.

I had barely made it halfway there when a voice called out to me, "Halt! Who goes there?"

It'd come from a group of four men at the opposite end of the bridge, and they were striding purposely towards us.

It was time to find out if our reception would be well received or not I thought, studying the postures of the men currently approaching.

"I'm the Captain of the Drassox guard, and I carry ill news from the south. I request urgent audience with

Duke Gerard!" I called back, hesitantly.

I saw one of the men's heads perk up at my reply.

"Captain Lothar? That you?" He asked.

I squinted to better make out his face, I liked to think it helped, and maybe it did, as I then recognised the slimly built young man with chestnut coloured hair coming our way.

"Ah, Tobias. Yes, it is, I'm glad to see you made it back safely. Did your cousin, Ezekiel, make it back with you?" I replied and started walking towards the group, with Del and the boy following shyly behind.

I didn't blame them for their trepidation, it seemed everyone we stumbled across bore us ill will as of late.

"Ay, he did. He's out hunting right now, helping harvest food for the camp," Tobias answered with a smile, reaching out to shake my hand as we met.

"Is Orin not with you?" He asked, looking about as we clasped hands.

Images flashed into my mind like a storm of the betrayal in Hiltsten, of the exact moment I saw Amond's sword rip through Orin's chest. It caused my heart to lurch in my throat.

I swallowed deeply to contain it.

"… No, sadly he's not Tobias."

My face must have betrayed my attempt at stoicism, as he didn't press the matter further, and instead offered a solemn nod in return.

"Well, this is Lieutenant Harold, and two of our

guards, Jakob and Felix," He said, motioning to each of the men that were accompanying him.

I offered my hand to Harold as befit his station, he reached back and grasped my hand with a firm grip. I'd never met him before, he had a short stocky build, and his hair had already begun to grey, making him appear older than I suspected he actually was.

"I'm pleased to meet you, Captain Lothar, your reputation proceeds you," he said looking me directly in the eye, and holding my grip for slightly longer than was necessary.

I was unsure if this was intended as some kind of slight, an attempt for him to feel tough, or a sign of genuine respect. The man was hard to read, and I didn't have time for such nonsense.

"Let's get off this bridge and back to the safety of the camp gents, follow me," Harold said letting go of my hand and breaking eye contact.

"By the way! I'm Delaney, and this is Kael. In case any of you rude sods were wondering!" Del exclaimed, stepping forward and interrupting loudly, before glaring at each of the men in turn.

I probably should've introduced her and the boy myself I realised, too late now.

I almost laughed as the men in front of me all shied from her gaze and awkwardly mumbled apologies. This woman, despite her unintimidating stature, never shied from a conflict, she was formidable in her own way, and that was something I respected, even with the attitude she gave me.

Our entourage crossed the bridge quickly, the guards on the bank shifting a section of barricade aside so we could pass freely into the camp.

This point of the Strunn was less than two hundred paces wide, a thin area of the river, and the reason it was chosen for the construction of the bridge. A shorter span meant less materials and with the quarry nearby, it was an ideal location.

There was only one more crossing I was aware of that allowed passage over the Strunn, a less impressive wooden bridge that was located over a day and a half's journey back the way we had come, a few hours trek north of Hiltsten.

As we entered into the camp, I noticed many people about and they all seemed to be busy doing something.

Men were chopping wood, workers were reinforcing barricades, animal carcasses hung from posts, ready to be harvested into meat for dinner. Guards patrolled the camp, and women were preparing numerous campfires, placing them about the area to provide warmth when the sun set, which wouldn't be long at all now.

While I looked around at the camp Lieutenant Harold stopped and addressed us.

"It would be improper for a commoner and a child

to attend a meeting with the Duke, unless they have news you are not privy to, Captain?" He asked.

I turned my attention to Del, she shrugged disinterestedly.

"I've nothing to add that you don't already know, I'll stay with Kael," she said bluntly.

I'd expected she would say this, she rarely let the boy out of her sight lately it seemed.

"I can go with them and arrange a tent for you all if you like, Captain Lothar?" Tobias stepped in and offered.

"That would be appreciated, thanks, Tobias," I answered, giving him a warm nod.

The boy looked at me worriedly and I motioned for him to follow Tobias, Del took his hand and guided him with her.

I watched them walk towards the tents and then turned back to face Lieutenant Harold.

"Alright, after you, Lieutenant," I said.

As we walked, Jakob and Felix took leave to return to their posts, wherever that were.

While I followed Harold towards Duke Gerard's tent, I couldn't help but feel anxious, the last time I attended a meeting with a Duke, I'd been beaten and taken prisoner, my friend had been murdered, and then an entire town was slaughtered.

I prayed this time would turn out better.

The camp was not that large, so after only a short

walk we arrived at a large well-constructed, square, blue tent with a single man posted at the entry standing guard. It was situated a short distance away from the many smaller, triangular shaped brown tents.

As Lieutenant Harold and I approached, the guard opened the flap and held it open for us to enter.

"After you, Captain," Harold said, stepping aside and waiting for me to enter first.

A standard courtesy to a higher ranked superior.

Well, here it goes. At least I have a sword this time, I won't go down without a fight, if it comes to that. I wished at that moment I'd asked Orin what he had told Tobias and Ezekiel about Zarek, it was obviously impossible now.

I entered the tent, a small fire burned in the corner, providing a dim light and warmth, while two men stood at a large wooden table, looking at a map then turned to face me.

I recognised the older slim man, dressed in ceremonious leather armour with a neatly trimmed white beard and hair to match.

It was Duke Gerard, he looked exactly the same as when I'd seen him last several summers ago. The other man took a moment for me to recognise, he appeared to have aged considerably more than the older man he was with.

His name was Rowan, a few summers younger than myself, he was my counterpart in Branwick. A

Captain and a reasonable fighter, his father and my own had fought together back in the day, although his had fallen in battle and not returned home. I'd met him once in the past and we'd shared a friendly sparring match with practice blades, men had gambled from both towns. It had proved to be rather one sided, with me beating him fairly quickly.

"Captain Lothar, what a surprise. I heard you'd arrived. Come, take a seat. We're going over battle plans, there is much to discuss and a set of eyes as experienced as your own is well received," Duke Gerard said to me, appearing pleased by my presence.

Well, that's a good sign so far at least I thought.

I walked over to the table and took a seat, Harold followed behind and the Duke motioned for him to sit down as well.

"Duke Gerard, Captain Rowan. Unfortunately, I bring grave news from the southern towns," I began, feeling the full weight of the news I was about to share flood over me like a rising tide.

"Mhm. I was afraid of that. Speak, Lothar," The Duke ordered, a grim expression settling on his face.

I took a deep breath, handed him the journal I'd taken from Gildred and told him all that I'd witnessed, leaving out the part that I knew I travelled with the boy the Order was looking for.

****

When I had finished speaking, each man at the table looked at me stunned, in utter shock, the mood inside the tent had turned to one of grief and sadness, for all the lives lost.

The Duke was the first to break the silence.

"So, you are telling me, that this Order of St Michael, led by this 'Zarek', have travelled north… through Arman, Ridgewood, Marlot, Drassox and Hiltsten, murdering countless people… all because they are searching for a child they think is possessed by the damned Devil!?"

I felt my face became even darker, if that was possible.

"Yes, that's what I've seen, Duke." I confirmed hesitantly, eliciting a gasp from Harold.

"Fucking religious zealots!" The Duke spat in disgust.

"These vermin sound like the devil to me," Rowan mumbled, his eyes staring vacantly at the table.

Harold murmured in agreement.

"What in the hells possessed that fool Roland to stay and not leave when you and your party did?" The Duke asked me, confused.

As much as I knew my answer should be a lie, I realised in that moment that I could not bring myself to use trickery that may result in the death of more people. These people didn't deserve that, and I couldn't wear it on my conscience, plus he would read about it in Gildred's journal anyway.

So, I decided to risk my safety and tell them the truth.

"I don't want to lie to you, Gerard. Roland believed the child the Order are looking for is the boy I travel with. He killed my man Orin and took me prisoner after I helped lead the defence against Gildred. The woman and the boy freed me, and we escaped just as Zarek arrived."

All three men looked at me at once, no one spoke.

I tensed preparing to defend myself, if need be, the tension running in the air felt as though it could be cut with a blade.

Suddenly Duke Gerard's face softened, and he broke the silence again.

"Relax yourself, Lothar. God's man—I'm not that fat coward Roland. I never thought much of that tub of lard, or his pile of shit advisor Herman. I don't hand over defenceless children to warlords to save my own skin. You're all safe here and I would appreciate your advice in the defence, no man here has more battle experience than you."

I felt my chest relax in relief at his words, but it didn't put my mind completely at ease, I recalled Duke Roland saying something similar to me when I had first arrived to Hiltsten.

No, I wouldn't drop my guard completely ever again.

"I appreciate that, Roland. I'm happy to go over your battle plans with you. As I said though, I encountered Zarek's scouts just south of here, he can't be far behind," I replied standing and pointing on the map roughly where I'd killed the men.

Everyone present looked where I was indicating.

"Are you certain of this location?" Rowan asked looking concerned.

I nodded confidently, my father had been very adamant that I knew how to read a map, right from the time I was very young.

"We don't have long then. Rowan, fill Lothar in with haste," Duke Gerard said.

***

I exited the tent a short time later sucking in a deep breath of fresh air, it felt as though a massive weight had been lifted off my chest now the meeting was out of the way.

The sun had set while I'd been inside and I noticed the fires around the camp had been lit to prepare for the cold night ahead.

The plan had been simple enough, I believed it would be effective, and it's what I would've done.

Duke Gerard's idea was to funnel the enemy onto the bridge, then using a column of shield bearers as well as the wooden barriers, trap them there while the archer's rained arrows from the sides and above. At only five abreast, the enemy would struggle to break through the defences.

To be honest, Zarek would be a fool to even try, but only a fool would underestimate that man's cunning as well.

I had advised the Duke of this, and about the use and effect of the blast stone in Hiltsten, it was agreed between all that the archers would be ordered to target any enemy wielding a crossbow with utmost urgency.

Prebuilt replacement barricades would be waiting nearby with workers, ready to be placed to fix any damage if a stone struck and erupted. Branwick's defence boasted sixty men at arms, made up of twenty archers and over forty guardsmen with a further twenty townsfolk armed and ready to fight.

Unless Zarek had another trick up his sleeve, an assault across the river would be devastating for his forces.

Yet, despite of all this, I felt racked with guilt. I knew we had to leave at first light, as much as it pained me to tuck tail and flee like a coward. The boy was changing, if Del was right and her priests could free him from Lucifer's grasp, then that is where I would take him.

Part of me had begun to wonder why I even cared and why I was making this my problem. I should stay here and help save these people instead, I know nothing of his ailment. What could I do to help?

Nothing.

And still, for some reason the thought of abandoning the boy fills me with emotions of thick dread, I have a persistent, deep urge, telling me that I must help him.

It's like an itch that I cannot scratch and I can't explain it.

"Captain Lothar?" A voice nearby called my name, causing me to look around, spotting Tobias waiting nearby.

"Tobias. How'd you go with Del and the boy?" I asked him.

"They're resting in a tent nearby, I've been waiting here to take you there. Are you ready?" He replied.

I nodded in agreement and began following him through the town. My body still ached as I walked, I felt it was an effort just to keep up with the younger, more sprightly man although I did my best to hide it.

I suspected I had suffered a broken rib back in the town. It hurt to breathe, and my twisted nose being filled with dried blood wasn't helping things either.

People gave curious glances as I walked through the camp. Like Drassox, everyone knew everyone here and a new face, especially one as battered as mine right now stood out.

I gave a few folks a courteous nod while we navigated our way about the maze of tents, they all returned the gesture.

Tobias stopped suddenly and turned to me.

"They're in that tent there," he said pointing a short distance ahead of us.

"I need to go, Ezekiel hasn't returned from his hunt out east yet, I'm going to go check up on him. I'll be at the barricades on the west side of the bridge later if you need me."

"I appreciate the help, Tobias," I replied, shaking his hand once more.

He started to walk away and then froze, looking back at me.

"I'm sorry to hear about Orin, Captain. He seemed like a good man," he said solemnly.

Then bowed his head and resumed walking. I stood for a moment thinking to myself. I am too Tobias, and not to just Orin. I've let so many others down lately.

And soon… I'll be forced to let everyone here down too.

Blocking out my thoughts, I slowly made my way to the tent.

As I grew near, I heard the boy's voice and paused for a moment to listen.

"… not leaving him! He's my friend, Del!" He yelled sounding upset.

"Kael, please keep it down. We can't stay here, we need to leave as the sun rises, with or without him," Del pleaded back quietly.

"No! We're all leaving together. Lothar wouldn't leave me, and I won't leave him either," I heard him say.

Rather than stand there eavesdropping like a sneak, I abruptly pushed the flap open and entered the tent.

They both jumped, startled at my sudden entrance, the woman wore an expression as though she'd just been caught pissing in the stew pot. We all stood there awkwardly, waiting for someone to speak.

The boy innocently broke the silence first, speaking with a matter-of-fact tone.

"Don't worry, Lothar, I told Del we aren't going anywhere without you."

"I heard you, boy. But Del is right though, it's not safe here. We're going to make for the mountains at first light," I replied.

I saw relief flood her face at this, but also something else.

A look of disdain aimed at me. Was there no keeping this woman happy?

I opened my mouth to ask what the problem was when a loud commotion outside interrupted me.

The three of us rushed from the tent together, all of the townsfolk and guards were looking out across the river and speaking in panicked voices. I didn't even need to look to know what had everyone so worked up, but I did anyway.

My eyesight may not be as sharp as it used to be, but even with the fading light I could still make out the silhouettes emerging from the path and stepping into the clearing on the opposite embankment.

It was him.

Zarek.

I'd hoped he wouldn't arrive until the morning, but he seemed hell bent on catching up. I could feel my blood begin to boil knowing he was so near to my grasp.

"He's over there, isn't he? …The man who killed Pa," the boy mumbled, and I realised he was standing closely by my side.

The question surprised me, I'd never spoken to him about Zarek. He was more observant than I gave him credit for.

"… Yes, he is, boy," I said back softly after a sigh, now seeing no reason in lying as I watched the figures form up on the far edge of the clearing.

It was a wise move, they were making sure to stay right back and out of range of our archers. I continued staring and noticed two men though, were making their way towards the bridge.

One carried a white flag, held high above his head, they crossed the clearing and apparently unconcerned, stepped straight onto the bridge and waited in plain view.

Something about this stunk.

I saw cloth hanging off one of the men flailing in the wind, a fucking white cape. It was most definitely him.

"Make way! Open the barricade," a gruff voice to my left shouted through a crowd of people, making them all scurry out of the way like startled rabbits.

As they made way I saw Captain Rowan. he strode through the opening with a small group of guards and the two of us made eye contact immediately.

"Captain Lothar, I hoped I would run into you on my way here, will you accompany me on the bridge?" He stammered.

Sweat was beading on his forehead, and his voice shook as he spoke, threatening to betray his façade of courage.

He was terrified, and I didn't blame him.

I can't leave them like this.

I began to answer when Del suddenly pulled roughly on my armour from behind, causing a sharp jolt of pain in my midsection, reminding me how tender my ribs were.

"What!?" I growled in frustration, spinning to glare at her.

"We should leave here now, we can't risk staying here to see how this unfolds, Lothar. There's too much at stake."

She spoke in a hushed whisper, but I heard the panic and urgency in her voice, the fear was evident on her face also.

She was right, I didn't know if her priests could do what she said. But I'd seen with my own eyes what resided in the boy, and I was at a loss how to combat such a threat.

The protective instinct that had been growing in me was becoming stronger with each passing day, it urged me to not allow Zarek to get a hold of him.

To protect him. No matter the cost.

No.

No, this is it I thought. No more running like a coward, I need to stop this madman once and for all, here and now. If I don't, he'll be on our asses all the way north to the commune. Out there on the bridge may be the best chance I'll get to send him to hell to join his companion. I won't waste the opportunity and I won't abandon these people to this fate.

"Give me a moment Rowan," I called back to him.

He slightly bowed his head to me and turned back to the men he was with.

I turned my attention to Del and the boy, I knew the boy wasn't going to like what I was about to say so I just said it.

"I need you both to head back to the tent and prepare to leave. I'll catch up to you when this is over."

As expected, the boy's eyes immediately opened wide with panic, and he began to object.

"We aren't leaving without you, Lothar, we can all

go now!"

Del put her hand on his shoulder to try calm him down, but he shrugged her off angrily.

I sighed and knelt, so I was at his eye level. He refused to look me in the eye, to try and hide the tears in his eyes.

"Kael, if I don't try to stop Zarek now, he will just keep coming. We have a chance here to save a lot of lives. I promise you, I'll find you both again. I said I'd teach you how to use that blade remember?"

He looked back to me with wet, bloodshot eyes and nodded slowly, it was hard to believe such an innocent child was capable of the things I'd witnessed him do.

"I already know how to use it. Just… just make sure you come back, alright?" He mumbled biting his lower lip to stop it quivering.

"A promise is a promise, boy. A man is only as good as his word. And I keep mine, now go," I replied to him, before looking to Del next.

"Make sure you get him there safely."

She nodded and I got the impression she was pleased that I wouldn't be going with them. I quickly shunned it from mind and turned to join Rowan where he stood waiting at the foot of the bridge.

"Let us get this over with, Rowan."

He nodded grimly, and then addressed the men he was with, "You lot, wait here. If things go south out there, lock the barricades behind us—they must not breakthrough."

The men murmured in reply, concerned but accepting of the order.

"After you, Lothar," Rowan said with a look of determination in his eyes, a look that reminded me of Elias when we'd similarly stridden forward to meet Zarek together.

Without hesitation I stepped out onto the bridge and let my feet guide me forward, the wind had picked up speed and I could make out Zarek's cape blowing wildly about as he also began to walk with purpose towards us from the opposite end.

The light of the sun had completely faded now, shadow had set in, and the only sound I was aware of was the water rushing past the pylons beneath us on its journey towards the mountains.

I didn't feel any nerves, I'd been waiting to meet this man again, my only regret was that my chance at revenge had come while I was injured.

As my father used to say, beggars cannot be choosers.

With Rowan on my left, I stared Zarek straight in the eye as the gap between us closed, he matched my gaze just like he had done in our first meeting, a hint of glee showing in his blue eyes. The wound I had scored across his forehead had been left unstitched, leaving a jagged, crusty, half healed wound that matched his ugly personality.

Truth be told, the wounds to my own head probably didn't look much better I thought.

"… Zarek," I growled through clenched teeth as we met.

My entire body tensed, making no attempt to hide my dislike for the filth standing before me.

A curious look washed over him, followed by recognition.

"Ah… so it is you… It would make sense that the one who escaped that wretched little town, would be the only man to land a strike on me in over a decade," Zarek replied, smirking and appearing completely unperturbed by my presence.

"Tell me, is the child here with you?" He asked.

Rowan took a step forward and interrupted.

"We aren't here to talk about children, turn around and head back the way you came, butcher."

Zarek scowled, a murderous look flashing over his face, so quick I almost missed it.

"But that is why I am here… interrupt my discussion with this man again, and the pleasantries will be over. Your life, along with them," he hissed, malicious intent dripping from his words.

The man next to him whispered something into his ear and I saw his lips curl into a faint smile as he nodded quickly.

Rowan laughed confidently, "The pleasantries ARE over, go back, gather your men and try to cross if you wish. Let's head back, Lothar. This discussion is finished."

"… Lothar, is it? Well, Lothar, you seem like the intelligent one here. Hand the child over, and everyone may live. Do not be a fool like your friend there—how many must die before you see sense? Is all this worth one boy's life?" Zarek said calmly, still refusing to break eye contact with me.

"There will be no deals here, scum!" Rowan shouted putting his hand on the hilt of his sword.

I glared, trying to burn holes in his eyes and didn't answer, I would offer this man nothing. Only death.

Eventually he sighed, his nose twitching in irritation.

"No matter, my tracker is very skilled. He will find the child's trail."

He looked to Rowan.

"And you… you were warned about interrupting me… you are aware this is not the only crossing over this river?" He continued suspiciously looking somewhere behind us off to the side.

Rowan spat on the ground.

"Pah! It'll take you days to send your force around. You think we'll still be here waiting by then!?"

"… Yes, it would. Unless I already sent them north when we were still in Hiltsten…" Zarek said.

And just like that, it all made sense.

The man next to Zarek holding the flag lowered it,

and immediately a flaming arrow shot into the sky from the bank behind him, leaving a trail like a firefly as it soared into the air.

I didn't hesitate to see what happened next, I punched Zarek full force in the mouth knocking him backwards. The man next to him charged forward and tackled me, sending us both crashing to the ground in a mess of tangled limbs with him landing on top of me.

Rowan bravely rushed forward, sword in hand to engage Zarek as he regained his composure.

Struggling with the man on top of me I heard shouts of alarm coming from the direction of the camp, followed by the unmistakable sound of battle as the missing half of Zarek's forces attacked from our side of the river.

The man on top of me managed to draw his dagger and was trying his best to put it through the armpit gap in my armour, my broken ribs shot pain through my body as I fought to stop him. Using all of my strength I pushed and flipped him over onto his back gaining the upper hand. The distinct clang of blades rang nearby from Zarek and Rowan as they fought not far from us.

I grabbed hold of my foe's hands and forced them up, and away from us creating an opening, then drove my elbow guard hard into his exposed face.

Once. Twice. Three times.

Deep gashes opened on his face, his right brow

hung grotesquely over his eye blocking its vision, while his grip weakened on the blade, allowing me to snatch it free and then drive it into his face with a satisfying wet thud.

I frantically rose to my feet and drew my sword, shooting a quick glance back to our camp as I regained my footing, a hectic battle was unfolding there as Zarek's force stormed the area from the nearby tree line and the men of Branwick fought back.

Rowan was falling to his knees when I swung back around, Zarek's blade stuck deep into his belly, protruding out of his lower back. Rushing towards the bridge behind them was the original half of Zarek's force, beginning an assault across the river in a pincer movement. Branwick wouldn't stand a chance, and I was trapped in the middle.

Time was short. This is it, I must kill him now.

With fury running through my veins, I charged forward while Zarek tore his blade free from Rowan's lifeless body.

Our eyes met, sharing pure hatred followed briefly by the clash of our blades for the second time, the ring of steel reverberating loudly across the free-flowing water.

I fought like a man possessed, every swing of my blade aimed to end his life before his men were upon us. But his sword was always there to meet mine, preventing the killing blow from finding its mark. I stepped back and we circled each other, sweat already dripping from both our brows while we breathed heavily and then resumed fighting savagely again.

Our steel smashed together and we locked in a vicious stalemate each staring into the other's eyes, I pushed his weapon to the side and head butted him square in the face knocking him back when something struck my right thigh hard, causing my leg to go dead and almost make me collapse.

I glanced down to see a bolt protruding from my limb, I growled to block out the pain, the momentary pause proving costly as I was kicked hard in the chest by Zarek, sending me stumbling wildly back…

Then I was falling, over the edge of the bridge and into the water with a splash. The heavy current and weight of my armour immediately began dragging me down, my last clear vision was of his smug face smiling down at me from the bridge above.

I fought to stay afloat, thrashing about desperately, my leg still refusing to work as my head dipped under the dark, murky water repeatedly, making me cough and choke more violently each time.

I knew this was it.

I've failed you boy.

My last thought being that I'm sorry, as my vision began to darken, and the water filled my throat.

CHAPTER 13

A BOY'S GRIEF

'He will wipe away every tear from their eyes, and death shall be no more, neither shall there be mourning nor pain anymore, for the former things have passed away'

"NOOOOOOOOOOOOOOOOO!!!" I screamed and started to sprint towards the bridge when I saw him fall, but I stumbled, my legs felt like they might buckle at any moment, like all the strength had left them.

I barely made it two steps before someone grabbed me roughly from behind, wrapping their arms around me tightly and my legs gave out. I fell to my knees sobbing.

He's gone. The water. It's too fast.

No one could swim in that… not even him. My

mind was jumbled, I couldn't think, and it was hard to breathe.

No, you're wrong, he's strong he'll be fine!

He promised you he'd come back!

The arms around me pulled up, trying to force me to stand.

"Kael! I'm sorry about Lothar, but we have to move. Now!" A voice pleaded to me, it sounded distant, like we were in different places.

I became aware of the muffled sounds of many other voices yelling all around me, mixed with the clanging of metal and painful screams. I recognised by now the sounds of a battle being fought.

I tried to do as the voice asked but my legs wouldn't move like I wanted them to, I couldn't stop staring at the water.

Searching, looking for a sign… any sign he was still there.

I expected Lothar's head to pop up at any moment and him to start swimming powerfully through the water towards us and say something like, 'Why are you crying, boy? I told you I'd come back.' But as more time passed, the sick feeling in my stomach only grew stronger until I felt like I would vomit.

I was small but I knew in my heart that no one could stay under the water this long.

"Kael, please get up! He's gone, we need to use the opportunity he gave us!" The person yelled, urging me to move.

I wanted to do as they asked, the voice sounded familiar and I knew it was right, but I just couldn't. All I could see and focus on was the water and images flashing through my mind of him stumbling and flipping backwards over the edge into the water. The dark water…

The darkness… it took him.

Suddenly I was lifted fully into the air, someone was carrying me, I could hear them puffing as they struggled to run.

"It's alright I have you, I'm getting us out of here," the person carrying me said while I felt tears run down my face, my eyes refused to stop staring at the water as we moved.

Still waiting, hoping, for his face to break the surface.

My tears made everything blurry, cloudy figures ran around the camp in all directions and the panicked voices grew louder.

"—get the people out of here! … bridge cannot fall! You lot, reinforce the eastern front!" Someone yelled giving orders and I saw a bunch of blurry figures nearby hurry away.

I ignored them all and closed my eyes tightly as the river got too far away for me to see clearly anymore.

The person carrying me began to puff louder as they grew tired but I kept my eyes shut and let them carry me along and tried my best to ignore the sounds of the battle, to block out the images of Lothar falling, and being swallowed up by the darkness.

***

I don't know how much time passed but when I finally opened my eyes, it was much darker, there was no moon out and it terrified me, I didn't want to be surrounded by the dark.

Bad things always happened there.

"Kael… I need… you… (huffing)… to walk… with me…" The voice said and I finally let myself recognise who it was.

Del.

"I'm going… to put you down… I—I'm… exhausted," she gasped, barely able to get the words out.

Del crouched down and placed me on the grass, then collapsed next to me flat on her back still puffing. I had no idea where we were, I didn't care either.

I hate this place. I hate everything. It's not fair, nothing is fair. He promised he would come back, and now he left me just like Mother did. And Pa too. They all left me!

I know I shouldn't cry, I'm meant to be strong, I'm always telling myself I have a sword now and that I'm a knight and knights don't cry, they're brave.

But it just hurts so much.

I want to wake up, but I know that I'm not dreaming… this is all real.

"Kael?" Del whispers to me making me look down at her, I can't make out her expression in the dark.

"Mhm…" I mumbled back, quickly realising it'd made me sound just like Lothar did when he wasn't interested in what I had to say.

She sat back up and spoke softly.

"I know you're upset, and I'm deeply sorry about what happened to Lothar. But he made me promise I would get you to the mountains, to keep you safe… I need to keep that promise. I need you to be brave and help me, please."

"I don't care about the stupid mountains!!" I yelled as loud as I could without thinking, causing her to flinch.

I didn't mean to yell at Del like that, I was just so angry I felt like I needed to get it out.

She sighed and lay back down on the grass, while I continued sitting.

"Well, we can't stay here. We can rest for a moment, but we need to move, Kael."

I ignored her and neither of us said anything for a while, choosing to just sit there surrounded by the dark, unable to do anything but stare into it.

I couldn't get away from it, I tried closing my eyes for a moment but it followed me, getting even darker, so I opened them again and when I did, it started showing me things I wanted to forget.

Images of Mother lying there, covered in thick blood on the floor of the town hall, the bodies of all the people I knew around her. Of Pa, being struck in the face by a bolt fired from a crossbow, and falling to the ground dead. Of Lothar, fighting on the bridge… and then disappearing into the water, swallowed whole by the dark river.

I watched these images flash by in the blackness, I tried to make them stop when I realised I could hear the chanting again, it was faint but it had definitely come back.

Or maybe it hadn't stopped since the last time I heard it, I couldn't be sure but it worried me. My heart begun to pound like a drum, in rhythm to the voices. It was like it knew what was about to come and I suddenly felt very alone.

I wanted the sun to come out again, I felt safe in the light.

Scared, I looked around me and searched the emptiness. It didn't take long before I saw it, and it made my chest thump even louder as soon as I did.

The faint orange glow had come back.

I knew inside it was the monster from my nightmares, it was still far off in the distance, but making its way towards me, flickering like a candle flame and with each flicker it was appearing closer.

"Del?" I whispered remembering she was next to

me, but too terrified to take my eyes off of the glow, even for a moment.

She didn't answer me.

"Del, do you see that?" I tried again, a little louder this time, realising I couldn't hear her puffing anymore.

I held my breath and waited for her to reply, I didn't dare try any louder than that, in case I got the monsters attention, but again she didn't answer me.

Why wouldn't she answer me? Was she asleep?

I wanted to look down at the grass for her, where I knew she was laying. But I was terrified if I took my eyes off of the monster for too long that it would move faster, as though my stare was the only thing keeping it back and it would charge as soon as I looked down.

My heart almost froze when I finally built enough courage to look and found the ground was empty, it was so dark I couldn't even see the grass anymore. Where there should've been grass there was just… nothing.

Del wasn't there either. She'd lied and left me too.

I was alone again.

The chanting became louder, closer. Close enough that I could easily make out the words again, they were the same as in my dream, but there was something else.

"… the light… **do not be afraid, Kael**… Accept the darkness and aid his plight… Vessel of treachery… **stay**

strong… Relinquish the light… **my child**… Accept the darkness and aid his plight… **fight**…"

What was that…?

I realised this time there was another voice mixed in, it wasn't chanting like the others, it was a woman, her voice shook as though it took great effort to speak. She sounded familiar even though I was sure I had never heard her voice before. Somehow it felt like with every word she spoke she was giving me strength, taking away my fear and I had a strong feeling that she was trying to help me.

I continued to stare at the thing flickering towards me, trying to slow it down with my eyes but it kept coming.

It was getting nearer, and I could make out its face again. The curled twisted horns like a ram and the large mouth filled with sharp teeth looking like it had a big wide smile on its face that grew wider when it saw me, like it was happy.

And its eyes… they began to burn even brighter, glowing orangey-red like when Rupert used to heat the steel up in the forge so he could hammer it.

The chanting became deafening once more but the woman's voice also grew a little louder.

"RELINQUISH THE LIGHT!! … **Stand and fight**… ACCEPT THE DARKNESS AND AID HIS PLIGHT!! … **Do not be afraid my child**…"

Again, I heard the woman's voice over the chanting

and my fear suddenly vanished completely. All that was left was a calm anger. I realised I HATED this monster in front of me.

Whatever it was, I blamed it for everything.

This is what trapped me in that dark closet, unable to get out while it took Mother and Pa and everyone else.

This is where I hid like a coward when I was too scared to be brave, like when Erik pushed me over in Hiltsten or when the men grabbed me in Branwick.

This is what took Lothar, dragging him off of the bridge and into the dark water to drown.

The darkness haunted my dreams and now it was coming for me because I was afraid.

Well, I wouldn't be afraid anymore, I'll make Pa and Lothar proud. I'm going to be brave and stop it once and for all before it takes anyone else from me!

I slowly rose to my feet, my knees no longer wobbled, and my hands didn't tremble anymore. I rose until I was standing as tall as I was able. The monster still towered over me as it came forward, only a few paces away now.

But I wasn't scared, I felt like a giant, I felt like Lothar.

We glared into each other's eyes, stinging heat came off of the monster and I could smell it's disgusting sharp odour, like rotting sour meat.

The chanting grew even louder, like the other

voices were trying to block out the woman's and they almost did.

I didn't care, I knew what I had to do.

I reached behind my back for my sword, and this time I found it was there, right where it should be. I wrapped my sweaty hands around the handle, squeezing it tightly to make sure I had a firm grip and began to draw it from the sheathe.

The monster was close to me now, but I was a knight, a warrior, and I would slay it.

For Mother and Pa.

For everyone who died back home.

And for Lothar.

I charged forward as fast as I could slashing downward like I practiced for hours against imaginary goblins…

… And suddenly everything around me vanished in a blinding flash like lightning had struck, so bright I had to shut my eyes to block it out, it was like staring straight into the sun.

Through closed eyes I saw the bright light die down as fast as it'd appeared. As I slowly opened them again, I noticed I was walking on a thin trail, with Del not far in front of me leading the way. It was cold and I had a blanket draped over my shoulders and I saw Del did as well.

What was going on, How had I been walking without knowing, had I been dreaming again?

I must have been… but it seemed so real.

"Um, Del?" I called out.

"Yes? What's the matter, Kael?" She replied without stopping or looking back.

"Where are we?" I asked, looking around, my eyes still stinging from the blinding light.

She stopped suddenly, looking back at me with an odd expression on her face.

"We're on the same trail we've been walking on all night, north of the bridge. Where else would we be?"

"Oh right…" I said and kept following her pretending nothing was wrong.

Something was wrong though, I wasn't sure if my dreams were even dreams anymore. Had we really been walking all night? I could see it wasn't as dark now, the light from the sun was beginning to peep over the horizon, although it still looked like it would be a while before it rose to daylight.

I don't know what just happened but I couldn't wait to be safe in the daylight again.

Maybe I'd I been sleepwalking again, Mother had told me I used to walk in my sleep sometimes, Pa had even found me in the stables once late at night, he said I must have opened the door while I was asleep.

But all those times I'd only gone a short distance, never like this. And I had never dreamed while I walked before.

I wish Lothar was here, I feel so lost without him.

But I knew I needed to be brave and stop thinking like that, that was how little kids thought, not knights.

My legs felt so tired maybe I really have been walking all night, but then again, they always felt tired lately.

I couldn't hear the river anymore, and I would be glad if I never heard it again. When I thought of the sound the water made all I could picture was Lothar sinking below it… I couldn't believe he was really gone. It made me feel sick in my stomach every time I remembered. I wanted him to come back so badly, to come with me and Del to the mountains where we would all finally be safe.

I followed along silently behind Del, she was walking really fast, it was exhausting to try and keep up with her and was beginning to make me angry.

Why couldn't she just slow down a bit!?

I thought about telling her but then she froze and put her hand up meaning for me to stop so I did.

I watched her crouch down and then wave at me to come crouch next to her. I tried to look ahead at what she was staring at and felt stupid that I hadn't noticed it until now, it was a stone house like the ones in Branwick and there was light from a fire glowing inside.

I did as she asked and crept forward to sit down next to her.

"Whose house is that, Del?" I whispered nervously

when I got there.

"I don't know, Kael, but we need food, so we're going to find out. Keep your dagger close and stay by my side, are we clear?" She replied sharply, like Mother used to when she didn't want any backchat.

I mumbled 'Yes' back to her thinking she didn't need to tell me like that, then followed her as she began to sneak towards the front of the house.

CHAPTER 14
BEGONE DEVIL

'Be alert and of sober mind. Your enemy the devil prowls around like a roaring lion looking for someone to devour'

She was so quiet, her feet didn't make a sound as we approached the porch, just like she had moved back in Hiltsten. I would've been impressed if I wasn't so upset.

I tried my best to copy but being so silent like that was harder than she made it look.

We neared the wooden door of the home, it looked pretty solid, I didn't think we would be able to break in if whoever was inside decided not to help us.

Lothar could've though…

Del stepped onto the porch first, as quietly as a mouse. But when I put my foot down on it, I made a light 'thud' noise and instantly froze, Del looked back at me with a scowl on her face.

"Who goes there??" A man's voice called out from somewhere inside.

I looked back at Del feeling a bit sheepish, she just shook her head and stood up from her crouch. There was no point in sneaking anymore now that we had been caught, I realised feeling guilty.

"We're refugees fleeing from Branwick, seeking aid. It's just myself and a young boy. Please sir, can you let us inside?" She called back, sounding much friendlier than she had lately, like she used to when we first met.

There was a pause from inside and then the sound of a deadbolt being slid aside. The door opened a crack, and a man's face appeared but it was half hidden by a thick brown hood. I could see a chain running across the door gap just below his head height.

"Eh. What could possibly cause folk of Branwick, to flee through the night? 'Tis a big settlement, and safe too," he said.

"What!? A large group of soldiers have been sacking all the towns south of the river—how could you not have heard of this!? Please, just let us inside," Del pleaded with the man.

She seemed really upset, it made me feel even worse for snapping at her earlier about the mountains.

I'd only been thinking of myself, and how hurt I was about Lothar… I hadn't thought that maybe she was just as hurt by losing him as I was.

"Alright, alright. One can never be too careful in these parts, miss, that's all. 'Tis very isolated here, news doesn't reach me in much haste, unfortunately. Forgive an 'ol man for being cautious," he replied, and the door closed, followed by the sound of the chain being removed.

It opened again shortly after, revealing a short man wearing dark brown robes. I could see him better now the door was open, he looked bald under his hood but it was hard to tell how old he actually was.

I don't know why but straight away I felt like I hated him.

Really hated him. Like something in me wanted to take my dagger and stab him with it, twist it into his guts until he was dead. My mind went blank when I realised what I'd just thought and I felt shocked, it didn't make sense because he hadn't done anything wrong to us.

Why did I just think that? Maybe he was a nice man. It would be good to meet someone nice for a change, like Hank, the old man we met on the way to Branwick.

He looked from Del to me and said, "Come inside, I can spare some food and water. The Lord Christ provides here, you're in safe hands friends."

Bile immediately rose in my throat, I felt sickened when that name came from his mouth and again, I had no idea why I felt that way.

I noticed Del hesitate after he spoke and look from him to me, studying me for a moment, before finally saying, "Come, Kael, we'll only be stopping a short while."

She looked back to the man.

"Thank you, I'm Del, and this is Kael. May I ask your name and why you're out here all alone?"

"Of course you may, I'm Father Benedict. Many years ago, I chose to take an oath of monasticism and live alone, to spread the Lord's word to those out of reach of the church. That decision led me here. But let us continue to chat inside, out of the cold, yes?" He replied and motioned us to follow, so we did.

The inside of his home was warm, a blazing fireplace filled the room with heat from the corner, a large bookcase stacked with thick books sat against the far side. I'd never seen so many books before, the stone walls felt like they did better than wood at keeping the cold out too. It was nice I thought.

Then something mounted above the fireplace on the wall caught my eye… two small bits of wood making a cross.

I didn't like it. I had a strong urge to walk over and tear it off the wall but the thought of touching it disgusted me.

"Here take a seat and I'll prepare you both some chicken pie I baked earlier," the man said smiling, taking my attention off of the cross.

He turned away and I followed Del over to the table, it was built of solid oak and very sturdy, just like the door.

I was getting an uneasy feeling in my stomach about being near the man, even about being near that cross on the wall, but the mention of chicken pie had my mouth watering, so I sat down next to Del.

While we sat there waiting, I noticed Del was staring at me like she was thinking something, it was beginning to annoy me, so I decided to ask her why.

"What are you staring at?" I snapped, the words coming out ruder than I'd meant them to.

She blinked and looked away.

"Nothing, I'm sorry. I wasn't meaning to stare, are you hungry?"

"Of course I'm hungry," I replied bluntly.

My stomach was growling, what kind of question was that?

Why wouldn't I be hungry, we hadn't eaten properly for days.

"Here we are, my famous chicken pie!" Father Benedict exclaimed loudly and broke the silence, walking back to the table holding two wooden bowls.

"Apologies, 'tis only warm," he said as he placed a bowl in front of me and then one in front of Del.

I nodded my head in thanks not wanting to talk to the man. The pie smelt delicious, the aroma filled my nostrils and made my mouth water. I picked up the fork resting in the bowl and used it to break off a large mouthful. It tasted just as good as it smelt and almost melted in my mouth.

Maybe this man isn't as bad as I keep thinking, he's being nice to us. Why am I not being nice back to him?

I sat and ate my meal in silence while Del and Father Benedict made small talk that I didn't care to listen to. It was hard to listen anyway with the constant chanting filling my head all the time.

Vessel of treachery, relinquish the light, accept the darkness and aid his plight. Over and over and over.

I was sick of it. But I ignored it and ate my food.

"Hmmmm hm hmhmhm, hmmhmmhmm"

I found myself quietly humming along without realising, as I finished eating.

I looked up from my bowl and Del and Father Benedict were staring at me.

"What… were you just humming child?" Father Benedict asked looking at me suspiciously.

"—It's nothing, just a tune he likes," Del interrupted rudely before I had a chance to respond.

"I can speak for myself, Delaney…" I growled suddenly feeling angry again—angry that this man questioned me, angry that Del answered for me.

Then I realised my voice had come out rough,

crude, not sounding like my own at all and it shocked me.

Father Benedict's face tensed when I spoke, his eyes narrowed for a moment and then softened.

What was happening to me, I feel like I'm changing.

The dreams, the chanting, my voice right now? Pa had told me about puberty once and that I would change when it happened, is that what this was?

"She meant no harm, Kael. By the way, Delaney is an interesting name… you say you both came from Branwick, yes?" Father Benedict said after a short pause.

Del had an odd expression on her face and then replied.

"Yes. Well, no. Not exactly. Kael is from Drassox, I met him when he came to Hiltsten. I lived there," she said, finishing the last mouthful of her chicken pie.

Father Benedict nodded slowly.

"I see… Would you both like to join me in a quick prayer? I believe it proper to thank the Lord for our food."

The word prayer… made my stomach do a flip.

Why should I thank anyone for damn food?

Del didn't seem interested in it either and an awkward silence started to fill the room.

"Oh, come now. Don't be embarrassed. 'Tis not hard, I will lead. Here, take my hands, we're all friends here," he said and reached out, holding a hand towards each of us.

Del looked uncomfortable but reached back and took his hand, lightly nodding for me to do the same.

I had a strong urge that I didn't want to touch him, the thought of it made the sour taste of bile rise in my throat again. I looked past Del and around the room, my eyes finding the wooden cross on the wall again and I hated the sight of it.

I hated that it was there. I wanted it on the floor where it belonged so I could stamp it into pieces.

This house reeked of something I couldn't describe. Something I know I didn't like. I wanted to leave now.

I became aware of the chanting in my head again and began to hum along to the tune once more.

Then I felt a sweaty hand clasp my own and it filled me with rage.

How dare this filth touch me!!!

My vision blurred and shook, my eyes stuck glued to the cross on the wall, unable to look away while I willed with all my mind for it to fall. To take its rightful place on the floor where I could stamp it into dust.

And then it moved.

Slowly, turning upside down. And dropping.

Hitting the ground with a heavy thud.

I felt the hand gripping mine tighten and I snatched it away as hard as I could, I felt my eyes narrow and glare at Father Benedict noticing he was also glaring at me.

"Why, are you leeching off this child, demon…?" He whispered slowly, his voice shaking.

I realised I was frozen in place, like I couldn't move and had no control of my body anymore.

And then without wanting to, I spoke.

"… Os… Claude. SACERADO."

My voice came out rough again, croaky and in words I didn't understand. And then I cackled a dry horrible laugh.

A laugh I've never heard before.

I felt terrified, trapped inside myself like it was some kind of nightmare that I was being forced to watch.

"Do not tell me to shut up, demon! You hold no sway in this house. I am a man of God," Father Benedict snapped back, like he understood exactly what I'd just said.

I felt my mouth stretch into a wide smile, so wide it made my jaw ache and the corners of my lips sting as though they might tear.

"This… child… is my vessel… MINEEEE… I am returning… PRIEST," I heard myself say over the chanting, and then I let out the same loud, evil cackle.

Del sat across from me silently, I could barely see her there with my eyes stuck staring at the priest unable to move them.

"What is your name, demon?" Father Benedict demanded, staring into my eyes.

I didn't answer, my smile just stretched even wider.

"I said tell me your name hell spawn!" He shouted at me.

I heard myself laugh loudly again, the chanting still going and then I whispered one word.

"… Lucifer… ha… ha… ha… ha… HA… HA… HA!"

Father Benedict's face sank when he heard this word, and he looked terrified.

He immediately reached into his robes and pulled out another cross like the one I'd seen on the wall, pushing it towards me and muttering under his breath.

I began to scream.

Loudly, louder than I've ever screamed before. Pain shot through my body, worse than anything I've felt in my life, like my whole body was in a fire. It hurt so much I wanted to cry but my body wouldn't let me.

The closer he came the more the pain grew, and then I heard Del shouting at him to stop what he was doing and jumping up out of her seat.

As I kept screaming the chanting drowned my voice out and I realised I was also laughing that dry horrible cackle at the same time, as though I had two voices at once.

And then I blacked out.

***

"Kael!"

"Kael, you need to wake up!"

"Can you hear me?"

Something lightly slapped my cheek a few times and I opened my eyes. Squinting, I saw it was now daylight but looked to be still very early morning.

As my vision focused, and I opened my eyes properly, I made out Del standing over me trying to wake me up. I was sitting outside on the porch of Father Benedict's house, but his door was shut.

"Del, what just happened?" I asked feeling very groggy still.

She reached down and helped me stand up, I noticed her hands looked like they had red on them.

"We were about to enter this house, and you fainted, Kael. I found some food and supplies inside while you were asleep because I couldn't wake you. We need to get moving though, I don't know how far behind us the soldiers are," she explained in a hurry.

I was confused, had I dreamt about Father Benedict and going inside the home? It'd felt so real.

"But... I went inside with you, Del, and there was a man in there, Father Benedict... and..." I stopped, unsure how to explain what had happened after that.

She put her hands on her hips and looked at me confused.

"Father Benedict?" She asked.

"Well… that's what he said his name was," I mumbled back.

"There was no one inside, you must have dreamt about him Kael, you were out for almost an hour. Anyway, we need to go now. We don't have time to discuss this here, it's not safe remember."

Then she started walking motioning for me to follow, I felt confused, but my dreams had been crazy lately, maybe I really had dreamt it and even though I'd just woken up I still felt exhausted, much too tired to argue right now so I followed after her. We took off towards the mountains that I could now see clearly in the daylight off in the distance on our left as we followed the trail.

CHAPTER 15
ROUGH AWAKENINGS

*'But they who wait for the Lord shall renew their strength;
they shall mount up with wings like eagles; they shall run
and not be weary; they shall walk and not faint'*

I awoke with my eyes fluttering open and blinding light filling my vision, the first thing that entered my mind was that I'd just vomited violently. A mix of salty, river water, and bile had forced its way up my throat and out my mouth so hard it strained my vocal cords.

With drool still dangling from my lips, I became aware of how much pain racked the rest of my body.

It felt as though I'd fallen from a cliff, every joint throbbed.

Next, it dawned on me that I was soaking wet and

freezing, the cold penetrated deep into my bones and my chest felt like it was filled with mucus.

I forced myself to cough a couple of times, trying to clear the rest of the congestion out while I rolled over on the black silt lining the riverbank.

"ACK'! ACCKK'! ARGHCCK…" I coughed again and then flopped back down flat on my back as I finished clearing my throat.

My chest was a little clearer, but I still felt like death frozen over. I realised that I could hear the sound of running water and then my nostrils picked up the musty rotting scent of mold and algae nearby.

I tried to concentrate and remember what had brought me here. It didn't take long for my memories to return and begin to flash through my mind. I remembered the camp the people of Branwick had set up, then Rowan and I walking out onto the bridge, Zarek and his lackey were coming towards us from the other side. We begin talking. And then suddenly I'm fighting for my life, wrestling with Zarek's companion. I see Rowan fall… Zarek tugging his blade free from his body.

Then I'm attacking him with everything I have, but it's not enough. Sounds of battle ring out. I'm running out of time…

And… a bolt hits me?

I look down at my thigh, the projectile is still there sticking out of me. Fucking hell.

It begins to throb now I've reminded myself of it.

I ignore it and keep trying to recall what happened next, I remember the wind being knocked out of me, and then I was falling. Stumbling backwards and off the bridge into the freezing water. I'm struggling to stay afloat in my armour, my leg is refusing to work as I collide with rocks, desperately trying to get a grip on them in the strong current, my hands failing to find purchase. I can't breathe.

Then, nothing.

Blackness.

The next thing I know, I'm waking up broken and battered.

I lay my head back again and realise I just want to go back to sleep.

I'm exhausted, beaten, broken.

No, not broken yet.

Part of me is telling me not to quit, to get up. So, I try to will myself to do it, but my body is so sore that it doesn't want to cooperate, it acts as though it has abandoned me and begs me just to let it rest.

I lay there peering up at the bright blue sky, slowly my eyes begin to adjust to the light and I don't have to squint so much. I notice a few dark, ashen clouds, hanging about but it's otherwise a nice day. Still early too.

A good a day as any to just close my eyes again and never wake up.

Argh. Fuck it, I have nothing left, everyone I know is dead.

Zarek's won. What can a single, broken, old knight do in the face of such insurmountable odds.

Do not be a coward, boy. You are not dead yet.

My father's words suddenly echo through my thoughts and I feel guilty. I know full well that he would roll over in his grave to see me lying here like this, snivelling like a whipped dog that I was beaten all while I still drew breath.

He would never accept any excuse off me when I didn't feel like training or working.

Do you think the enemy could give a shit if you are sick or tired?

He would say that, then drag my carcass out of bed and give me a kick, forcing me to get up. I remember hating him for it at the time but as I grew older, I understood.

Then understand now. Get up and be a man.

The boy needs you.

The boy…

Kael.

Did him and Del escape?

Fuck! I told them to flee if anything happened to me, they're probably on their way north to the mountains right now and that maniac will be following them.

I scolded myself and felt embarrassed for

forgetting about them while I lay here feeling sorry for myself. I need to get up and make sure they are safe.

But first, I have to remove this godforsaken bolt from my bloody thigh I thought as I sat back upright and noticed it still protruding from my upper leg.

Reaching down I tenderly begin to probe the area around the wound, pressing lightly to see how bad the damage is, the wound is tender but from what I can see it has completely missed the bone, which bodes very well for my health.

I roll further onto my side and see what I hoped I would, the head of the bolt is visible out the back.

Luckily, I have some skill in treating wounds, and I know this is going to make the removal much cleaner and easier.

Generally, when an arrow had not passed through completely, more damage is done cutting the flesh to remove it, and I really didn't want to have to cut my flesh either.

Looking on my belt I spotted my dagger, still in its sheathe. The very same dagger I'd taken from Frederick all the way back in Hiltsten and then retrieved off the brigands in Branwick.

Reaching down I drew it, I felt a deep dread for what I was about to do. But it had to be done.

I began using the sharp blade to carefully cut the feathers from the shaft whilst trying my best not to wobble it too much and cause myself unnecessary agony.

The time for that would come soon.

A short time and a few curse words later, I'd successfully managed to shave the flights from the shaft. The clotting around the wound was disturbed and it'd begun to lightly bleed again, not that it mattered.

It was going to be worse shortly.

I paused for a moment gazing at the shaft sticking through my flesh, the time I was dreading had arrived. I knew what I had to do and it had to be done, I just wasn't looking forward to it.

But, I suppose there is no better time than the present I thought with a sigh and placed the leather strap that ran across my chest from my sword sheath into my mouth, clenching my teeth tightly onto it.

I pushed the edge of the dagger blade underneath the head of the bolthead, hooking the broad tip firmly. It stung as it irritated the wound, but I'd already committed to the task.

The pain was irrelevant. This was about survival, I couldn't walk with a fucking bolt in my leg.

Taking a deep breath and using all my strength, I quickly pulled up and away from my body, groaning while the shaft harshly slid its way through muscle and flesh, I felt the wood fibres trying to grip inside the wound as I forced it free, the blood inside of me providing enough lubricant to allow it passage. It gave a satisfying shallow 'pluck' sound, as it popped free from the wound. The relief was almost instant.

"Pah!" I spat on the ground next to me and chucked the broken bolt aside, glad it was out of me.

Sliding my dagger back into its sheathe I began to take note of my surroundings and realised for the first time I was close to the feet of the mountains. I must have been swept a considerable distance upstream as I couldn't see the bridge nor the camp at all anymore.

I slowly rose to my feet, placing weight on my injured leg gingerly, to get an idea of the damage. I was surprised to see it was not as bad as I thought, tender yes, but I could walk well enough. My broken ribs caused me more discomfort than my leg right now, but I wouldn't allow a bit of discomfort to stop me.

I'd studied maps of Blightreach many times, I knew if I kept the mountains on my left and followed them north from here, I should meet up with the road eventually.

So long as Del and boy escaped the camp in time, that's the route they would've taken.

I felt wet, cold and sore but I was alive, that was more than so many others could say right now I thought and began trudging up the riverbank towards the drier ground, where the grass begun to grow.

***

It didn't take long for me to find the road I was searching for, and what I found worried me. I could see hundreds of indents pressed into the earth, all clustered tightly together. They were footprints and there was a lot of them. Even the grass on the sides of the road appeared flattened and trampled. I had enough tracking knowledge from my time hunting and scouting to recognise when a large group had recently passed through an area and that's exactly what this was.

It had to be Zarek's men, and if he was still heading north then it meant he had not yet found the boy.

Which meant he and Del had escaped.

I felt a surge of relief wash over me and rose back to my feet.

He's still alive, I haven't failed him yet.

Since I'd been walking again the pain in my body had almost vanished entirely and it shocked me. I had lost my limp from the bolt and my broken ribs no longer ached when I inhaled air. I knew I should be in a lot more agony than I was currently feeling, it was as though something was keeping my pain at bay. But it wasn't only my lack of pain that baffled me, I also felt like I knew exactly where I was going, like I was being guided along a path I couldn't see and at the same time it was energising me the further I walked upon it.

Like so many things lately, I can't explain it, but I felt younger. I knew what I had to do and I was beginning to wonder if something divine was intervening. I had no explanation for my devotion to helping the boy, but I'd now accepted that it was something I had to do no matter the cost.

"Aaaaarrrrwhooooooooooooooo!" A loud familiar howl suddenly cut through the trees around me, snapping my mind back to the present.

The howl had been distant, but still close enough to cause a shiver to run down my spine. I knew straight away what it was.

There was no mistaking the creature that made that sound, and I now believed wholeheartedly that its presence was no coincidence. I needed to move faster and put some distance between it and myself.

With that in mind I chose to double my pace and continued following the long winding road north. I felt defenceless with a only a dagger to defend myself. If the beast comes though, a dagger is better than nothing, I'll do my best to make it regret attacking me.

***

I'd been walking for the better part of half the day when I saw the house appear in the distance, it stood alone, isolated and out of place here deep in the wilderness.

A very odd place for one to choose to live. Its grey, stone walls stood out among the greenery of the grass and trees, made more obvious by a very faint smoke trail that sifted out into the air above through a chimney on the roof, showing signs the fire inside was almost out, but still smouldering.

As I trudged closer, I began to make out more details. On the front of the building sat a small wooden porched area which was sheltered by a veranda. The door was quite impressive, made of solid oak, it sat tightly shut. Whoever had built this home was a skilled carpenter, the way the wood had been worked was expertly done.

If the owner was the builder, it seemed odd that a man like this had chosen a life of solitude, his skills would've been in high demand in any of the nearby towns.

I stepped up onto the porch and almost instantly a feeling of sadness and dread passed over me, and somehow, I knew a terrible thing had occurred here.

Death was around, I could feel it deep in my bones.

The hair on the back of my neck stood on edge, I looked around the porch searching for a sign that might warn me if danger lay inside the home, but nothing appeared amiss. Nothing except the feeling of dread that lingered, refusing to pass.

I stood there a moment hesitating, considering my options.

Eventually my curiosity won out, maybe my trepidation was unwarranted. Fuck it, there's only one way to find out.

"Is anyone there?" I called loudly enough for someone inside to hear but quiet enough to not attract unwanted attention.

Silence followed as I waited anxiously for a reply, but none came. I waited a moment longer and still nothing.

My heart began to thud faster as I quickly made the decision to open the door, reaching out with a clammy hand I grasped the door handle, my other hand clenching around my dagger preparing to draw it if need be.

I turned the doorknob and it gave a rusty squeak as I did so, making me cringe. I slowly pushed inwards to reveal the interior.

Immediately my nostrils were assaulted by the tangy metallic taste of blood. Lots of it. The amount that told me someone had died here, and brutally.

"Hello?" I called out in a low voice, although in my mind I didn't believe I would receive a reply.

My eyes scanned the dim interior, the open doorway lit up half the room while a fireplace on the other side gave out a faint glow which struggled to produce enough light to reveal the other half. I could see enough to make out a table on the dark side of the room and a large bookshelf sitting against the far wall but that was it.

I stepped cautiously inside, careful not to make too much noise even though I knew anyone in here would already be well aware of my presence.

"If anyone's in here, reveal yourself. Now. I won't ask kindly again," I called, my tone firmer to let them know I wasn't in the mood to be trifled with.

Still, no reply came.

The feeling of dread had heightened since I entered the room, and the further in I walked the stronger the scent of death became, something dark had occurred here I was certain.

I approached the centre where the table lay, two chairs on opposite sides had been pushed out and left, each had an empty bowl in front of them. A third chair had sat at the end but now lay fallen on its back, and beyond it I could make out a dark shape resting still on the floor.

Even in the dark, I recognised a body when I saw one.

I walked towards it and hunched over the figure where it lay, as I did so my feet slipped in a wet liquid that had pooled on the floor, it'd been nearly invisible in the dim light. I barely regained my balance, saving myself before falling completely and muttered a curse, scolding myself for my clumsiness.

I tried again, squatting down successfully this time, immediately I could make out the features of the body laying beneath me.

It was a bald man in mahogany brown robes, his throat had been viciously cut open with a blade. Deep slash wounds crisscrossed his face, opening his cheeks wide enough to reveal white bone underneath. He'd been stabbed repeatedly, all over his body. Even his eyes had been stabbed, it looked as though his attacker had gone into a frenzy.

Something about it seemed oddly familiar and then I realised why. The man Del had killed in Hiltsten when she freed me, he had been brutalised in a similar fashion.

Could she have done this? The longer I looked at his mutilated corpse the more it certainly looked that way.

Something in his hand caught my eye, whatever it was he'd been clutching it tightly when he died. Then the rigour mortis had set in and stiffened his joints, forcing him to hang onto the item after his soul left his body.

I reached down and gently pried his lifeless fingers open, pulling the object free to examine it.

It was a small cross, attached to a set of rosary beads. This man had obviously been a Christian priest.

What would have made the woman kill this man? This didn't make any sense. Surely a priest could've helped the boy, that was the whole reason she wanted to take him to her commune in the mountains in the first place.

I gently placed the cross over the man's head and around his neck, positioning it on his chest. It would have to do instead of a funeral I thought and rose back to my feet to look around further.

I walked to the other side of the table, as I stepped near to the fireplace my foot kicked something in the dark making me stop.

I reached down to pick it up.

It was another cross, larger than the one the priest now wore, rather the size you might mount on a wall. Holding it I turned back to the table and that was when I saw something that made my blood run cold.

Deep claw marks were gouged into the table area in front of one of the chairs. As though someone had sat there, and clawed into solid oak with their fingernails, something no human being should be able to do.

Because, it had not been a human that sat there.

No, it was a demon.

Lucifer was beginning to take hold of the boy. I realised that it was not dread I could feel in the air. It was pure evil.

And this entire home reeked of it.

"AAAARRRRRRWHOOOOOOOOOOOO!" The hairs on the back of my neck stood up as another howl cut through the air interrupting my thoughts.

This time it was much closer, I was running out of time. I needed to move now.

CHAPTER 16
LOSING HOPE

'Do not throw away your confidence; it will be richly rewarded. You need to persevere so that when you have done the will of God, you will be richly rewarded'

I was struggling to keep up, trailing a few paces behind Del as I followed her. Every step I planted felt harder than the last since we'd turned off the main road and onto a narrow dirt path that spiralled upward, high into the mountains a few hours ago now. This journey felt like it'd never end, even though she'd told me it wasn't much further.

My mind felt muddy, exhausted, like I was half asleep or in a daze and the longer we walked the worse it got. It was taking all my concentration just to focus on putting one foot in front of the other and not fall asleep. I didn't want to sleep, I was terrified to fall asleep again. Every time I almost did, I saw flashes of the darkness… and the monster's face was there, waiting for me.

I couldn't let myself fall asleep.

I would've missed the narrow track if Del didn't point it out, it was overgrown, and barely noticeable. At the start it'd been almost flat but that had changed fast, and it became steep, then the air had grown colder the higher we climbed.

Not that I cared though, I was so hot I could barely feel the cold, like when I used to get sick, and Mother would say I was burning up with a fever.

Sweat poured from my brow, stinging my eyes when it ran into them, it felt like a fire was raging inside of me, keeping me warm on purpose. I knew I should be cold, it was windy and Del had wrapped a blanket around herself to block it out, twice she'd asked me if I wanted my own blanket, but both times I'd told her I was fine and she just shrugged.

The mountains looked different up closely than they had when we were further away. Now, they just looked like steep hills.

The trail was all brown dirt when we started, but now it had begun to turn white from the snow. I'd never seen snow before, and I would've been more excited about it if I wasn't missing Mother, Pa and Lothar like I was.

Since Lothar had fallen I felt so much more alone, not just alone but hopeless. Lothar had been the one to save me from the dark closet when everyone else was gone, I thought he was so strong that nothing could hurt him. But I'd been wrong, I knew now that no one was that strong. His death felt like a bad dream I couldn't wake up from and no matter how hard I tried to block it from my mind it just kept coming back.

Only Del was left now, and she hadn't spoken much since we left the house. Father Benedict's house.

That was the other thing that I couldn't stop thinking about. Del said I'd been sleeping outside and never even gone in there, but I was so sure I had. I could remember exactly what it looked like inside, the taste of Father Benedict's 'famous' chicken pie, and what happened in there… it just seemed too real to only be a dream.

Since then, the chanting in my mind hadn't stopped either, not even for a moment. It was faint but it was always there, and it scared me.

Something was happening to me, and I had no idea what it was or even how to describe it.

"We should be at the commune before nightfall, Kael," Del said, turning her head back to me and breaking the silence between us.

"Good. I don't know how much longer I can walk, it's so steep," I replied, panting.

"It is. The commune is on the mountain peak, so

it's quite the climb, but we'll be safe there. Here, drink some more water," she said, pulling a goatskin bladder from her pack and passing it to me.

I took it from her hands thirstily, from the weight I could tell that it was almost empty. I took a small swig, it was cold but did nothing to stop the burning inside of me.

I offered it back to her, but she shook her head.

"No, I'm fine. You drink it all, you're sweating so much you need to replace it."

She was right, I was sweating a lot and didn't need to be told twice so I lifted the bladder to my lips again and swallowed the rest of the water, my dry lips and throat thanked me for it.

She took the empty bladder back from me and stored it back in her pack and then pulled her blanket tightly around herself again with a shudder.

"Del, what's happening to me?" I blurted out as she turned to start walking again.

Her head jerked up and she stopped in her tracks.

"… What do you mean, Kael?"

A burst of anger shot through me, what the hell did she think I meant? I was starting to think she knew more than she was letting on and I was sick of being lied too.

"You KNOW, what I mean. Tell me," I replied through clenched teeth, and put my hands on my hips.

She breathed a deep sigh.

"You've been through a lot these past few days. You've witnessed things a child shouldn't ever have to see. Things that can take a toll on anyone, especially a boy as young as yourself. I'm taking you to some people that can help you and keep us safe. I promised your mother long ago I would look out for you, and I promised Lothar too."

I stared at her and felt tears well in my eyes as she mentioned Lothar's name, I sniffed and looked away trying to hide my wet eyes.

She just stood there waiting for me to reply.

"How can you be sure we'll be safe there though?" I asked finally, while using my shirt sleeve to wipe my eyes dry.

"Because I know the people there and they're prepared to protect us. Just trust me, Kael, it'll all be better soon. You'll see. Come, let's keep moving, Zarek isn't far behind. Stay close to me," she said, taking my hand into hers for a moment, and looking into my eyes.

I stared back at her and slowly nodded.

She gave me a light hug, let go of my hand and then started walking again. I watched her for a moment and slowly began following once more up the steep trail.

I wanted to believe she was right, and it would all be better soon but a feeling of doubt inside my heart was making me question her promises.

Why did you have to leave me Lothar?

CHAPTER 17

A DIVINE ENCOUNTER

'The Lord is faithful, and he will strengthen you and protect you from the evil one'

"AAARRRWHHHOOOOOOOOOOOOOOOO!!!" Another loud, bellowing howl, cut through the air around me once more.

It was getting close now, the cursed creature had been following me for some time but thus far, had thankfully chosen to keep its distance.

Occasionally when I glanced back into the woods, I'd caught a glimpse of its thick black fur darting amongst the foliage in the distance. It was black as the darkest night, and I would be lying if I said it didn't concern me and cause my legs to quicken their pace.

Still, I was well aware that worrying wouldn't help

me, so I ignored it and pressed forward as I'd done since I awoke on the riverbank this morning half drowned.

I knew it was no longer a matter of if the beast attacked anymore, but when. And I was as ready as I would ever be.

For reasons unknown to me, my body had returned to full strength, like that I was ten summers younger. All my aches and pains had vanished, the wound on my leg while still there, felt surprisingly numb and hindered me in no way, apparently by some miracle not of my making. I wasn't complaining, I would need all the help I could get when the time came.

The tracks had been easy to follow so far, Zarek had no one left to challenge him and therefore, made no attempt to hide his movements. No one except me, although I doubted that would've worried him, he probably thought me dead and if he did then, I'd make it his downfall.

The man had bested me twice now, before this was over, I swore to end his life regardless of the cost. I would die before I allowed there to be a third time.

It was getting late into the afternoon, the sun had begun to dip towards the horizon but there was still some time of daylight left and I planned to use it. I was nearing the mountains and had been keeping a close eye out for a path that would lead me up into them.

It would be cold when the sun set and travel through the night nigh' on impossible, unless I wanted to risk freezing to death, which meant I would need to find somewhere safe to sleep eventually.

Eventually, but not yet.

I stopped walking for a moment and reached into my satchel to remove the waterskin I'd found in the priest's house earlier. His dead body flashed through my mind, I didn't feel guilty about taking the water, he was hardly going to use it anymore, but I was still confused as to how he'd met his fate.

I tugged free the wooden cork and took a long scull of the cool water inside, feeling it run down my throat quenching my thirst.

While I stood there listening to the sound of my own gulping, it suddenly dawned on me how eerily quiet my surroundings had become. No birds or insects chirped anymore, and even the woods themselves seemed as though they'd become deathly silent. It was like every living thing around me had suddenly become terrified to make even the slightest of sounds.

Not a good sign.

I felt the hairs on the back of my neck begin to stand on end, my every sense screaming at me that I was being watched. I froze and stopped swallowing, still holding the waterskin to my lips and listened intently trying my best to hear a sound. Anything that would break the eerie silence.

I waited.

And then it came, with the crunching of twigs and a deep, low rumble from not far behind me.

Fuck. Not a rumble, a deep throaty growl.

A growl that I knew came from a dire wolf.

I snapped into action and reached down for the dagger on my belt, letting go of the waterskin. Time appeared to slow, my mind begged me to move, and I knew I had to act fast. I didn't hesitate, the trees blurred into one as I spun to face the threat head on, but I wasn't quick enough.

The rotten odour of wet dog overcame my nostrils as a large, heavy, weight hit me hard from the side, sending me tumbling away into the bushes. I recovered quickly and bounced back to my feet with surprising agility, bringing my dagger to hand.

The time had come.

The wolf wasted no time charging for me again, but this time I was ready. Swiftly stepping back out of range of its snapping jaws I slashed downwards reflexively, slicing the top of its skull wide open revealing white bone as the skin parted. It issued a loud yelp and retreat backwards in shock.

We stood there, ten paces apart circling each other.

The wolf, slowly let a low growl escape its snarling lips as it pawed at the cut on its head, clearly surprised it had ended up second best in the surprise exchange.

"You like that, fucking cursed spawn! You aren't preying on children now, come on!!" I bellowed loudly, trying to feign that I wasn't scared.

Perhaps more to convince myself than anything else, while inside my heart felt like it was trying to leap from my chest.

I gripped the blade of my dagger with sweaty palms as hard as I could, knowing to lose it would be the end, the entire time keeping my eyes locked with the animal in front of me.

Its own eyes bore back into mine with nothing but pure hatred and murderous intent as we continued slowly circling, daring each other to make the next move.

"Well, what are you waiting for demon. I haven't got all fucking day," I spat, attempting to bait it into attacking.

Praying on a hope that I could use such a moment to launch a counterattack and make it pay again.

My eyes shifted slightly to my dagger that I held defensively in front of me, hells be damned I wished it was a spear right now. I scolded myself for not making one when I'd had the chance.

Fuck it, beggars can't be choosers.

"GRAHH!!" I growled loudly and feinted forward with a short stab, again trying to tempt the creature into snapping but it smartly recoiled, just out of range.

I tried to antagonise it several more times as we

continued to circle, but it refused to take the bait. Instead, it just hunched there, poised, and prepared to pounce at the first opportunity.

Staring with its dark, soulless eyes.

Eyes that showed an unnatural intelligence for a cur and were as dark as the hair that covered its body, hair that right now stood upright in a line down the centre of its back, making it appear even more menacing.

The wolf knew I couldn't escape and seemed content with waiting for the right moment to attack, the right time to tear me to shreds and feast on my flesh.

I was at a severe disadvantage in this fight, and I knew it.

The tension in the air was palpable, being this close with no protective shelter between us made me feel very exposed and realise just how massive this beast really was.

Its head, even hunched low to its shoulders as it were, sat over my waist height and was easily twice the size of a normal wolf.

Standing at full height on all fours it could only be a head shorter than myself. Strong corded muscles rippled underneath its coat, and its tendons were visible also, pulled taut like a bowstring ready to be released.

Ready to propel the mouthful of razor-sharp teeth

for my jugular.

The worst thing though, was the smell of its breath. It stank like it'd been eating rotting meat, as though it feasted on corpses. The smell was overpowering to the senses making it difficult to concentrate.

A stringy glob of drool oozed from its mouth as it no doubt hungrily, predicted the meal to come while eyeing me off.

Standing there waiting the silence was deafening, my heart continued to beat wildly in my chest like a drum and my forehead ran freely with a nervous sweat.

I knew that to try to run, to show any fear whatsoever, would be certain death. I had no intention of it anyway, it wasn't in me to tuck tail and flee, I was prepared to fight to the death.

A rustle in the bushes somewhere behind the wolf broke the focus between us, making its ears perk up, tilting slightly in the direction of the sound, homing in on the disturbance for a moment.

Whatever it heard it didn't like, as it reacted by suddenly spinning its entire body to face whatever had made the noise while releasing a loud, angry snarl. The creature had quickly decided that whatever was coming was a bigger threat than me. A stupid mistake for a stupid animal.

I prepared to take advantage of the moment but what I saw next made me pause in my tracks.

The bushes nearby suddenly parted, revealing gleaming white fur and an enormous set of antlers that came crashing through the shrubbery at an astonishing speed, seeming hellbent on destroying anything in their path.

I recognised it straight away.

The majestic white stag had somehow, returned. I'd been sure the wolf had killed it, yet here it was unharmed before my very eyes. Immediately I was overcome with a sense of calming and thoughts to not to be afraid, that all would be fine.

I knew the stag only wanted the wolf. And so, I did the only thing I could to help it win the battle this time.

I lunged forward and planted my dagger down hard, firmly driving it into the wolf's back, right where I could see the bumps of the creature's spine. I felt the blade hit something solid, likely bone, before sliding in with a satisfying crackle as it wedged in and forced the vertebrae apart, severing the mongrel's spine. It yelped a loud screeching wail and then its back legs collapsed underneath it, apparently unable to hold its own weight anymore, mere seconds before the stag closed the distance.

The charging stag was a ferocious sight, forcing me to dive out of the way as it skidded forward, lowering its head underneath the wolf's chest and then in one powerful motion, flicking upwards and catapulting the demon high into the air while at the same time lacerating its chest open when the antlers made contact.

The wolf unable to break its fall since I had severed the use of its back legs, hit the ground with a heavy thud and let out another low painful whine. The stag showing no hesitation or mercy pounced and charged forward again, smashing its antlers into the wolf's face and sending it skidding across the ground once more, violently colliding into a nearby tree trunk.

I rose to my feet, recovering from my frantic dive and backed up, giving space to the two behemoths.

The wolf was still whining but valiantly tried to rise once more to defend itself. It was a brave but futile attempt.

The stag seeing this, immediately charged once more, this time squashing the wolf against the trunk so hard that it shat itself and faeces littered the forest floor where it lay.

Whether this was from the pressure of the charge or fear of the end I don't know, maybe it was a bit of both.

The stag stepped back triumphantly, releasing the pressure and letting the wolf fall back to the ground, free from its crushing antlers.

Clearly defeated, the wolf didn't try to rise again after this last attack, although I doubted it could even if it wanted to. Its breaths were now coming out rapid and shallow, likely taking in its final moments.

With a heavy snort, the stag rose high on its back legs and came down heavily onto the wolf's head with its two front hooves completely obliterating its skull.

The visceral crack and crunch of bones was clearly audible as its hooves connected, finishing its arch enemy off and silencing the great beast forever.

The final blow the stag dealt instilled in me flashes of a memory when I'd done similar to a man not long after I rescued the boy from the town hall, a time not long passed which almost seemed an age ago now.

I stood there frozen, staring at the great stag in shock. It still had its back to me and its attention seemed to be fixated on the broken remains on the forest floor in front of it, as though it expected the beast to rise up once more although I was sure that couldn't be possible.

It roughly prodded the carcass with its massive hoof but garnered no response.

Although I sensed the stag meant me no harm, I couldn't help but feel uneasy that any sudden movement could set the animal off and cause me to suffer a similar fate.

So, I waited a moment longer, almost holding my breath to keep as silent as possible and just watched it.

The stag prodded the carcass again, harder this time and I heard the broken skull 'click' as the shattered bones moved around inside the skin. The dire wolf was most definitely dead there could be no doubt to that, but the stag still made no effort to leave.

In my mind I knew the longer I stay here the further ahead Zarek was getting, I was hoping the stag would leave so I could retrieve my dagger, but it wasn't moving, which I figured meant I should while it was still interested in the wolf and hope it stayed that way.

There was no point in risking my life over a dagger, it was time to go. I carefully took my first step back towards the road, which I could still see only a short distance away.

Once I was on it, I would continue following it to the northwest and hopefully find the trail into the mountains Del had told me about in our travels.

I took another step, staying careful to remain as silent as possible, still the stag gave no reaction and I relaxed a little.

Unfortunately, it was my third step that did get the stag's attention, causing it to turn around and face me, making my blood run cold as it glared into my eyes.

I instantly froze.

I noticed its eyes had an oddly human intelligence to them but still, my whole body tensed, preparing to defend myself if it came to it. Even though I had no weapon I'd fight tooth and nail if that is what it came to.

You will not need to do that.' A beautiful feminine voice suddenly echoed in my mind, as clear as my own thoughts.

I jerked, startled.

What the fuck? Am I losing my mind? I thought staring at the stag. Yet somehow it no longer appeared to be glaring menacingly at me, it looked… almost friendly.

'No, you are not, Lothar. Please, you must listen to me. I do not have much time. You need to get to Kael, he is not safe.'

I heard the voice in my mind again and the stag lifted one of its front hooves then gently tapped it on the ground.

"Is that… you talking?" I asked out loud, half feeling like a mad man.

Maybe all the beatings I'd taken lately had muddled my senses and driven me mad.

'Your senses are not muddled, and you are not mad. I have healed your injuries, but my power has grown weak in death. I cannot help you again.' You must go now. Kael needs you," it said.

Suddenly, my miraculous recovery made sense.

"Who are you!?" I demanded, stepping forward.

The stag looked back at me, a gleaming, luminous glow beginning to radiate from its pure white coat.

'My name is Mirella.'

Mirella? The boy's mother.

That made no sense, the last time I seen this creature it had tried to charge the boy. Her child.

'I was not charging at my baby. I saw Lucifer, standing behind him in shadow. The wolf attacked me to protect its master. Please hurry, Lothar. Save my child, only you can. You have been chosen to be his guardian…'

She started turning away from me and the light grew brighter.

"Wait! What do you mean I've been chosen as his guardian!? How am I meant to save him from the fucking Devil!?" I shouted, taking another step forward toward her.

She looked back to me.

'You must find a way, guardian.' And with those final words the glow became a blinding light, so bright it hurt to look at and I was forced to shield my eyes.

And just like that, the light vanished. When I was able to see clearly again the great white stag was gone as though it had never been there.

I looked forth in shock, unable to believe what had just happened, and I may not have believed it, if not for the proof all around me, in the form of the trampled grass, and the mangled, deceased body, of a large black dire wolf which still had my dagger sticking out of its lower back.

CHAPTER 18

THE COMMUNE

'Those who worship false gods, turn their backs on all God's mercy'

"Vessel of treachery! Relinquish the light! Accept the darkness and aid his plight! Vessel of treachery! Relinquish the light! Accept the darkness and aid his plight!" The voices sung around me so quickly that the words started to sound all jumbled together.

Somehow, I was alone in the blackness again and the monster was coming for me. It was the only thing in the dark that I could make out and I wished it would disappear.

Why was I back here? When would this stop happening to me?

One moment, I was walking behind Del in the daylight and the next, I was here again.

The orange glow blazing around the monster's body lit up the terrifying face that kept haunting my dreams. Its curled horns stuck out from its ugly head, all twisted like the roots of an old tree… and that wide evil grin stared at me, filled with sharp pointy teeth that looked like they could tear me apart.

I wanted to be brave and fight, to draw my sword again like last time, like Lothar would if he was here.

Like he always had, until he fell.

Arghhh! I want to kill it once and for all! I hate it!

I wanted to but I couldn't, because I couldn't move. My body was frozen stiff and it wouldn't do what I wanted it to, I was helpless and could only watch while it came for me.

Why did this keep happening to me, what did it want from me? Why won't it just leave me alone!

"Kael?" A faint voice echoed somewhere nearby, but when I tried to open my mouth to reply, my jaw or lips wouldn't move.

I couldn't take my eyes off the thing coming my way, its face was getting clearer with every step it took and when I finally saw its eyes, the smile on its face grew bigger, like it knew it was finally going to get me this time.

I begged my legs to move, I begged my hands to reach for my sword, but they ignored me.

The monster let out a long, deep growl, while it kept on walking forward, slowly gaining on me.

It was close now I could smell its putrid breath again, it stunk like wet dog. The air that came from its mouth hit me straight in the face and was so hot it burnt my cheeks and nose.

I was terrified, it felt like I couldn't breathe. I wanted to cry but I couldn't even make myself do that.

It had me this time. It was going to eat me. Slowly.

My body started shaking uncontrollably.

"Kael!" The voice called my name again, shouted it this time.

It was Del. She was coming for me!

Hearing her voice made me realise I wasn't alone and some of my terror left me. The monster seemed annoyed it was being interrupted and its smile turned to an angry snarl, it went to reach for me, opening its mouth wide as if it was going to swallow me whole when suddenly its movement slowed, like it was held back by an invisible force.

Then out of nowhere I felt my shoulders being squeezed, and I wobbled back and forth, like someone had grabbed me and began to shake me.

"Kael!"

All around in the darkness I saw small, bright stars start to light up and glow, then swirl like a storm of fireflies spiralling around the monsters reaching arm until that blurred into the swirling mess of light as well.

I squinted and squeezed my eyes shut, terrified I was going to be taken away with it as well, but somehow it was over just like that as fast as it had begun, and I could see normally again.

My eyes tried to focus, and I blinked to clear them, looking around dripping with sweat and breathing hard.

Del was standing in front of me with her hands on my shoulders, shaking me.

"Snap out of it, Kael. Breathe," she ordered, her voice sharp as she pointed ahead of us.

"We're here, at my home. Just a little further and it'll all be over alright? Stay with me," she pleaded, letting go of my shoulders.

Exhausted, I mumbled "Yes," and we started walking again.

I was finding it hard to keep my eyes open and my head felt heavy and sore, but I pushed myself to stay close to her.

We'd arrived on a clearing atop the mountain, the view from up here was like nothing I'd ever seen, everything below looked so small. In happier times I would've loved being up here, but this wasn't happy times.

Not far in front of us I could see a tall stone wall that ran all the way across the clearing, right to the mountain's edges. It looked like it stopped us from going any further, I couldn't see much past that except the roof of a tall building a way back.

There was a big wooden door in the middle of the wall and Del seemed to be taking us towards that. I hoped she knew how to open it because I couldn't see any handles.

As we got closer, I started to feel unsure I wanted her to open it, it was like something inside of me was saying I should run as fast as I could back down the mountain without stopping.

I didn't feel the cold, but I couldn't stop myself from shaking.

The chanting in my head had gotten louder now too, it just wouldn't stop, I hated it. It came out even faster and the words had become really hard to make out, I just kept doing my best to ignore it even though it was almost impossible now.

I knew I needed to stay brave, I was with Del, and she wouldn't let anything bad happen to me and I wouldn't let anything bad happen to her either. She was the only friend I had left.

I wasn't losing anyone again.

I couldn't.

When we made it to the big wooden door Del stepped forward and drew her dagger making my heart jump in my chest worrying we were being attacked, but it turned out she was just using the hilt of it to bang on the door.

I nervously counted the thuds as she knocked in my head, trying to use them to block out the chanting, I was trying anything now to make it stop.

'One. Two. Three. Four. Five. Six.'

Del waited a moment and then banged again.

'One. Two. Three. Four. Five. Six.'

I watched patiently, but still no one answered.

She tried it one last time.

'One. Two. Three. Four. Five. Six.'

The final thud echoed in my head, droning out the chanting for a second which I was happy for, and Del took a step back from the door.

"Maybe no one's home?" I whispered after a moment, but she rudely shushed me.

I was about to tell her to shush herself when the wooden door clanked heavily from the other side making me jump, it sounded like something was being moved and I started to sweat nervously even more than I already was.

The door slowly started to swing open with a long, loud creak. It could use some oil I thought to myself, and then stepped closer to Del, unsure what was going to be waiting for us on the other side.

I didn't trust anyone anymore, people were all so mean.

I hated them. I hated all of them.

I went to draw my sword just in case, but Del reached back and stopped me, putting her hand on mine, "Calm down, Kael. You won't need that, I know these people. Trust me."

I listened to her and put my hand back down, even though I wasn't fully convinced, then waited. When the door finally opened, six men in dark leather armour like Del wore were waiting, steam was coming from their mouths from the cold as they breathed, and all of them had thick black robes on over their armour, probably to keep them warm from all the snow and wind.

I felt like I should've had my blanket on too, but I was just so hot I couldn't stop sweating. I didn't understand why I wasn't feeling the cold, it was strange, it looked like it was freezing up here, but I felt like I was on fire inside.

Burning. Like the monster's breath.

The man at the front of the group stepped forward and bowed his head, I noticed he looked a little older than Lothar and had short hair with a long, thick, grey beard.

My chest hurt every time I thought of Lothar, I wished he were here, I missed him so much.

"Delaney, you've returned from your post. You look well. I hope for your sake though, that you show with good reason," the man said, and it almost sounded like he was threatening her.

His eyes glanced down at me when Del replied.

"Vesper. Yes, and I wouldn't have unless my task

was complete, I must see the Grandmaster at once. Time is short, the Order of St Michael has been on our tail for days. I tried to lose them before ascending the mountain path but failed, I fear they're on their way here as we speak. You must prepare the men," she finished, bowing her head back the way he had.

Vesper frowned and whispered something to one of the men with him. The other man nodded and quickly ran off towards the big building behind the wall, then Vesper turned back to face Del.

"We knew it would come to this, Delaney, and we are ready. Do you know the size of the approaching force?" He asked, but Del shook her head.

"I can't be sure, Vesper. A man we'd travelled with heard rumours of one hundred strong, but many have since been killed fighting with townsfolk to the south."

He made a clicking sound with his tongue and stared at me. "Let's hope it's less than that. You're positive that this is the child though, Delaney?"

Del put her hand on my shoulder protectively.

"There is no doubt, Vesper. He is here among us."

I had no idea what she was talking about, so just stood there, listening to the two of them talk.

"I hope for your sake you're right and haven't brought the Order upon us for nothing. Now make haste, the Grandmaster will be awaiting you, Delaney. Let him know that I am preparing the defence. I'll grant as much time for the ritual as I'm able."

"I'm not wrong, Vesper, I promise you. I will let him know. Good luck brother, and glory to the chosen few," she said.

"Glory to the chosen few," he replied back to her, and I noticed the other men said the same thing as well, almost as one.

With that, Vesper stepped aside, nodding for the rest of the men with him to do the same.

Del turned to me and said hurriedly, "Come on, Kael. We're almost safe, hang in there just a little while longer, okay?"

Exhausted I nodded and started to stumble along behind her still feeling like I might fall asleep again at any moment.

I was worried that if I even blinked, I might open my eyes and be in the blackness again and it terrified me.

I didn't want to be here in this place either, but I trusted Del knew what was best for us, I just needed to hold on like she said.

"Oh. And, Vesper?" Del said as we began to pass through the doors.

"Yes, Delaney?" He replied impatiently.

"The one leading them, is a man called Zarek."

Vesper's frown deepened, and I could tell he knew Zarek's name and didn't like hearing it. He wiped his brow with the back of his glove, and nodded again, then began yelling out orders to his men to begin preparations.

Del moved fast but I did my best to keep up with her as we crossed through the door in the wall, once we were on the other side I was amazed to see that there was pretty much a small village the size of Hiltsten hidden up here!

It only had one road and from what I saw it led straight from the wall to a really large building right in the middle of the town. Stone homes like the ones I'd seen in Branwick were scattered around us and I remembered Del said they had a quarry here as well, so it made sense they would be similar.

The sight of the large building at the end of the road got my attention, I'd never seen anything like it, it was gigantic. It was so amazing it actually made me wake up a little and almost forget the voices singing in my head for a moment.

It reminded me of the stories Pa had told me of massive buildings that used to be around before the Great War, he called them castles, I think. He said only the most important people were allowed to live in them.

While I followed Del towards the building, my mind started to wander back to a better time. A time when Pa was telling me stories about the castles from before the Great War, before all the horses were killed and people didn't have to walk everywhere. I would sit on his knee listening in awe thinking how amazing it'd be to ride atop one of these animals, the fireplace burned warmly and Mother would be cooking dinner listening to his stories with a smile on her face.

Everything was just the way it used to be.

I asked Pa if he'd ever ridden a horse before and he just laughed, then told me they were all gone before he was born. He told me how his father had ridden them many times and told him about it when he was my age. Mother called to us that dinner was ready, and I turned my head to look at her.

As I sat there, I became aware the room had grown dim, like the fire was beginning to go out, I expected Pa to get up to add another log, but he didn't move.

Shadows started to flicker over Mother's face and her smile fell away from her face. Her expression looked odd, but I couldn't understand why.

She was Mother but not Mother anymore.

I opened my mouth to ask her what was wrong but when I spoke no sound came out, my heart began to beat wildly as I realised what this meant.

I had fallen asleep and was dreaming again. I had to be.

I turned to Pa for help, but his face started to change as well, except much more than Mother's. The whites of his eyes turned red, and his mouth started to stretch into a wide smile, so wide I saw his lips tearing open. His teeth grew long and sharp and his skin became scaly like a lizard. Horns began to pop through his forehead, ripping the skin open as they forced their way out and turned him into the monster from my dreams.

I tried to scream, to kick, to fight my way free, but I was frozen in place on his knee, held by something I couldn't see. I moved my eyes to look at Mother and saw she was holding a long thin knife in her hands, still with that same odd look frozen on her face that made her seem like a stranger.

I watched in horror while Mother slowly put the knife to her throat and began sawing back and forth.

Straight away, blood poured out of her neck, tears ran down her face and her eyes didn't leave my own the entire time.

The monster next to me that used to be Pa began to laugh, a deep, evil cackle that sounded nothing like him and seemed to mix with the chanting in my head, making it even louder.

I felt tears running down my own cheeks and then warmth between my legs like I wet myself.

I wanted someone to save me, but I was all alone.

Suddenly, I heard the sound of voices cut over the monsters cackling.

"Ah, Initiate Delaney. I had word that you had returned. And with great news it appears?" Someone said, and my eyes fluttered open, waking me from my nightmare.

I blinked and looked around trying to remember

where I was, if I was really awake and not still trapped in a nightmare.

The castle maybe? It looked like I was inside of it now, it was dark and I didn't like that, I wanted to be back in the sunlight where I felt safer.

"Grandmaster Ravak," Del said, bowing.

"I've returned at great haste… and with the child."

She put her hand on my shoulder and smiled at the old man in front of us. He looked like he was a hundred years old, and he was dressed in funny black robes. I could see there were other people around us as well, they all wore dark robes like the ones the men wore outside except these people didn't have leather armour on underneath.

They were all looking at me and smiling, and in the middle of us all was a large stone table with four chains coming from each corner.

Something seemed wrong.

No, something was definitely wrong.

I looked up at Del nervously but the man spoke again before I built the courage to ask her what was happening.

"Are you sure this is he, Delaney? How can you be certain?"

Still bowing, Del replied.

"I am, Grandmaster. I, with my very own eyes have borne witness to his absolute power, to his ruthlessness. There is no doubt left in my mind… this is the one we seek."

What? Who do they think I am? What is going on right now?

Everyone around us gasped and their smiles grew wider, some of them clapped and a few even mumbled 'glory to the chosen few' like I'd heard the Vesper man outside say.

The Grandmaster, looking pleased, raised his hand after a moment, and they all stopped cheering, quieting down.

"This is most welcome news. You have remained true to the meaning of your name, Delaney, you truly are… the descendant of the dark challenger!"

Del blushed and bowed her head again, looking the happiest I had ever seen her, like she might cry.

"You shall be remembered in our annals for all eternity. Initiate Delaney, the one who returned our dark lord to us. Our powerful Prince—Lucifer, will finally return… AND LEAD THE CHILDREN OF SAMAEL TO PROSPERITY!!" The old man yelled loudly, and another round of cheers and clapping went up in the room.

Suddenly, I was grabbed by two of the men in robes and I panicked, I knew I should never have come here.

"Del, stop them! Tell them to stop! Please, help me! Please!" I screamed while they started to drag me over to the stone table, but she just ignored me and kept looking at the old man, with happiness on her face and tears of joy in her eyes.

"Your act of betrayal will be the catalyst needed to strengthen Lucifer's will over the child's soul, Delaney, and aid him in crossing the final circle—the circle of treachery! You alone have exceeded anyone's expectations and truly brought glory to the chosen few," the old man continued.

"Thank you, Grandmaster! Thank you!" Del said, her voice breaking now as she spoke.

I looked around with tears in my eyes, I wasn't strong enough to break free from the men and I didn't want to try anymore. How could Del do this to me? She was my friend.

No, she isn't. You have no friends.

Lothar was your only friend and he's dead and gone just like Mother and Pa.

"Tonight, my brethren, we shall meet our Prince! Prepare the summoning ritual at haste. Glory to the chosen few!" Another cheer went up as they started chaining my wrists and ankles to the stone table in the dark building.

I didn't fight back, I just began to sob.

CHAPTER 19

THE GUARDIAN ARRIVES

'Behold, I send an angel before you to guard you on the way;
and to bring you to the place I have prepared'

Zarek and his cohorts tracks had remained easy to follow, even easier since I'd begun to ascend the mountain path.

It had been easier to spot than I expected even as the ground quickly became dusted white with snow, which only grew thicker the higher I climbed until eventually the dirt no longer remained visible.

I'd fully intended to stop and rest along the way, to wait for the morning sun to rise and ensure I was at full strength for my arrival at the Commune.

However, in the time since my interaction with Mirella, I had experienced a feeling of utter indefatigably and almost felt possessed by a deep and powerful urge to hurry without further delay, that the boy needed me now and time was running short.

It was an unsettling feeling, one that wouldn't allow me to rest with a clear conscience. And so, I pressed onward throughout the dark of night, allowing the glow of the full moon to light my path, my mind a little more at ease now I knew the demonic dire wolf no longer stalked my flank from the shadows.

The wolf, its blood still hung upon the blade of my dagger, now dried it had crusted thickly, making it fit tight in its sheathe.

A grave reminder of how close I came to becoming the beast's dinner.

Had the stag—Mirella—not shown up when she did, I held severe reservations that I would've survived the clash.

You need to hurry, Lothar.

A voice in my head urged me to hurry, as it had done numerous times since beginning to ascend the mountain. I couldn't tell if it was myself thinking it or if something else was invading my thoughts and trying to spur me on.

It didn't matter to me either, I couldn't deny the urgency I was feeling, the growing dread that I wouldn't make it in time, that I would fail to be there to save the boy before Zarek arrived.

The thought made me feel sick in my stomach.

Determined to not fail him, I forced myself once again to increase my pace, shedding any thought of trying to save some strength for the battle I knew lay ahead of me.

I would be ready to fight regardless of my physical condition. My mind would not waiver, Zarek will die.

He *must* die.

"BOOOOOOOM!!!!!"

My hands instinctively sprung up to cover my ears as a deafening sound rang through the air around me.

A second, less intense sound echoed nearby making me look around for the source—and quickly dive out of the way as a large chunk of ice detached itself from the cliff face above me, violently crashing to the ground where I'd been standing only a moment prior and shatter into a shower of smaller chunks when it impacted the ground, leaving a small crater on the snow covered path.

What the fuck was that?

But as soon as I thought the words, I already knew what it was. Something I'd heard before.

Something that caused my heart to race and my hands to tremble.

Blast stone.

And if Zarek was firing blast stones, it meant he'd arrived and was wasting no time laying siege to the Commune.

I hoped the people there had some kind of

defensive ability and were not just a group of peace-loving religious fanatics.

Although, if the woman was anything to judge by, then maybe they had half a fighting chance.

Still…

God damn this to hell. Move fucking faster old man!

With that in mind, I began running, pushing myself through the thick, boggy snow and up the steep incline, embracing the burn in my calves and thighs and abandoning any slither of a thought for self-preservation I may have had remaining.

Judging by how loud the blast had been, I knew I must be close, or at least it had sounded close.

Very close.

Trekking restlessly throughout the night I believed had allowed me to close the gap between us, I prayed I would arrive before Zarek's forces were able to breach whatever they'd fired the Blast stone at.

As I crested the incline I'd just forced myself to run up, I realised just how close I actually was.

Atop the hill, the area instantly opened up into a wide expanse, high atop the mountain itself.

It was the summit.

And barely two hundred paces out, on the field before me, illuminated by the bright glow of the moon, I witnessed a ferocious battle taking place.

The remainder of Zarek's forces were marching

forward in a shield wall formation towards a large stone wall that ran all the way across the expanse, right to the edges of the cliff face from what I could make out in the dim light.

Pieces of splintered wooden gates lay in the middle of the stone wall surrounded by rubble, and Zarek was directing his forces towards the opening. I could make out a group of robed defenders standing valiantly behind the shattered wreckage, preparing to engage Zarek's men when they arrived.

Flaming arrows rained down onto the shields of Zarek's men while they trudged forward, fired by defenders of the commune perched atop the stone wall. Voices and shouts of panic could be heard coming from both sides.

I had no idea how I would breach the compound without being seen but the good news was my arrival had gone unnoticed, and I planned to use it to my advantage.

Crouching and keeping my frame low to the ground so I did not cast a silhouette from the moonlight above, I stalked forward, drawing my dagger as I crept, silent as death itself.

As I made my way forward, I stumbled upon a cache of supplies. I realised Zarek must have left them here to retrieve after his attack. Foolishly believing no one would pursue him and likely convinced of his impending victory he'd not bothered to make any effort whatsoever to hide them.

A foolish move, powered by his ego, no doubt.

I scoured over the goods, most of it was his men's personal effects. Loose items such as, diaries, clothing and some food and water. Nothing useful.

I lifted a blanket up and found something I did need though, a sword. I quickly put it into my sheathe and then gave a final, quick search over the area before I prepared to move on but one more thing caught my eye as I turned to leave.

A glint of metal catching the light above giving itself away.

Reaching down I found a bundle of rope, with a sharp, metal, three-pronged hook attached to the end.

I couldn't believe my luck, it was a fucking grappling hook.

My prayers had been answered.

Someone must have forgotten to grab it before the assault, no doubt an error made by some inexperienced, nervous recruit. A recruit that probably wouldn't see the morning sunrise if he continued making mistakes like this.

Tough luck, I should be thanking his stupidity.

I looped the bundle of rope over my shoulders and carried on skulking my way across the open field, bee-lining towards a secluded section of the wall near the mountain edge. It appeared a safe distance away from where the melee was about to take place.

I was almost to the wall when I heard the fighting begin, Zarek's men had closed the distance managing from what I could see, to suffer minimal losses by the Communes archers. The clang of weapons ringing together and striking shields was intertwined with battle cries and screams of agony.

It was clear even to my veteran ears that both sides were fighting viciously for their causes, refusing to give an inch of ground to the other.

Blocking out the painful cries of anguish, I unloosed the grappling hook from my shoulder and prepared to throw it atop the wall. I'd never used one before, there had never been much need around Drassox. It couldn't be that hard though.

I laid the rope neatly to the side of me and began swinging the hook in a small circle, allowing it to build momentum.

The metal hook made a gentle 'phoom, phoom, phoom' sound as it picked up speed along its arc until finally, I released the hook.

Whether through beginners' luck or some latent unknown skill, my first throw made it clear over the wall.

I began reeling in the slack and let out a sigh of relief when I felt the hooks grab and hold sturdy atop the stone construction.

I gave myself a quick final check over to be sure all my belongings were secure, before I started to climb over the wall.

It wasn't easy wearing armour but after a bit of a struggle I clambered my way up the wall before my arms gave way and got a leg up securing my path into the compound.

The battle was still raging, when I dropped free, landing safely on the other side. So far, it appeared like the people that lived at this place were more than holding their own against Zarek's men.

Zarek better not die before I find him.

Please hurry, Lothar, you are almost out of time.

The voice again. It sounded like Mirella.

Fuck.

Alright, I just need to focus on finding the boy, then I'll worry about Zarek.

I retrieved the grappling hook just in case and took a quick survey of my surroundings. I could see the two groups were still fighting a short distance away, although the battle sounds had begun to lessen which could only mean one thing, that the number of combatants was dwindling.

Shifting my attention elsewhere, I saw random homes lay scattered about the area, lacking any discernible pattern, and a single road cut through the compound from where the battle was taking place. I followed it along with my eyes to a large, tall structure in the distance, it was unlike anything I'd seen before. It resembled a relic that was left from the old days, surviving destruction only by remaining hidden here high in the mountains.

It was built like a fortress, or at least, what I knew of them from my father. Large granite blocks made up the walls and a second story balcony ringed with stone barricading overhung the front of the structure. From where I was stood, I could see two window openings up there that leaked a faint orange glow from within. Candlelight.

Below the balcony, two large wooden doors stood as the only visible entryway inside.

For some reason gazing upon the building made my skin crawl, filling me with a thick sense of dread. The full moon sat high in the sky, casting its ashen light down from above penetrating the clouds and faintly lighting the cold stone walls giving the whole structure a dark and foreboding appearance.

The boy was in there, I could feel it in my bones.

But something was terribly wrong.

Squashing the urge to turn back and charge headfirst into the battle to find Zarek and slaughter him like the dog he was, I pressed onward toward the ominous fortress until the sounds of the melee unfolding behind me grew too far away to make out.

There was not a soul in sight as I passed the numerous houses littering the area, all were either fighting at the gate, or taking shelter elsewhere I presumed.

Or maybe they were all fighting.

It didn't matter, I was only here for the boy.

A short while later I arrived at the doors to the structure, I tried to open them but unsurprisingly found they wouldn't budge, likely having been barred from within. This came as no great shock considering the settlement was currently under assault from armed invaders.

Still, it angered me inside, I needed to get in and I needed to do it now, the urgency racing through me had only heightened the closer I drew to this place.

I banged on the doors, partly in frustration and partly in hopes that someone would come and let me in—it didn't work which only frustrated me further. I glanced around, scouring the exterior for a way in, some kind of weakness I could exploit.

There was only one possibility as far as I could see.

The balcony. I knew it was going to be a difficult climb, I'd need to lose my armour, there was no way I would make it with the extra weight. I'd struggled to get up the wall earlier and there I was at least able to kick my way up the stone, this would require a free climb up the rope.

Just the thought of being without my armour made me feel exposed though.

But I knew it had to go so reluctantly, I laid the grappling hook down onto the ground and removed my breastplate, pauldrons, and tassets. Keeping my gauntlets, boots, and leather gambeson on for protection, the gambeson would help against a slash but do little to deter a full-fledged blade thrust.

Beggars can't be choosers, it's still better than nothing.

I bent down retrieving the grappling hook, shocking myself how much lighter I felt.

It suddenly dawned on me that I hadn't removed my armour in quite some time, since this all began.

Since… the massacre at Drassox.

My heart sank as I pictured the faces of all those I had lost, but then I quickly shut it out. The boy was still alive. It wasn't too late to save him at least.

I still have time.

Feeling more determined than ever, I uncoiled the grappling hook once again and began swinging it in a circular motion as I had done before, allowing the weighted head to build momentum.

"Phoom, phoom, phoom," it whistled, building up speed.

I timed the release, and the grappling hook sailed up into the air, clanging against the stone barricading but failing to grab hold of anything before it clumsily tumbled back down, thudding to the ground near me.

"Fuck!" I cursed, a little louder than I'd meant to.

I quickly looked around to make sure no one had heard me, luckily no one seemed to be around still.

Kael needs you now, Lothar.

Yes, I fucking know—I'm trying!

Taking a deep, calming breath, I repeated the process and lobbed the hook skyward once more, and again it clanged against the barricading, but this time, it fell over onto the balcony itself.

I slowly drew in the slack and pulled hard on the rope, the grappling hook lifted up and then I felt it grab firmly onto something above.

Success! I'm coming boy, hold on a little longer.

I gave my armour one last sorrowful glance, then began shimmying my way up the rope, lifting with my hands and pinching the rope between my boots, quickly propelling myself upward now that I was free from the excess burden of weight.

A short time later I was pulling myself over the barricading and planting my feet safely on the balcony, puffing heavily.

Catching my breath I didn't take time to congratulate myself for my efforts because the moment I stood, I was hit with an intense aura of evil, so thick I felt that I could smell it. Taste it. It permeated the air like a cloud, in a way that words can't explain. It was the presence of evil.

I drew my sword.

There was a brown wooden door before me between the two narrow window openings, I tried the handle and to my relief it turned, and the door opened freely. I wasted no time slipping inside and as soon as I did, I heard voices.

There were multiple and it sounded almost as though they were humming together, or chanting. The words were too muffled to make out so I ignored them and pressed on.

I was in a corridor, illuminated by sconces on the walls. To the left I could see the corridor ended so I went right, gripping my sword handle tightly, I followed the sound of the humming.

The words started to become clearer as I drew closer to the source, but they were still not clear enough for me to make out the words yet.

A tight spiral stairwell appeared before me, without hesitating I began to make my way down, watching my shadow flicker as I passed the flame of a wall sconce.

"… treachery… rel… … … … light… … … … … ness… … …" I could now almost make out the words and somehow the tune sounded almost familiar, like I'd heard it before.

Sweat beaded on my forehead and I urgently pushed on, creeping cautiously down the stairs until their descent ended at an iron reinforced door. The voices were coming from just beyond it, the stench of evil had grown so thick it was almost overpowering now and making me feel nauseous.

Clenching my jaw and preparing myself for the worst, I turned the handle and pushed the door open.

"Vessel of treachery, relinquish the light, accept the darkness and aid his plight."

In the middle of a large room, illuminated by candles, six figures in dark robes stood in a circle holding hands around a stone table while chanting the words.

Words I'd heard the boy mutter once.

The boy, who right now lay chained by his wrists and ankles on the stone table.

My vision swirled as I saw red and felt my rage begin to simmer.

"WHAT FUCKING DEVILRY IS THIS!!?" I bellowed across the room, causing all of them to stop chanting and snap their heads in my direction.

They looked back to one of their number, a man that was clearly much older than the others and a brief awkward silence ensued.

"Stop him at once! The summoning ritual is almost complete, The Prince has nearly returned to take his rightful place among us, buy any time you can!" He yelled, breaking the silence and ordering his minions to attack me.

Immediately, one that bore a slightly smaller build than the others turned and ran like a coward while the rest drew daggers from beneath their robes and began advancing toward me.

The summoning ritual?

They're summoning the demon. That fucking bitch

Del must have been betraying us all along to lead the boy here.

I'm going to murder her. How could I have been so blind?

That's it! All these demon worshippers will fucking pay.

Revelling in the opportunity to unleash my rage, I raised my sword and stormed forward, ready to send these vermin to hell to join their Prince.

CHAPTER 20

TRAPPED IN THE DARKNESS

*'In righteousness shall thou be established, thou shalt be far
from oppression; for thou shalt not fear; and from terror; for
it shalt not come near thee'*

The men had tied me down and started chanting the words that kept haunting my nightmares.

As soon as they started chanting everything around me had grown dark and the darkness had come back.

I didn't care anymore, I was too upset to care.

Del was meant to be my friend and she had betrayed me.

I had no one anymore, everyone I met wanted to be mean and hurt me. Why was no one nice!

I couldn't stop crying, I just want someone to come and save me but there was no one left. Why did you all leave me?

Mother?

Pa?

Lothar?

Anyone!?

I'm sorry!

I'm not really a brave knight, it was all pretend, I'm just a small boy and I'm scared… I want a grown up with me.

"I don't want to be alone anymore," I mumbled out loud, sitting down, putting my face in my hands, and sobbing.

I could feel wet tears streaming down my cheeks and into my hands.

"… Vessel of treachery, relinquish the light, accept the darkness and aid his plight…"

The chanting was loud and I could hear it all around me, I had no way to get away from it, so I just kept my face in my hands and whimpered. Why can't they just shut up!

"**VESSEL**," a deep scary voice suddenly cut over the noise, and I realised I could feel heat coming from above me.

I was too scared to look and see where it'd come from, I kept my face in my hands and tried my best to pretend I didn't hear it. I silently prayed it would just leave me alone and go away, while I pulled my knees close to my chest and made myself into a ball. But it didn't go away.

Instead, it spoke again. Closer this time.

"**FINALLYYYYYYYY**," it rumbled, its voice was deeper than anything I'd ever heard before, deeper than even Lothar's voice.

It terrified me, I was paralysed with fear and it was hard to breathe.

I felt the wind from its breath move my hair from above, and the smell of rotting meat came with it.

My whole body trembled, deep down I knew what was talking to me, I knew what I would see if I opened my eyes.

I knew it was standing right over me, but I couldn't bring myself to look.

I was weak, knights don't hide like this.

I just wanted to disappear, to be safe in Mother's arms with Pa and Lothar nearby, but I knew I was stupid for wanting that because I was all alone. And they were all dead.

"**LOOK UPON ME, VESSEL!!!**" The voice cracked in the air like thunder, sounding even angrier.

It was so loud it hurt my ears and made me sob even harder.

"**YOU ARE ALONE. NO ONE CARES ENOUGH TO HELP YOU. ACCEPT ME.**"

I squeezed my eyes shut as it began to laugh, the

evil cackling mixing into the chanting.

Please just go away…

"J—just leave me alone!" I suddenly burst out and opened my eyes, quickly wishing I hadn't.

Inches from my head was the terrifying face of the monster, its scaly skin, twisted horns, and pointy, jagged teeth, looking even more terrifying now it was so close.

I felt a warm wetness begin to seep between my legs and my whole body shook even more. I wanted to jump back in fear, to get away but as soon as my eyes had met the monsters, I'd became stiff as a tree. I couldn't move at all, my heart sank. I knew it was finally going to eat me, slowly chew with its razor-sharp teeth and swallow me bit by bit.

"YESSSSS, LOOK INTO MY EYES VESSEL. RELINQUISH THE LIGHT. ACCEPT THE DARKNESS AND AID MY PLIGHT!!!" It smiled showing its fangs and its voice grew louder until it became a deafening roar.

I felt it inside my head, it hurt so much that I screamed in pain and the monster cackled loudly again.

And then something happened, it recoiled in shock and a voice suddenly yelled from somewhere in the darkness making the chanting instantly stop.

"—WHAT FUCKING DEVILRY IS THIS!?"

It was a voice I recognised and for a moment I

thought I had imagined it. But somehow, I knew in my heart that I hadn't.

It was real.

And it was Lothar's voice.

Lothar was here? He'd come back for me!

I couldn't stop myself from letting out another sob but this time, it was from joy at hearing my best friend's voice.

He was here! Lothar was alive, I knew he wouldn't leave me!

I tried to hear his voice again but the one I heard next came from someone else.

"Stop him at once! The summoning ritual is almost complete, The Prince of Treachery has nearly returned to take his rightful place among us, buy any time you can!"

The monster in front of me stood tall with rage on its face and let out a screeching roar of anger, before grabbing me roughly by my shoulders. Its grip was like a vice, the touch burnt my skin, and its eyes blazed red like burning hot embers.

I heard the sounds of fighting begin all around me, metal clanged, and men were screaming in pain, but I couldn't see anything through the black. It was like when I'd been trapped in the closet again but this time I wasn't scared anymore.

None of the screams sounded like Lothar.

He was here to save me, and I felt hope again.

CHAPTER 21
GOOD VS EVIL

'Yay, though I walk through the valley of the shadow of death, I shall fear no evil; for thou art with me; thy rod and thy staff they comfort me'

"Guuurghhhhh…" A slow wet gurgle slithered its way out of the old man's throat while I ripped my blade free from his feeble chest.

Blood poured from the wound, and he dropped to the floor like a weightless sack of shit. Fitting.

All around me, the five men he'd ordered to 'stop him at once!' lay just as lifeless on the cold stone floor. Some were missing an arm or a leg, while another's head had been completely decapitated from his body, his blood now steadily pooling with that of his companions.

Satisfied I'd fulfilled my promise of sending them to hell to meet their Prince I turned my attention to the boy, his small frame still rested upon the stone table, chained and unmoving.

My heart rhythm began to beat faster and my hands grew clammy as I proceeded forward, stepping through the thick puddles of blood towards him.

The stench of evil had quickly subsided when my presence caused the chanting to abruptly end, dispelling like a cloud almost immediately.

I silently prayed this was a good omen, but I couldn't shake the feeling that something was still amiss.

"… Boy? Can you hear me?" I called softly to him, hesitantly.

Fearing what I might find.

As I neared the table, I held my breath and looked over his body for wounds, blood or anything that might indicate he was injured… or worse.

The thought of it made me feel nauseous.

I'm here now, please be alright.

I can't fail you too boy, I can't take failing someone else.

Glancing over him, I felt my chest relax and allowed my lungs to exhale in relief. I couldn't see any injuries, his short, black hair was stuck to his forehead with sweat, his pants were dark as though he'd wet himself in fear, but it seemed he had no physical injuries. I noticed he looked very pale, but not deathly so. I dared to hope, that maybe I'd made it in time.

"Kael. Can you hear me, boy?" I tried calling to him again but still, he didn't respond in any way.

Damn this place, I'm taking you out of here boy.

I reached down and started to undo the bolt on the metal shackles that had been secured around his little ankles, it dawned on me that the shackles had been designed for a child.

These fucking animals, they're as bad as the Order.

While I was fiddling to undo them, I saw he had grazes where the metal had bit harshly into his skin, likely from struggling as the wretched cowards forced him down, onto the table.

I felt my anger begin to rise momentarily, but it quickly settled when I saw the butchered priests' corpses out of the corner of my eye.

I undone his ankles quickly and moved on to his tiny wrists, they also had suffered similar grazes.

I felt my face grow hot and growled under my breath, if I could kill them again, I damn well would.

I should've been here earlier.

One of his wrists shackles I was able to release easily, but the other was giving me trouble, the pin was stuck. I drew my dagger and used its edge to pry the pin out successfully.

I sighed once more, looking down at the poor child

before me and replaced my dagger back in its sheathe.

"Alright, boy. I'm taking you out of here," I mumbled, half to myself since I knew he couldn't hear me, and then lent over, gently picking him up.

Holding him close to me, I turned and started to walk.

"You are safe no—," I barely took one step, when I was blasted heavily by some unseen force that threw me, the boy and the body of the dead priests wildly through the air in all directions.

Their bodies smacked hard against the walls with bone shattering thuds, while I tumbled along the floor with all the wind knocked clear out of me.

Stunned, I lay there for a moment coughing in pain.

"Argh…" I let out a moan and rolled over onto my back still spluttering and gasping for air from the force of whatever had just launched me across the room like a child's toy.

Heaving large gulps of air to refill my lungs the first thing I became aware of was the nauseating stench of evil.

It had returned a thousandfold, filling every inch of the room.

My eyes cautiously scanned the room, the first thing I noticed was that the flames of the candles illuminating the room had stopped flickering. Still burning, yet they stood perfectly still, as though time itself had come to a stop.

This could not be good.

Forget the candles, find the boy. Make sure he's all right.

A quick glance around the room is all it took me to find him, he was standing but twenty paces away.

Facing me, with his eyes closed and hands by his sides, a shadow radiated from him as though his body cast darkness like a fire did light. It resembled a living thing that wanted to reach out and devour the entire room, the frozen candles the only thing fighting a losing battle to keep it at bay.

None of this was what made my blood run cold though, that was reserved for what towered proudly behind the boy, its large hands clamped upon his shoulders.

It—or he—stood at least a full foot taller than myself, broad and muscular with skin scaled like that of a reptilian, a thick set skull with gnarled, twisted horns, protruding from his head. Steam billowed from a mouth full of daggerlike teeth. And eyes, burning like red hot iron fresh from the forge, radiated pure intense hatred as they looked upon me.

There could be no doubt who this was.

Lucifer.

The Prince of Treachery himself had broken into the realm of the living.

Seething with hatred of my own, I rose unsteadily

to my feet, determined to stand tall and meet his dominating gaze but the moment our eyes locked together, and I looked into his burning red orbs my mind was rapidly overcome with the most terrible images imaginable and my courage evaporated.

Images of everyone I'd ever known, and all those that had died, suffering eternal damnation in the fires of hell.

Unspeakable tortures were being suffered upon them by all manner of creatures. Their voices pained my ears as they screamed and begged me one after the other to save them, yet no matter how hard I tried I could do nothing but gaze on, frozen in terror and held in place by an unseen force. Their screams turned into words of anger as they cursed me for not helping them, cursed me for watching on like a coward as they were ripped limb from limb, eaten by demons, raped, murdered and torn apart repeatedly over and over and over.

Seconds passed, yet it felt like an eternity.

Then he spoke, the vile smell of rotting meat accompanying his voice.

"A GLIMPSE OF WHAT AWAITS YOU IN MY DOMAIN, MORTAL," it came out in a deafening bellow, so loud that I dropped to my knees, my ears ringing in pain.

Kneeling there, I was overcome by a deep, unnatural feeling of terror, that further pummelled me into submission making me feel helpless like a child in the face of such an entity. The far reaches of my mind were still screaming at me to be defiant, to rise and fight, but my body refused to listen.

The shadow surrounding the boy began to extend, as though it fed off my fear. I watched while it slowly crept its way towards me, slithering like an army of snakes over the floor and along the walls. The small, candle flames, instantly going out one by one as they were overcome by the darknesses touch.

I wanted to resist, I tried to force myself to get up and fight, I struggled with every fibre of my being, but the wave of terror was unfathomable, dominating.

Unholy.

It was paralysing.

I fought with all my willpower to resist the effects, I begged my legs to stand, for my hand to draw my sword, but it was hopeless. I could do nothing in the face of such an adversary.

I am just a man.

And I've failed.

My heart sank and I began to stop fighting back.

And then… just as all will to fight was about to leave my mind and body, when I thought all was lost.

I felt it.

A tiny ray of hope.

It began to trickle into my mind, rapidly growing and pushing back against the overwhelming terror that had taken hold of me.

It cleared my mind of all self-doubt and the air itself became charged with energy, the ceiling above me lit up brightly, illuminating the area beneath it and forcing the darkness to retreat. In the centre of the light, I saw a glowing ball begin to materialise, shining brighter than the brightest star. It slowly floated down through the ceiling and descended toward the ground, stopping at my head height. I gazed at it in wonder as it hung in the air protectively, between me and the demon prince.

Lucifer roared a guttural scream of pure hatred, but did not advance. Instead, he seemed to be recoiling from the light, almost scared, while he pulled the boy back into the shadows with him for shelter. It was as though to stand before the luminescence before us was causing him great pain.

The orb floated there in front of me for a moment and then a voice emanated from within it.

It was both soft and commanding, calming yet powerful.

It rang with supreme confidence.

It was… angelic, divine and holy.

"GUARDIAN," it said.

"W—who are you?" I stammered, nervous to be so close to what I sensed was a very powerful being.

The orb floated closer, I could feel it scrutinising me and it paused before replying.

"I, AM THEE ARCHANGEL. COMMANDER OF HEAVENS ARMIES, SAINT MICHAEL."

My heart leaped into my throat when the being stated its name. Could it really be? Surely he'd come to banish Lucifer once more!

"…So, you've come to defeat him, to help me save the boy?" I finally replied, hopefully.

"NO. I AM NOT HERE TO FIGHT MANKINDS BATTLES."

I felt a sudden surge of anger at his answer.

"What the fuck do you mean! You've defeated Lucifer before, you're God's most powerful angel, the leader of his damn armies! If not you, then who!?"

As the words left my mouth, I felt a pang of guilt speaking to such a divine entity like that, but I could really use some fucking aid right now!

"IS THOU READY, TO FULFIL THOU RIGHTFUL ROLE?" He replied, ignoring my outburst which only caused me to have another.

"What fucking role!? I can't fight the Devil, I'm just a man!"

"THOU HATH BEEN CHOSEN TO BE THE CHILD'S GUARDIAN. NONE BUT THOU, CAN STOP LUCIFER'S RETURN. MAKETH HASTE AND STRIKETH FAST, BEFORE HE CROSSES THE FINAL CIRCLE OF HELL AND RECOVERS HIS TRUE POWER."

Guardian angel? I can't fight something if I can't

even move!

"Oh, and how the hell am I supposed to do that!? I'm no match for a Prince of Hell. You could end this yourself with ease!" I shouted back, frustrated with his lack of help.

I felt a calming sensation rush over me and my anger dissipated.

"I SHALL GRANT THOU A BOON, GUARDIAN. DO NOT FALTER AND USE IT WISELY, IF THOU FAIL, ALL OF MANKIND WILL SUFFER."

As the archangel finished speaking, the orb that was he started to fade.

"A boon?"

"Wait! What do you mean a boon!?" I yelled stepping forward.

But my protests were ignored as he continued to ascend above, slowly disappearing through the ceiling as suddenly as he'd appeared.

The light that accompanied him however remained, still shining brightly and keeping the darkness at bay until he was completely gone from sight, and only then did it begin to move. Slowly at first, towards me, floating through the air and rapidly speeding up until it quickly blended into a blur, rushing through my body, filling every fibre of my being and flooding my veins with its purifying warmth, the feeling was indescribable, as though I had been reborn.

The terror that previously overcame me rapidly evaporated, forced out and replaced by the indomitable feeling of supreme confidence, of fearlessness, of the familiar will to overcome any foe that stood before me.

I could feel holy strength pulsing throughout my body.

The power of an Archangel now surged within me, empowering me to stand and fight.

A heavenly boon.

I finally understood what I needed to do.

I looked onward and saw Lucifer stepping forward from behind the boy, now holding a large flaming claymore, the blade glowing red hot from the fire enveloping it, licking its way along the dark, demonic steel. The boy stood behind the demon in his trance, staring straight ahead while the darkness once again began to crawl its way towards me.

Unperturbed and confident in my newfound power I reached over my shoulder and drew my own weapon, surprised when it felt light as a feather, an extension of my own arm surpassing even the feel of my late father's sword, now broken and lost.

As I brought the weapon in front of me, I saw it'd now changed, replaced by a weapon of unparalleled beauty. A pearl white handle with a beautiful golden cross-guard and pommel was gripped in my hand, attached to a gleaming blade of the highest quality, intricate inscribed patterns spiralled along its length from which radiated a brilliant light, casting its glow all around me and stopping the spreading darkness in its tracks.

Lucifer roared in fury when he saw its illumination, so loud the building around us shook.

As the quake settled, he looked to me and spoke calmly.

"I OFFER YOU ONE CHANCE AT MERCY, MORTAL. JOIN ME AND I WILL MAKE YOU A GOD AMONG THIS PLANE. FIGHT, AND YOU WILL SUFFER FOR ETERNITY."

I could feel his trepidation, he wouldn't use deceit to save himself from his fate, I would not grant it.

"Your treachery won't work on me, demon. And even if it weren't lies, my answer is no. That boy is under my protection, release him. Now," I ordered with conviction in my voice.

"YOU CHOOSE DAMNATION. SO BE IT… MORTAL," he spat the last word out hatefully.

And with that, he raised his fiery blade and began to stride forward, accepting his challenge I walked forth to meet him.

The darkness retreated from the light of my blade as I marched, closing the gap between us I kept my eyes locked with Lucifer's, now protected from his paralysing mind tricks.

He still towered over me, but I felt no fear, only

supreme confidence, even as his huge, muscular, arms swung the heavy claymore down upon me, attempting to cleave me in two straight down the middle. Calmly, yet in a blur, I blocked the blow, matching his strength and stopping the burning blade instantly as though he was a mere man. A brief look of shock passed over his face, then he snarled and kicked me hard in the chest causing me to skid back across the floor all while keeping my balance perfectly.

I smiled back at him then quickly charged forward again, using my superior agility to narrowly duck under his blade as he tried recklessly, to once again to decapitate me. His blade passed harmlessly overhead, as I countered with a strike of my own, my blade biting into his exposed thigh, easily cutting into the thick scaled flesh making him let out a grunt of anger and attempt to correct his attack direction, but I was already retreating out of the way.

He glanced down at the wound on his thigh, dark blood trickled from the open wound.

Steam billowed from his mouth and his eyes burned even hotter, then he roared once again in rage.

"INSOLENT WRETCH! YOU WILL SUFFER UNIMAGINABLE HORRORS! YOU WILL BEG AND BEG FOR MERCY!!"

His anger only grew my confidence, and my calm.

That's right, get angry.

Get reckless.

With a grunt he charged forward unleashing a frenzied attack, swinging his blade in wild arcs that forced me to back up, slipping and parrying the blows as I did. Calmly, I waited for an opening. As my father had taught me, anger leads to recklessness and recklessness leads to death on the battlefield.

For a Prince of Hell, his swordsmanship was failing to impress me. No doubt without his full power and minions to do his bidding, he was a just an average swordsman, a demon praying on a defenceless child's fears using mind tricks and cowards' tactics.

I blocked a side slash and used the momentum to drive my shoulder heavily into his chest, knocking him backwards. He stumbled far less gracefully than I had done when he kicked me.

We locked eyes once more and he snarled, letting out a low growl, then pounced forward, closing the gap between us again and swung another heavy downward blow like he'd done earlier. A one trick pony, just as I'd hoped.

I'd been waiting for this and side stepped into safety, allowing his claymore to whistle down past my shoulder, then drove my sword upwards, under his open ribcage. The magnificent blade passed like a hot knife through butter and out his upper back with little to no resistance, I rapidly retracted it and once again sprung back to a safe range, anticipating a follow up strike.

It didn't come though.

Instead, he stumbled back on wobbly legs, reversed his grip on his sword and slammed it into the stone floor to hold himself upright from falling over.

Thick dark claret poured from his rib wound, oozing onto the floor and adding to the pool of blood from his feeble priest's.

A fatal blow.

Breathing heavily, he started to speak again.

"... I WOULD TEAR YOU... LIMB FROM LIMB... WERE I... AT FULL POWER..."

I slowly edged my way forward.

"Blessings to me that you're not then, demon."

He coughed and spat blood, his legs quivered, and then he dropped to one knee unable to support his heavy weight. His grip on his sword loosened, and the massive weapon clattered to the floor beside him, immediately extinguishing its flame.

"... FINISH IT THEN. MORTAL," he said in a low rumble.

Again, spitting the word mortal, although the defeat in his voice sounded clear now. Still, I continued approaching cautiously, even kneeling he was close to my height.

As I neared striking range, I raised my sword and pointed the tip at his heart, preparing to deal the final blow, to cast Lucifer back to the depths of hell where he belonged.

"DO IT," he growled again through gritted teeth.

I pulled back to thrust and suddenly his muscular arm snapped up to grab my throat as fast as a serpent's strike.

However, this was the Prince of Treachery after all, I was no fool, and I was ready.

Turning my blade in the blink of an eye, I sliced sideways and cut clean through his forearm severing the hand that made the mistake of reaching for me, he opened his mouth in a howl of pain and anger for a moment and recoiled, shortly before I retracted my swing and plunged the tip of the blade cleanly through his black heart.

The effect was almost immediate.

Lucifers eyes fixated on me with pure hatred, and then he exploded into pieces in a shower of gore, covering everything in the room with blood, guts, bone and bits of his scaly skin. Only a puddle of muck sat where he once kneeled.

I stood looking around at the carnage for a moment in utter shock, claret and small chunks of meat dripped from me from head to toe.

Then the entire room went pitch black, even my sword no longer spreading its purifying light.

My body tensed, my senses springing to action expecting another threat. Yet, it only lasted a moment and then the darkness began to dissipate, the room grew brighter, the candles rekindled and began flickering once again.

A cold flush washed over my body and I felt the archangel's power and supreme confidence start to melt away as rapidly as it'd entered me.

And just like that, I once again, felt like just a man.

Glancing around me I saw all sign of Lucifer had vanished, as though he'd never existed. The dead priests remained where their bodies had struck the walls, but the gore that had splattered everything from the demon had now completely disappeared without a trace.

And then my eyes came upon the boy, lying on the floor motionless where he'd stood in a trance only a short while ago and I suddenly felt sick with panic.

"KAEL!!" I shouted and began sprinting over to him.

CHAPTER 22
THE END IS NIGH

*'The beast and his vassal kings will make war on the lamb,
and the lamb will conquer them'*

"Kael… I'm here. Wake up, please. Please don't be dead…" I heard his voice, but it was much clearer than it'd been before and he sounded really worried.

Hearing his voice made me less afraid, I couldn't feel the monster's breath on me anymore so I stopped clenching my eyes so tightly. I didn't open them yet though, I was still a little worried I'd see its horrible face right there staring at me if I did.

But I hoped…

Something or someone pressed their fingers lightly against my neck for a moment and then I heard him speak again.

"I'm taking us out of here, it's alright, boy. It'll be alright…"

I felt large, strong hands trying to pick me up, reaching under me and I carefully peeked, opening my eyes just a little to see who it was. Even in the dark room I recognised the long brown hair and dirty bearded face almost straight away.

"Lothar!" I shouted, opening my eyes and he jumped in fright as I wrapped my arms around him.

I felt him quickly relax and then he hugged me back.

"Yes, it's me, boy," he replied, then stepped back, looking at me.

I looked around the room and saw there were bodies lying everywhere in the room.

"Lothar, what happened? I was trapped in the dark and…"

"It's a long story. We can discuss it later, but not here," he answered.

"Alright," I nodded.

I couldn't believe he was really here, tears started filling my eyes as I remembered the last time I had seen him.

"I—I seen you fall into the water. I th—… I thought you were gone…" I said trying hard not to cry right there in front of him.

He smiled at me and then laughed shaking his

head.

"It'll take a bit more than that to get rid of me. How're you feeling though?"

I thought about it for a moment. I felt good, great actually, my head felt clearer, and I couldn't hear the chanting anymore for the first time in days.

"I'm good. What happened to your armour?" I asked noticing he didn't have it on anymore.

I hadn't seen him out of it since we left Drassox, and he looked different without it on.

He frowned like he was annoyed for a moment.

"Argh. I had to leave it outside. Anyway, are you able to walk? We're not safe yet, we need to leave this place."

"Yep, I sure can. Let's go," I said as he helped me stand up.

"I'm glad you're alright. Oh, and before we leave, I believe this is yours," he said, bending over and picking up something shiny from the floor and handing it to me.

My sword!

"Thanks! Also have you seen Del?" I asked, putting my sword back in its sheathe, happy to have it back.

"… No, I haven't. And she better hope we don't cross paths again. She betrayed us, Kael. Forget about her. Now, come," he grumbled, looking around the room, then walking towards the exit.

I thought back to how she'd let those men grab me

and chain me to the table and felt my shoulders droop, I thought she'd been my friend, but Lothar was right.

She had betrayed us. I have no friends.

Well, that isn't true anymore, Lothar is here again!

I smiled to myself and followed silently behind him, my best friend in the world. He walked faster than I remembered, like all his injuries didn't hurt him anymore, he was so strong.

One day I'll be as strong as him.

We made it to the doors, and I watched while he easily lifted the heavy wooden cross bar out of its catchers, then threw it to the side with a loud crash that startled me.

"Stay close to my side, Kael, and do not stray, we need to move quickly out here alright?" He said and glanced back at me.

I nodded then he drew his sword—I realised how nice it was and wanted to ask where he'd found it—but before I could he slowly started to push the doors. Sunlight streamed in as the crack in the middle opened up and it made me squint, my eyes had gotten used to the dark candlelit room but boy was I glad to see the sunlight again.

Lothar paused and looked around before stepping out into the daylight, I did as he told and stuck closely by his side.

I wasn't planning on leaving him again, from now on wherever he went I was going too.

"… Well, well, well. Look who it is! And praise the lord, is that the child there I presume?" A voice suddenly shouted out of nowhere, a voice with a familiar funny accent.

A voice I remembered hearing in Drassox when I was locked in the cupboard.

Lothar spun in the direction it came from, I saw his whole-body tense up, and a big frown came over on his face. He looked angrier than I'd ever seen him and ready to fight.

My heart started to race, I tried telling myself I was safe, Lothar was here now as I hid behind him and peeked to see who it was.

"Zarek," Lothar grumbled, his voice coming out in a deep growl.

"Indeed, nice to see you too Lothar. I trust your swim was not too discomforting. In any event, you have something I want. Hand the child over and be gone from my sight. No one else needs to die," the voice replied.

"Wrong, Zarek. There is just one last life that must be extinguished," Lothar replied in a very serious tone.

I followed Lothar's gaze and spotted it came from a man walking out from behind a nearby building with two other men that looked almost exhausted.

I recognised the one that spoke from the bridge, it was the man who kicked Lothar over.

So that's Zarek I realised.

The voice I'd heard back in Drassox was him.

He was the one who'd killed Mother, and everyone else that had hidden in the town hall. Well, he was responsible anyway.

I hated him, just hearing his voice again made me mad.

"Go away! Leave us alone!" I shouted out angrily from behind Lothar, pulling my sword out and trying to act scary even though I couldn't stop my body from shaking.

"Stay calm, Kael," Lothar mumbled without looking at me.

This made Zarek laugh loudly, while the others that were with him stood there just watching.

"Fool, this is not a situation to be calm. Damn this, I have no time for debating. Both of you, kill the child. I will deal with the blasphemer personally," he ordered to the two men.

And then he began to walk forward but stopped after a few steps when he realised his friends weren't following him, they still hadn't moved and were now looking at each other.

Zarek spun around, looking very annoyed.

"Did you two imbeciles not hear me? I said to kill the child."

Lothar hadn't moved and waited in front of me holding his sword low watching the three men.

"L—lord Zarek, it's just that…" One of the men

stuttered.

"Just what, Camran?" Zarek replied, using a tone like Mother used to when I was about to be scolded.

The men looked at each other again and this time the second one answered, louder and more confidently than the first.

"What we're doing is blasphemy, Lord Zarek! He's just a child! We've slaughtered countless innocents in this 'holy' crusade—how can our actions since we left the monastery, not have condemned all our souls to hell?"

I saw Lothar's muscles relax a little bit and it made me think it was alright to relax too but I didn't trust any of these men.

Zarek sighed and took a couple of steps back towards his two friends.

"We are doing God's work, and I am his messenger. Lucifer is trying to use this child to sway you from our righteous path when we are so close to victory. All of our brothers died for this, we are the last of our order. Do not let their deaths be in vain. Kill the child, remove his head and burn his remains."

The men looked at each other again, back and forth.

Moments passed and then the loud one suddenly started shaking his head.

"No. No. No, we can't do this. This isn't God's work. I'm sorry, Lord Zarek, I can't kill anyone else in his name. It isn't right," he mumbled, and I saw tears welling in his eyes.

Then his sword dropped from his hand, landing in the dirt.

The second man mumbled something with tears in his eyes as well and then he dropped his sword too.

Zarek stood there looking at them, I could feel his anger growing by the second.

"… I will not tolerate insolence," he mumbled.

Then he sprang forward almost in a blur, swinging his sword in a wide arc that cut the closest man's throat making him fall backwards grabbing at his neck to stop the bleeding, the second man jumped and went to run but Zarek was already swinging for his throat as well.

He tried to turn away from the sword but it caught him hard in the side of the neck and almost cut his head completely off making it flop over sideways, he stumbled and reached up to hold his head but then quickly fell to the dirt as well kicking his leather boots around on the sand while he bled everywhere.

Zarek turned back to us still smiling widely, the men behind him were gasping and making gurgling noises as they died.

"Apologies for the delay, Lothar. Unfortunately, good help is hard to find, shall we finally end this?" He said looking straight at Lothar still smirking.

Lothar sniffed heavily, eyeing Zarek before he

turned and told me bluntly.

"Stay out of this, Kael."

What? No! We're a team.

He went to move, and I grabbed his arm.

"No! I can help you!" I cried, starting to shake.

I can't lose him again!

Zarek watched us, standing there still smiling, waiting.

Lothar glanced back at him then knelt down next to me.

"You need to trust me, Kael, I'll be fine, but not if I'm worried about looking out for you. I know you're strong and one day you'll be strong enough to help. But right now, you'll only get in the way. I haven't let you down yet, have I?"

He knelt there looking into my eyes and I knew he was right.

I wasn't strong like him yet and he was right, he hadn't let me down ever so I sniffed back my tears and nodded, letting go of his hand.

"No, you haven't," I answered, rubbing my eyes.

"That's right, and I don't plan to now. It's almost over, stay strong," he said winking at me.

Then he turned back to face Zarek.

"Do not worry, boy. You will join him in hell after I slaughter you both," Zarek called out, and laughed loudly again.

Lothar glared at him but didn't react or say another

word, he just stood up tall, raised his sword and left me unable to do anything but watch, trembling, as he walked away from me towards Zarek.

CHAPTER 23

A MAN'S HONOUR

'You have armed me with strength for battle. You'll find, the more difficult the battle, the more strength you'll have. Your strength will always match what you are up against'

The sand crunched beneath the leather soles of my boots as I strode forward, the acrid smell of smoke and blood hung faintly in the air, stinging my nostrils.

I could feel the boy's gaze burning into my back, casting an aura of trepidation behind me.

I tensed but refused to look, being worried that to see the fear in his face might dull my senses.

I couldn't allow weakness to take hold of me, it served no purpose on the path I now tred.

With each step, the edges of my vision darkened,

narrowing like I was entering a tunnel. Yet the tall, armoured figure in the distance remained razor sharp, focused, denying the darkness that was slowly creeping into my sight.

My hearing grew muffled until the only sound I was aware of was my boots thudding the dirt and my own beating heart.

Its rhythm was not panicked, but steady and calm.

Peaceful.

All of my senses were now heightened, like that of a predatory animal, finally with its prey in sight. A familiar feeling.

My mouth watered, salivating at the chance of redemption.

I'd been waiting for this moment since this nightmare began.

To have the one that has caused so much suffering finally within my grasp.

The one who slaughtered Elias.

Catherine.

Lord Edmund.

And Joan…

The one who killed all the people in Drassox I had once called friends.

I miss them all dearly. Their names forever seared into my memory, the mere thought stinging my mind like poison darts.

And now, there he stood but a stone's throw away.

The one who'd made the boy an orphan and ordered the people of Hiltsten and Branwick butchered like cheap cattle.

The one, called Zarek.

His beady eyes watched me as I neared, a smug smirk etched upon his face. A face forever tarnished by an ugly half healed wound that ran jaggedly across his face. A wound I'd given him upon our first meeting, a time that felt a distant memory now, aside from the pain it caused me to recall it.

He appeared weary, his armour that I'd once marvelled at now filthy and battered, yet the expression on his face was one of relish. He'd waited for this moment as long as I.

With the gap between us closing, I saw his mouth moving, forming unintelligible words that my muffled hearing forbid from ever reaching my ears. It was a small matter, nothing he could say would alter the events that were about to take place.

His mouth stopped, and then he raised his sword and moved to meet me.

"CLANG!!!"

His strike came in a blur, yet somehow through instinct alone, I blocked it. The deafening impact of our swords meeting rang through the air, instantly causing my hearing to return.

With blades locked together, we poised there glaring at one another and he began speaking once more, his voice straining while he struggled to hold my blade at bay.

"… Once you are nothing but a gutted corpse… I am going to carve that wretched boy's heart from his chest and burn it—just like I did to your entire godless, cesspit of a town!"

My blood started to rise making me bite down and clench my teeth. I fought back against the boiling anger, forcing myself to ignore him, and then using a surge of strength, shoved his blade aside while attempting to slam my shoulder into his chest as I'd done to the demon.

But Zarek was too agile, too experienced, his footwork flawless. With the skill of a dancer, he gracefully sidestepped out of the way causing me to stumble forward off balance as my shoulder failed to meet its target.

He wasted no time using the opening to attack with a slash for my head. I heard the boy gasp in concern, just as I instinctually dove low, rolling underneath the blow and tumbling roughly onto the dirt but managing to quickly compose myself and get back to my feet.

"How lucky," Zarek muttered, still smirking, although a hint of annoyance was evident in his voice.

"Do not worry, it will all be over soon," he continued, as he reset his footing to attack again.

Smug fool.

I didn't wait for him to lead again, instead

springing forward I lashed out with a combination of furious attacks of my own, first for his neck, then reversing my swing I aimed for his mid-section before shifting to launch a third strike for his knee. But for every attack I threw his blade was there to catch my own, the parries causing a symphony of clangs to ring through the air around us.

"Stop!! Just leave us alone!" The boy yelled from somewhere behind me in distress.

Zarek snickered, his eyes flickered past me for a split second. "Silence your forked tongue, devil! I will see to you shortly."

"Your business is with me!" I shouted furiously, and rushed him again, thrusting my sword forward in a lunging stab at his mid-section.

Prepared, he expertly parried the attack to the side with a flick of his wrist and swung his mailed fist towards my exposed face. I saw it coming a moment too late and tried to slip my head to the side to reduce the impact, but his fist still connected to my mouth with a crunch, making me stumble back uttering a surprised grunt.

Tasting the familiar, coppery tang seep into my mouth I spat to the side and saw a piece of broken tooth fly out with the bloody glob.

Zarek wasted no time using the brief pause to press his assault, swinging his weapon with reckless abandon at my face.

I defensively raised my own sword and our blades met once more, the heavy impact causing them to violently bounce apart and force us both to adjust our grips mid clash to further trade blows.

The boy continued to protest as we fought, his panic and fear rising, yet his voice was becoming barely audible over the increasing intensity of the melee.

Zarek and I separated once more, both panting heavily.

Sweat poured from his brow, and I could feel my own running down my face, dripping from my chin in a steady stream.

We slowly circled a few feet apart, scuffling our boots in the dirt, each man's eyes refusing to leave the others as though to break contact for even a moment would spell one's defeat.

Pure seething hatred was etched upon his face that no doubt mirrored my own. He was too skilled, I had to end this now before I made a mistake.

I noticed his body tense as he prepared to launch another assault, telegraphing his actions and right before he did, I took a chance.

And flung my blade at him as hard as I could.

In shock and confusion, his eyes broke from mine and reflexively followed it as it hurdled the short distance through the air towards him, flinching he tried to parry it away.

Taking advantage of the sudden opening, I charged, slamming my full weight into Zarek's chest right after the weapon clashed harmlessly into his parrying blade.

A sharp exhale of air hissed from his lips as the wind was knocked out of his lungs and we both went tumbling through the air in a mess of tangled limbs. Crashing heavily across the hard dirt I used my strength to make sure Zarek took the brunt of the fall with me landing on top of him, his sword clattering somewhere nearby from the force of the charge.

The dust clouded both of us, stinging my eyes and clogging my nostrils but I did not slow my momentum, I'd gained the upper hand, and I would not waste it.

Now both disarmed, I grabbed for his neck while he cursed at me and tried desperately to swat my hands away, my left-hand locking onto the neck opening of his chest plate, using it as a handle I began to rain blows on him from above with my other fist. He tried to block but multiple punches connected cleanly, opening up a deep split above his left eye which poured blood onto his face no doubt clouding his vision, yet he continued to fight back.

I grimaced when my next blow was deflected and my knuckles crunched into the steel of his pauldron, the bones surely broken.

Zarek continued to struggle, his hands reaching

down towards his waist, frantically trying to lift me off, a desperate move that left his face completely unguarded.

I unleashed on him, blocking out all senses, now consumed with my desire to end his life and started to land more thudding blows with my broken fist, feeling the mangled bones contort as they made contact with his bloody face.

HE killed them all.

"THUD."

He deserves to die.

"THUD."

He will not harm the boy.

"THUD."

I became faintly aware of a wet trickle seeping down my side that made me take pause, confused I glanced down and saw what he'd been reaching near his waist for.

His dagger.

Now sticking in my side, halfway through my gambeson, only slowed by the thick leather, deep but not deep enough to kill.

Yet.

I frantically grabbed hold of his hand to stop him driving it any further into my innards, struggling against each other I looked down at his bloody face, our eyes meeting while we both grunted in pain.

"It... Ends... NOW, ZAREK!" I stammered

through gritted teeth and spat blood straight in his face, causing him to recoil.

"THWACK!" In the next motion I smashed my forehead down onto his face with all the power I could muster.

His nose exploded with a spray of blood and a jagged bone broke out of the skin forcing him to let out a low guttural moan. Instantly like I expected his grip on his dagger loosened allowing me to wrap my hands around his and pull it free from my side. Squeezing his hand onto the hilt, I slowly repositioned it above his face as he fought to stop me but failed.

I saw the fear begin to creep into his eyes as the blade inched closer to his cheek, quickly growing more and more pronounced as the tip moved into position over his eye.

His lip began to quiver, and the smell of piss and shit wafted into the air. And then, he spoke.

"P—please! Stop! I am a servant of God, I am doing his will!" He cried timidly, his voice no longer smug and arrogant.

And finally, I meet the real man.

A COWARD JUST AS I THOUGHT.

My brow furrowed with intensity and images of all the people he had killed once again flashed before my eyes as I slowly forced the tip of the dagger down toward his face.

He tried to resist, gasping as his strained muscles

begged for oxygen. Then he tried to beg as he realised he no longer had the strength to stop the inevitable.

And finally, his panicked begging turned into screams of agony, followed by a slow, wet, gurgling as the blade slid deeper and deeper into his eye socket until it passed clean through his brain.

And just like that, his screaming stopped.

Silenced once and for all.

CHAPTER 24

HIDDEN SURPRISES

'The righteous stand in bold faith against adversity while the wicked flees in fear'

I realised I was holding my breath and let out a long puff of air.

Lothar was still crouched on top of Zarek, holding tightly onto the handle of the dagger. Zarek wasn't moving anymore, his feet had stopped twitching a while ago, but Lothar didn't seem ready to let go of him yet.

I decided to walk closer, careful not to make too much noise.

"Lothar…?" I mumbled quietly when I got close enough, but he didn't look at me.

I waited a moment nervously and then tried again.

"Lothar, are you alright? …Is it over?"

I looked to Zarek, and my stomach lurched. His head was covered in blood, and the dagger was stuck all the way down to the hilt in his eye, I knew he had to be dead. Lothar's face was also bloody though, and I could see a dark wet stain starting to grow on his side.

After what felt like forever Lothar sighed, and keeping his eyes on Zarek he started to stand back to his feet.

"Yes, boy. It's finally over… we're safe," he grumbled.

I felt a massive flood of relief and ran forward, throwing my arms out and hugging him tightly. He seemed to wince like he was hurt but then put one arm around me as well.

I felt so happy I could cry but tried to hold it in, quickly burying my face in the rough leather of his gambeson so he wouldn't notice.

My hand touched the wet patch on his side, and I felt like being sick when I realised it was blood. He was hurt.

"Are you going to be alright?" I asked, hoping it wasn't bad.

He snorted almost rolling his eyes, and then a faint smile showed on his face making me feel better.

"Of course I'll be alright, boy. I promised, remember?"

I felt embarrassed and looked away.

"I know… I was just worried is all."

"Well, you don't have to. I'm fine. Now, are you ready to leave this place?" He asked.

Heck yes I am!

I looked up at him and nodded my head quickly.

"So am I, lets mov…"

He started to say 'move' but his voice trailed off and his eyes darted over to a wooden building next to the castle we had come out of.

I hadn't really noticed it before but now I did I thought it kind of looked like the big wooden barn we'd had back in Drassox for the pigs and sheep.

I knew that wasn't what had gotten Lothar's attention though, something inside was making a soft tapping sound.

"Lothar, no!" I blurted, out grabbing his arm when he turned to walk towards it, "Let's just go!"

He frowned at me, then spoke calmly.

"Kael, everything is going to be alright."

I had a bad feeling, I didn't know why. But I trusted him, he'd never let me down before. So, I put my head down and followed closely behind him towards the barn.

Well… what I hoped was a barn at least.

He bent down and picked his sword back up on the way and then held up his hand for me to stop when we got closer to the doors. I watched nervously as he put his ear against them to listen.

I stood waiting but my patience didn't last long so I leaned closer and went to ask him what he could hear but he sharply turned his head and went "Shh!" then frowned at me.

Fine, he's back to rude Lothar.

He put his ear back to the wood to listen again, I turned my head and took a quick glance to make sure Zarek was still where we'd left him, my muscles relaxed a bit when I saw he hadn't moved even though I would've been pretty surprised if he had.

"Stay behind me, Kael," Lothar said, making me spin back around to his direction.

My heart was still racing about going inside, but I knew better than to argue with him once he'd made his mind up about something by now, so I did as he asked.

The doors creaked loudly when Lothar began to push them open, making me jump and move closer to him for protection.

The sunlight streamed in and lit up all the dust hanging in the air inside making it hard to see clearly, but what I could see looked just like a barn. I was right after all.

We carefully stepped inside, there was hay on the floor that crunched underneath our feet but I ignored it because of what I was seeing straight ahead, not twenty paces away standing behind a thick wooden fence the same height as my head.

I can't say I've ever seen anything quite like it, but I

realised I knew straight away what it was. Something I'd only ever heard about in the stories that Pa used to tell me while we sat huddled around the fireplace with Mother at home. Something, I never thought I'd ever see in my life.

"Lothar, is th—that a…" I stuttered as I spoke, struggling to make the words and get them out.

"… Horse," he finished for me.

"And yes. It is, Kael."

He kept walking slowly towards it, unable to take his eyes away from it just like me. I could tell he was as amazed as I was by what we were looking at. It was beautiful.

Massive and over twice my height easy, with muscles that bulged from under its shiny brown skin.

Well hair, it was covered with short shiny hair.

It stood staring back at us with its long face, and gently tapped its front feet on the ground, which I noticed didn't have toes but were hoofed, kind of like the sheep or pigs we used to keep but bigger.

As we crept closer it let out a funny sound, pushing air out its nose and moved its head like it was nodding at us.

"Hrrrmphh."

The horse's dark, brown eyes looked at Lothar and then at me and I could see it didn't want to hurt us, it was all alone and probably just wanted to get out of this place as much as we did. It just wanted friends as well.

Lothar sheathed his sword and lightly reached out his hand towards its face, it didn't flinch and let his palm touch it on the cheek. I wanted to touch it too, but I wasn't sure what it would do. I looked up at Lothar and he nodded at me that it was okay, so I carefully reached through the fence and started patting its shoulder since I couldn't reach its face.

It was warm, the soft hair ran through my fingers, and I could feel how hard its huge muscles were.

"Woah, it's so big, Lothar!" I blurted out with a wide smile on my face.

"She sure is," he replied, smiling back at me.

The horse seemed calm, happy that it'd finally met some new friends.

"Do you think that maybe… maybe we can take it with us?" I asked hopeful he would say yes.

"Her, Kael. And yes, she's coming with us."

My smile grew even bigger hearing him say that and I continued patting her shoulder.

"Will we get to ride her? You know how right?" I asked him as he started unlatching the gate to her enclosure.

He looked at me and seemed to think about it and then shrugged.

"To be honest, No. I don't, but it was common for everyone to ride them back before the Great War so it can't be that hard. I'll figure it out, my father described it to me once."

He sounded unsure but I believed him, he could do anything and one day I would be just like him.

"You want to come with us, girl?" I asked her while Lothar went into the enclosure.

"Hrmph," she made the funny sound again, this time softer than the last, and I giggled.

"Hey, Lothar, I think she said yes."

He just raised his eyebrows at me and muttered, "I hope you're right," as he entered her enclosure.

I watched from outside the fence, he reached out and grabbed the short rope that was attached to her face and lightly pulled, asking her to 'come' which she did straight away and I opened my mouth in surprise.

"Woah. I was right she did say yes!" I said while she started to follow him.

"I guess you were," he chuckled back.

Her feet made a soft tap with each step as she followed behind him and out of her enclosure to my side of the fence and I realised just how big she really was.

"So, what now?" I asked nervously.

"Well. Now we climb onto her back, but I'll try first just in case she panics. Stand back a bit, Kael."

"Alright," I answered, taking a few steps back.

I was happy to just watch first anyway, she was just so big, I wasn't sure how she might act when we climbed on her.

Lothar took one more glance at me to make sure I was out of the way then he turned back to the horse, and my eyes widened in surprise when he just climbed straight up onto her without hesitating. They widened even more when she didn't even flinch from him on her back, it was as though he weighed as much as a feather to her. I gasped a little louder than I meant to but he ignored me, he seemed focused on keeping his balance and I didn't blame him, he was really high up.

He took hold of the ropes attached to her face, then gently tapped her sides with the heels of his boots and she began to walk forward, I watched him pull the rope to the right side when they neared the doors, and she turned around and came back towards me.

"Woah! Lothar, you're actually riding her!" I shouted to him excitedly.

He nodded biting his bottom lip to hold back a smirk and then turned again, doing a couple more laps, riding her up and down the barn a few more times before finally, he pulled back on both ropes, and she stopped not far from me.

"So, what do you think, boy? Would you like to ride a horse?" He said, looking at me with a smug grin on his face.

I smiled widely and nodded my head, then waited while he climbed back down from her.

Once he was back on the ground, he waved for me to come over and I did, struggling to hide my excitement.

This was going to be so much fun! I couldn't believe I was going to ride an actual horse. Pa would never have believed this, I wish he were here to see us.

Lothar crouched down so we were the same height and looked at me seriously now.

"Listen to me, Kael. She seems like a calm animal so I'm going to lift you onto her first and then I'll climb on after you. If she panics or goes to run, you are to pull back on the rope like I did as hard as you can, alright?"

"Yep, don't worry. I got this, Lothar," I said, trying to sound more confident than I felt.

He stared at me hesitantly for a moment.

"Okay. Now turn around, it'll be easier to climb on," he replied.

I did as he said and turned so I was facing her, I felt his hands grab under my armpits and then start to lift me off the ground.

My feet left the dirt, and I started rising, I reached forward to get my hands onto her back to start climbing, when suddenly I heard quick footsteps behind me and someone cried out.

Lothar let out a grunt, stumbled, and dropped me back to the ground making me fall over.

"Thwack," something made a wet plucking sound.

"You fuckin' bastard, you killed them all!!" A high-pitched voice screamed loudly.

"Thwack," another wet plucking sound echoed, followed by Lothar grunting in pain again.

I spun and climbed back to my feet as fast as I could, desperate to see what the heck was happening.

There was Del standing over Lothar, who was now on one knee holding both of his hands against his side as well as one of Del's and she was wrestling to pull her hand free from him.

Both of their hands were covered in dark blood that dripped onto the ground.

"Die you fucking pig!" She screeched at him again scratching at his face with her other hand drawing blood on his cheek.

"No!! Del, stop!!" I yelled.

This can't be happening. I felt sick inside.

It was as though time had slowed almost to a stop.

Like I was seeing a nightmare.

Do something Kael stop being scared for once in your life!

Why isn't Lothar fighting back!?

Why can't I move? I want to help but my body won't move!

"… Run, Kael" Lothar said, his voice coming out strained.

No! I won't run!

Move! Why can't I move! He needs me!

Blood spurted from his side and Lothar collapsed backwards dragging Del down on top of him.

They kept fighting until she managed to pull her hand away from his side and I saw she held a dagger in it. Raising it up high above her head she tried to plunge it into Lothar's neck, he pushed his palm up to stop it and the blade went straight through his hand but stopped short from his face.

My legs felt weak, my chest suddenly tightened and I felt like I couldn't breathe anymore.

She was killing him. No, please no.

"Kael, go. Now," he said again, gritting his teeth and I could see they were stained red.

No.

No. No.

No. No. No. No.

I kept repeating it in my mind over and over while I watched them fight unable to stop it. I reached up and put my hands over my head wanting to block it all out, praying it wasn't real.

But it was.

No. No. No.

My fingers touched the hilt of my sword.

NO.

I wrapped them around it, clenching my fist and pulling it out. I began slowly walking towards them while Lothar struggled to hold the dagger from his face.

Her back was to me, and Lothar was focused on stopping her. I glared at her hair while I crept forward, slowly raising my sword and tightening my grip even more on the hilt.

"LEAVE. HIM. ALONE!!!" I screamed as loudly as I could and then thrust the blade deep into her neck with all my strength.

CHAPTER 25

WOUNDED HERO

''All of life has a beginning and an end. We can rest in the fact that he has created both'

Sharp pain radiated through my jaw as I clenched my broken teeth and struggled to block the dagger, but it was quickly dwarfed by the agony I felt when the blade passed through my hand. My energy was fading fast, she'd stuck me deep in the back more than once, I just needed to hold her off long enough for the boy to escape.

I glanced at him, tears were streaming down his cheeks and his small frame quivered violently.

"Kael, go. Now," I stammered out, gritting my teeth to try to hide the pain in my voice.

I glared back into her hysterical eyes, willing my

body for more strength, my anger rising in me like a storm.

She was not getting him, I won't allow it.

Unfortunately my body was betraying my will, exhaustion was taking over and her blade was inching closer toward my chest.

Closer and closer.

I pushed my palm up, the only thing saving my life right now. Pain erupted down my arm, but I didn't care.

She cannot have him.

I looked up at the tip of the dagger closing in, the fucking irony wasn't lost on me. I was about to face the same fate I'd just given that maggot Zarek.

"Thwwrrrt!" And suddenly, just when I thought it was over, a sharp metal point emerged through her scrawny neck, spraying thick blood onto my chest in arbitrary squirts.

Her grip on her dagger released as she tried to paw desperately at the piece of steel protruding from her throat in a futile attempt to stop her life force spilling out.

I saw my chance, mustering what little fight my body had left I ripped her dagger free from my hand and plunged it deep into the side of her head, clean through her skull.

It was a sudden end, her whole body instantly stiffened, giving a slight jerk before her hands fell limply to her sides.

Then she breathed out her last gurgle of air through a throat filling with blood.

I grunted as I heaved her carcass to the side and she hit the ground with a hard thud, never to rise again.

Letting my head drop back to the dirt I sighed a heavy breath of air myself, my whole body wracked with pain.

You're not dead yet so quit your winging.

My father's voice echoed in my head, his typical saying when he was pushing me to my limits, and even in my current position I almost laughed to myself.

No, not yet old man.

A faint sniffling snapped me back to reality and I started to sit back up, ignoring the many protests my broken body screamed at me.

The boy stood nearby, still trembling with his face in his hands trying his best to hold back his sobbing.

"Kael," I said calmly, while rising gingerly to my feet, but he didn't look.

I carefully stepped towards him, pressing my hand to my side. I could feel the blood leaking from my wounds, but this wasn't the time to check how bad they were. I knew they were bad without looking anyway, I didn't want to see just how bad.

"Kael, I'm here," I said again softly, and this time

reached out and put my other hand on his shoulder.

He slowly parted his fingers and peeked out.

"Y—you're hurt, Lothar, and it's all my fault! I took too long a—and…"

"…I'm sorry!" He cried and started sobbing again.

I knelt in front of him, mentally blocking my pain out.

"No. It's not your fault, Kael."
I reached up and gently pulled his hands from his face and looked him in the eye.

"None of this is your fault. And I'll be fine, it'll take more than that to get rid of me," I said and winked at him, trying my best to sound strong amid the creeping doubt in my mind.

It seemed to work. A glint of happiness, or maybe it was hope, shone in his eyes. Whatever it was, he stopped crying.

"R—really?" He stuttered and used his shirt sleeve to wipe his eyes.

"Really. Now, are you ready to ride a horse?" I grinned.

***

The boy's excitement about riding the horse had died down after the first few hours of our journey. As we travelled back down the mountain, exhaustion had finally caught up to him not too long ago. He'd been sleeping soundly since, so I did my best not to wake

417

him. I could feel my strength leaving me just a little more as each hour passed us by.

The bleeding hadn't stopped and I could feel the horses back had become slick with it long ago, the wet made my ass slide on her as we navigated some of the more treacherous terrain.

I'd done my best thus far to hide the blood from the boy, he would only worry and get upset, but there was now so much it was becoming difficult.

I didn't want him to worry.

I could definitely use a rest though, seeing him sleep so soundly made me long for a nice warm bed… and maybe Joan to keep me company like those cold nights back in Drassox.

That would be nice.

It's just a dream though, a nice thought to accompany me down this mountain.

All that really matters is I get him somewhere safe.

"Where are we?" His voice suddenly snapped me from my thoughts, while he let out a long yawn and rubbed his eyes.

I shifted forward on the seat to make sure I was over the worst of the blood.

"Ah, you're awake. Well, I think we're almost at the bottom of the trail…"

Fuck. Just speaking was beginning to feel like an effort.

You aren't dead yet.

No, not yet old man.

"Wow, it's so much faster riding her huh, Lothar?"

"It sure is," I answered.

The gentle rhythmic 'tap, tap, tap' of the horse's hooves was almost lulling me to sleep.

Not yet.

"We need to come up with a name for her don't you think?" He asked turning his head back to me.

My brain felt foggy, clouded. I had to concentrate to answer.

"… Yes, I think you should, Kael."

"Nooo, not just me. I said we. Do you have any ideas?"

Ideas. Do I have any ideas…

Yes. You do.

"Maybe…" I replied squeezing my eyes shut and opening them wide, trying to wake them into staying open.

They were starting to feel like they were made out of lead.

"Really?" He said turning his face again to try and look at me.

I paused, focusing my thoughts.

Yes… really.

"How about… Mirella…" I slurred.

"Like my real Mother? Hm. Yeah, I like that. Do you like that girl?" He said reaching forward and rubbing her head.

She let out a soft 'hrrmph'.

"See that? She said yes, Lothar," he exclaimed, smiling.

"… I saw… she sure did…"

And then my vision fluttered, my tunnel vision took over and I felt the wind rushing by my face.

"Lothar, no!" I heard the boy shout out.

I'd momentarily passed out and fallen from Mirella's back, looking up from the floor I saw the boy was about to start climbing down to help me.

"… S—stay… there, Kael," I groaned, rolling onto my side.

"What!? No, I can help you back up!"

I shook my head and started standing to my feet, my legs shook violently as they struggled to hold my weight.

"No! I won't be able to lift you back on her. Just give… moment… to catch… breath…" I stammered breathlessly.

My vision was still swirling, sweat poured from my forehead and I felt nauseous. And cold.

I knew I was dying.

"Um… Lothar, who're they?"

They? My brain snapped just enough out of the fogginess for me to look ahead of us, scanning the trail.

The first thing I realised was that we'd made it to the bottom, finally. The second thing was that up ahead, I could make out a large group of people coming towards us, at least twenty. Maybe more.

I heard a few shouts and knew they had spotted us as well.

My heart sank. They must be soldiers Zarek left behind, the prick had left men to mop up any that tried to flee the commune. I can't say I'm surprised, I'd have done the same in his position.

Only one thing left to do.

"Kael, stay… on, Mirella."

My words came out weak.

I raised my bloodied hand and reached behind my back, closing my fingers around the hilt of my sword.

One final fight.

You aren't dead yet.

No, not yet…

"What? No! Get back on Mirella! We can just ride the other way!" The boy shouted, panic rising in his voice again.

"You're to ride hard to the North, Kael. Do not look back, no matter what," I said without looking at him.

I heard him protest but still I didn't look back, and I couldn't make out his words anymore.

I prayed he would do as I said. And for the last time, I began to march forward to meet my foes.

My feet felt like oak, each step a struggle against the numbness trying to overcome them.

My sword felt heavy, threatening to pull itself from my grasp.

My vision blurred further, and a cold sweat dripped from my forehead pooling on the ground before me.

My hearing had muffled, as though I was back in the river, tumbling helplessly through the heavy current once more.

I felt lightheaded, nauseous, weak.

But my mind, remained unbroken. It knew what I had to do.

This would be my final stand.

I would buy the boy as much time as possible.

His voice continued behind me, but I couldn't make out what he was saying. All the people approaching me were blurring into one single swirl of bright colours.

Good, at least now I only have to attack one target. I raised my sword, my muscles ached but I was ready.

"Lothar! Is that you!?"

"Duke! Get the Duke down here! It's Lothar and the boy!"

Who is this? They're saying your name.

I squinted my eyes, trying to force the swirl into focusing so I could try make out the faces before me.

The voices sounded familiar.

"Lothar, are you alright? It's Harold," the part of the blur closest to me said.

Harold?

I tried to place the voice but struggled to focus my

thoughts.

"Lothar, it's Gerard, what the hell happened!? Where have you been?"

Gerard… Harold…

The names slowly began to form memories in my mind, and I realised I recognised the voices.

"Duke… Gerard… Lieu… tenant… Harold…" I mumbled.

"Yes, Lothar. I'm with the survivors from Branwick. Are you alright?" He asked with growing concern in his voice.

"I… promise me…" My voice trailed off.

The blur started to come closer.

"… look… after the boy… he is… special…" I mumbled.

"Of course, Lothar. Maria, come here now!" He replied getting more frantic.

Good.

He.

Should be.

Safe.

Now.

My sword slipped from my hand, its weight finally overpowering my remaining strength and I felt a hand reach out and gently touch my shoulder.

"Maria, hurry with the bandages! Lothar needs help now!" Duke Gerard's voice echoed, like he was someplace far away.

Then my legs finally lost the battle they had been fighting, and I was falling. I felt a gentle thud as my back hit the dirt.

Lying there a comforting warmth quickly spread over my body and down my limbs, I felt no pain anymore. Just numbness.

It was the deepest sensation of relaxation I've ever felt.

I heard Kael shouting and became aware of people standing over the top of me, looking down all talking at once although I struggled to make out the words.

I felt a small weight land lightly on top of me, holding me. And then his voice breaking up as he spoke.

"Lothar! Please get up, you said you were alright! Don't leave me! Stop pretending please!"

I struggled to find the energy to reply but I tried anyway.

"I'm sorry… Kael… Stay… with these people… safe now…"

I couldn't be sure if my words came out clearly or not, my hearing and vision was fading.

Everything beginning to glow a blinding white.

It looked so serene. Perfect.

Suddenly a beautiful voice began to speak to me. A voice I recognised, and as I looked around me, she appeared out of the white glow, a warm, happy smile, upon her face.

"Guardian, you have done everything I knew you could. You have saved my child and given him the chance to learn to use his powers to help others in need. You saved him from damnation and succeeded where no other mortal could."

I silently listened to her speak and as I did, I began to see everyone I'd lost start to materialise in the distance behind her, all my friends and loved ones from Drassox.

Elias, Catherine and Lord Edmund stood there among many others waving happily. Even my father was there, and Joan, looking as beautiful as ever. They all looked excited to see me again.

Welcoming me to join them.

"You have completed your task and earned your place in heaven. Take my hand and come with me. Let your suffering end," she said extending her hand closer to me and waiting for me to take it.

I went to clasp her hand but paused to glance back, in the distance I saw the people of Branwick huddled over my broken, bloody body. The boy clung onto me sobbing hysterically, begging me not to leave.

"How… can you be sure he will be safe now?" I asked hesitantly, looking back at the boy.

I didn't want to leave him, we'd been through so much together… I cared for him deeply.

The thought of him alone, to fend for himself in this violent world scared me to death.

Her face softened as though she'd read my mind.

"You have sent Lucifer back to his prison, within the frozen lake Cocytus. It will be a long time before he can return. The Order has been crippled. The boy now has a chance to grow up and master his abilities. In time he may face adversity, but you will always watch over him and protect him."

She paused for a moment.

"You are, and always have been, his Guardian Angel."

I glanced back to Kael once more, it hurt me to know I was leaving him, but somehow, I also knew she was right.

He would be upset and mourn my death, but in time I knew he would recover and become who he was meant to be. He was strong, I knew that.

I had done my duty and protected him.

And I would never stop watching over him.

So, without further hesitation.

I reached out and took her hand.

***

The lady, Maria crouched next to me, she'd cut Lothar's gambeson off and was using her bandages to wipe the blood from his wounds, but it seemed useless. No matter how much she wiped, the blood just kept coming back.

Lothar wouldn't answer me since he'd closed his eyes, I was doing my best not to panic but I couldn't stop my body from trembling.

I kept telling myself he was strong, nothing could kill him. He promised me he wouldn't leave me.

Suddenly Maria's hand slowed in wiping the blood and she looked to the man standing above us, I saw him faintly shake his head and my chest tightened, I felt my lip quiver.

Maria's hand froze, she paused and looked at me, then gently put her hand on my shoulder.

"He has passed away, Kael… I'm so sorry, but there's nothing more I can do. He… Lothar… is in a better place now…"

My mind went blank. I tried to make sense of what she just said but I couldn't make it make sense, so I just snapped.

"No!! You're a liar!" I yelled and angrily shrugged her hand off of me.

"You're wrong! You're all wrong!! You're liars!" I screamed, putting my hands over my head and pulling my hair.

No, no, no! It can't be true.

You can't be dead.

You promised you were alright!

You promised me!

Tears streamed down my cheeks making everything grow blurry while I looked down at him.

My friend. My protector.

It can't be true…

I was all alone again. I had lost everyone!

I lay my head down on his chest and began to sob.

Please don't leave me, Lothar.

You can't be gone, you can't be.

Please come back. Please come back.

Closing my eyes tightly I started whispering it over and over again, I felt like I couldn't stop myself. And then, I started begging his wounds to heal, willing it with everything I had.

I blocked out everything around me.

Please come back. Please come back. Please come back.

I imagined his injuries slowly closing, his blood going back into his body. I tried to force it to happen.

And then…

Suddenly a warm, fuzzy, sensation began to run over my body, I could feel it running through me, spreading from my chest and down my arms, into my hands then… into Lothar.

I could see it in my mind. It looked like glowing colours speeding along and blurring into one.

I pressed my face harder into his chest.

I heard someone nearby let out a surprised gasp and then others did the same. I ignored them and tried to hold onto the feeling, it felt as though if I didn't, I would lose grip on it, and it would slip away forever.

I clenched my eyes and concentrated harder, wrestling inside myself to hang onto it for as long as I could and push it into Lothar, the people around started murmuring in hushed voices to each other.

I clenched my eyes tightly and shut them out.

Please come back. Please come back. Please come back.

"Gerard, are you seeing this?" Maria's voice echoed, it sounded distant but near at the same time.

"I… think so…"

"It… his wounds, are they… really… closing?" Someone else mumbled.

I refused to open my eyes to look, instead focusing even more to try to hang onto the fuzzy feeling, but it was getting harder and harder to hold on and I could feel it draining me.

I struggled and fought, terrified to let it go, somehow knowing to let it go was to let Lothar go. But I was losing the fight.

My head was pounding, the pain becoming almost unbearable, but I hung on, refusing to let go.

Please come back. Please come back. Please come back.

He was leaving me. I could feel it. I had been too late.

And then, I lost hold of it completely and the world spiralled out of control and turned black.

EPILOGUE
A CHANCE TO START OVER

'Do not be overcome by evil, but overcome evil with good'

Three days later…

I stood there still as a statue back in Branwick, staring at the big chunk of stone that marked Lothar's grave.

I'd memorised every sharp edge and mark on the rock, I hadn't taken my eyes off of it since it was put there on top of him.

I couldn't believe he was really gone, I had cried until I couldn't cry anymore and now, I had nothing left. I felt empty.

So, I just kept standing there, staring in silence. I

had no idea how long I'd been there, it was like time didn't matter anymore.

Nothing mattered to me now.

A few other people also stood nearby, staring at their own rocks that marked their loved one's graves, but I was too upset to really notice. I knew it was wrong, but all I could think about was him.

We had buried a lot of people here today and everyone was sad. Gerard had promised me once things in the town were settled, and things were back up and running he would teach me how to chip the stone into shapes, and I could carve Lothar a gravestone that he would've been happy with.

I said I would like that, but it hadn't done anything to take this feeling away.

Maria had told me that in time I would feel like myself again, but I wasn't so sure. I couldn't stop thinking… if only I'd tried to help him before he'd fallen… if I'd stopped Del faster… maybe… Maybe he would still be here.

I felt like I hadn't helped him enough, and this was all my fault.

I could feel my eyes trying to tear up again, and I grew angry at myself.

NO.

No more crying, he wouldn't like that.

He would want me to be strong. I would be strong. Just like he was.

I crouched to one knee and put my hands on the stone.

"I miss you, Lothar… you were always there when I needed you. I'm going to try my best to be brave, I promise. One day, I know I'll see you, Pa, and Mother again."

"… And I'm going to learn to control my powers, to make sure I never lose anyone I care about again… I won't be scared anymore. I'll be strong, just like you and Pa were."

I slowly stood back up and bowed my head.

"Goodbye, Lothar. I won't forget you."

Just before I went to turn away, I felt a cool gust of wind pass over me, wind that carried the familiar scent of… of him.

And for the first time in days, I felt hope.

Then something gently squeezed my shoulder.

I spun, as quickly as I could, but no one was there.

Just Branwick in the distance.

My new home.

A chance to start over.

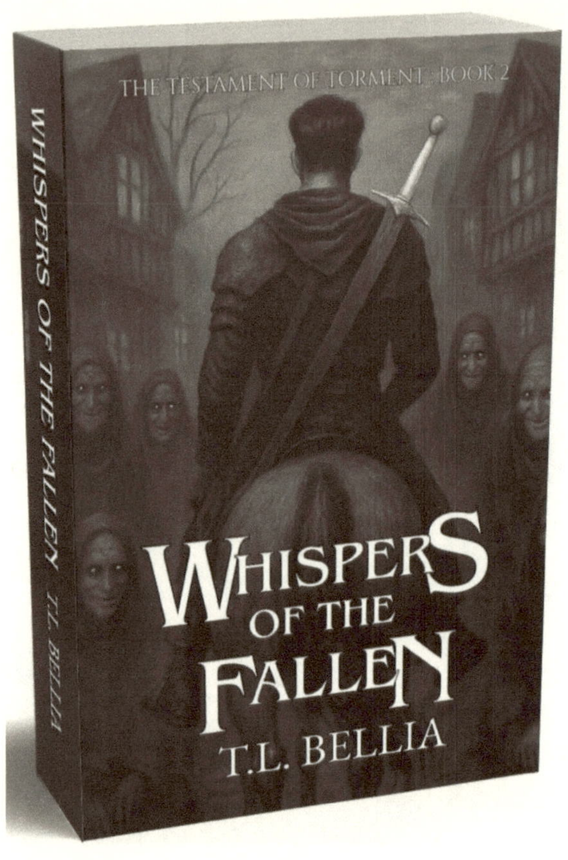

…Continue reading in Book 2 of the Testament of Torment, Whispers of the Fallen - Out Now!

About the Author

T.L Bellia resides in Perth, Australia and began writing Beneath the Ashen Sky in mid-2024 while employed as an Emergency Services Officer.

Being an avid reader and fan of grim stories, he decided to try his hand at writing his own novel and Beneath the Ashen Sky was born.

When not writing he can be found hiking, fishing, gaming ,or hanging out with his Cat, Chester. He  also has a keen interest in Boxing and MMA, having trained extensively in Boxing for many years.

If you enjoyed '**Beneath the Ashen Sky'** please leave me a review on Amazon – it really helps!

Continue the Journey in Book 2 in the Testament of Torment Trilogy - **'Whispers of the Fallen'**.

Out Now on Amazon and Online Retailers!